CW00499492

INTUITION

Also by Peter Jinks

Hallam Foe

INTUITION

Peter Jinks

review

First published in 2003
by Review

An imprint of Headline Book Publishing

10 9 8 7 6 5 4 3 2 1

ISBN 0 7472 6943 2

Typeset in Perpetua by Palimpsest Book Production Limited,
Polmont, Stirlingshire

Printed and bound in Great Britain by
Clays Ltd, St Ives plc.

HEADLINE BOOK PUBLISHING
A division of Hodder Headline
338 Euston Road
London NW1 3BH

www.reviewbooks.co.uk
www.hodderheadline.com

Thanks to Charlotte Mendelson, Amy Philip and Lucy Ramsey at Headline, Natasha Fairweather, Linda Shaughnessy and Rob Kraitt at AP Watt, Ruaridh Nicoll, John MacKenzie, Geraldine Murray, Henry Chapman and very much Lucia.

One

The soft hiss of the coach brakes woke Magnus instantly, but
he did not open his eyes. Instead he raised both sets of
fingers and touched his face. As he feared, nothing had
changed. The skin was numb. Someone else's. He let his
fingers drop again and sighed. It had been like this ever
since he received the bad news two weeks before; as if the
information had jolted him half an inch out of alignment
with his own body, along with the entire world, which
now seemed artificial, like a stage set. Perhaps this was
only to be expected, he had told himself at the beginning.
Shock did such things. He could tell almost anyone that he
felt 'totally numb' and they would not be surprised. On
the contrary, they would forgive the cliché and prepare
the next concerned question. But if he told them that
he was half an inch to the left of the Magnus they were
looking at? Literally? It was not the same thing at all.

So he had decided not to tell anyone about his freak
malalignment and hoped instead that it would pass of its
own accord. The days that followed the bad news were

insanely full of activity and things to deal with, but still, every time he woke and at many other times during the day, often unconsciously, his fingers would creep up and dab the skin of his face in the hope that it had become his own once more. For two weeks now, the situation had remained stubbornly the same: he could touch and feel himself, but he couldn't feel himself be touched. As with the face, so with the rest of his body. Arms, legs, flanks, nipples, genitals. All felt as if they had been mysteriously laminated. Only the fingertips – ten precious pads of sensate skin – provided reliable information.

On the plus side there was no pain. There was no nothing. Cold baths and pinching had no effect whatsoever. Nor did abstaining from cigarettes and alcohol – a foolish experiment that he rapidly abandoned, although he did switch to a low-tar tobacco brand and reduced his booze intake as a precaution. Perhaps, he speculated, he was suffering from a medical syndrome with an Eastern European name attached to it, or maybe a pupil had spiked his glass of water with LSD. Unlikely, though. And if these strange symptoms really were caused by pure, straight emotion – which felt like the obvious explanation – how was it that the government allowed anyone to drive under the influence of grief?

But there had been no time to grieve yet. How could he when he was racing through a transit lounge, shouting at an official, or trying to make an international call from a payphone in Rundu? He hoped that he did not look as odd as he felt. People, he noticed, had been keeping their distance. Nobody sat next to him on the coach – even though he couldn't have looked as bad as most of his fellow passengers – and the flight into London, by chance or design, had left another empty seat beside him. These things made him a little paranoid. He did not want people to know that he found them disturbing and unreal and that their bodies had acquired in his mind a grotesque lucidity. Everything was amplified to an almost unbearable degree: their smells, their sniffs, their scratchings, even their sweating. Faces held a particularly revolting fascination. The knobbly features and open pores resembled wood fungus while beneath their unlikely shapes he imagined the brain as a grey, unappetising nut. One way or another, people must have picked up on it.

So, he felt alienated: from himself, from other people and from everything else too. A coach was therefore not a good place to be. After so many hours spent in enclosed spaces he felt increasingly claustrophobic. This was partly why he had decided to keep his eyes shut until he heard the doors open. In the meantime he tried to allay his panicky impatience by thinking of something else. Unfortunately but inevitably this led back to the phone call, the one that had delivered the bad news, the one that had made him numb.

He had expected it to be his girlfriend Felicity – or, more precisely, his ex-girlfriend. They had argued the night before, broken up and walked out of the restaurant in opposite directions. But he didn't believe that she was serious, and was hoping to hear her repentant voice on the end of the line, hoarse from a sleepless night. But it was Father. Their conversation was brief and strangely banal in tone. The banality of people organising a stay in purgatory. He remembered his actions vividly from his then entirely new, half-inch-to-the-left perspective. First he had put down his mobile phone. He had lain back on the bed, then checked the time on his Mickey Mouse bedside clock (the white gloved fingers indicated that it was a little before seven in the morning). First he phoned Felicity who didn't answer or wasn't there. Then he phoned work, claimed compassionate leave, booked a flight, phoned Felicity's mobile (no answer), packed some things, phoned Felicity again (nope), left his rented accommodation in Shepherd's Bush, and took a taxi to the airport. He boarded the first of two aeroplanes, passed through several time zones and booked into a cheap hotel in the hot, surprisingly tidy city of Windhoek, Namibia. There he located the relevant offices, gave up on Felicity and, over the course of several days, bulldozed his way through some African bureaucracy – the only time when his numbness had found a use for itself. Then he had come back, disoriented, frayed but more or less in one piece. Give or take half an inch.

The coach seemed to be stationary now but the engine continued to shudder in neutral. Resisting the urge to open his eyes, he wondered if they were going to have to move to another stand, but then the engine abruptly stopped. The doors clunked open and the sounds of the city broke into the cabin, followed by some cool, tainted city air. His eyelids would not open easily – they were gummed together – but by applying some saliva he succeeded. The view, as expected, was ugly. He blinked and straightened up. Through the misted glass of the window the coach station presented itself, a depressing panorama of queues and ticket offices and a shabby pub away to the right. Time to move, before everyone else did. Edging his way out of the seat on unreliable legs, he crabwalked swiftly down the aisle and just managed to avoid the crush, to his intense relief.

Inevitably, however, while waiting to collect his rucksack from the luggage hatch, Magnus found himself jostled and closed in. It was too much. He longed to get away. The last leg of his long intercontinental journey had been easily the worst, albeit the least eventful, punctuated by burpers, crunchers, toxic farters and the steady drone of all-night student large-talk. He did not want to hear about the Baltic authors, whoever they were, ever again. The travellers who still circled the hatch made him think of an awful orchestra warming up: plucking their underwear, tuning their catarrh.

Finally he got hold of his rucksack. Mobiles started ringing behind him as they left the station and Magnus decided that he must avoid that hideous throng. He put his head down and made his way towards the bus-only exit. Almost immediately a Musselburgh-bound double-decker hooted at his back and he was obliged to lob his rucksack and then vault – or, as it transpired, urgently flop – over the metal barriers on to a paltry slice of kerb. There he cowered, just catching a glance through the side-doors of the driver who, with ardour in his eyes, was declaiming something in his direction. Poetry? Magnus straightened up and swiftly checked that his bag was out of the path of a second bus whose hydraulics guffed directly in his face as it passed. Amid the aroma of oil and rubber he fancied that he could identify the trapped wind and accumulated foot odour of a thousand overnighters. Reminded of several jaw-clacking snoozelets that had punctuated his journey the length of England and beyond, he turned away and found that his face was inches from a reflecting window. It appeared that someone had rolled his eyeballs in a mixture of blood and egg-white. He looked closer at himself, appalled, fascinated, and pushed his wire spectacles higher up along the bridge of his sharp nose. He was trying to interpret the Oriental calligraphy that had been scored on his cheek in the form of a sleep-mark: Japanese, perhaps, for dog breath. With his sickly yellow tan he looked even worse than the orchestra; maybe he was the conductor.

Without much hope Magnus tried to rearrange his hair, which reminded him distressingly of a bad eighties band. It was flat on top and appeared ferociously backcombed at the nape of the neck – the result of having wedged his head for eight hours between a wet window and the headrest. He managed to snag his rucksack on the barrier, then inched his way along the kerb towards the promise of broad pavement. Objective achieved, he paused and blinked painfully. Edinburgh's luminous grey light wasn't the problem. He was stunned by the noise and vibrations that echoed horribly where he was standing in the exit arch. A third bus came honking past and he decided as a matter of priority that he should get out, as far away from public road transport as his puffy feet would take him. He got to the pavement, crossed the road, survived, and did not savour his first proper view of the open square with its saint on a high column, radiating taxicabs. This wasn't the district that interested him. Instead he turned right and headed down the hill, over Queen Street – equally savage with traffic – and towards the relative quiet of Dublin Street. At the top he paused to admire the Forth estuary and beyond it, far away, illusory tranquillity in the form of Fife. The hills were still blurred with morning mist. The sun never finished its job over there.

Magnus knew that the Georgian part of the city where he was heading would be unchanged: protected from time by World Heritage Site planning orders. He had once been vaguely contemptuous of it on metropolitan terms – 'site' was just the word for this strangely unboisterous, un-ugly place. Now the buildings' tomblike greyness, which used to oppress him, seemed graciously well judged. The roll-call of street names signalled his approach to that special part, whose invisible boundaries were defined by the three points. They were called (according to street or crescent) India, Bellevue and Drummond. Joined together, these nodes – each significant to his dearly departed, since they had been marked down on a map he found among her things – described a sharp triangular slice. One he knew, while the other two were mysteries. Even though the purpose of those three Biro ink dots was most likely banal, such tiny details, since the news, had acquired an almost mystic significance. During an emotionally precarious Namibian night he had calculated that the distance it enclosed came close to a square kilometre. A square in a triangle. Nice. This geometry of death, of mathematical precision applied to the last great human mystery, appealed to his sense of the arcane.

There were several practical reasons for Magnus being in Edinburgh. He had to report back to his parents, he had to extort some money from them, and he also had an idea to leave teaching in London permanently and start a business here. There was a letter, too, that had never reached his sister and that he intended to return to its sender. But in truth they were all subordinate to a vaguer, more potent need: to nurture his memories of his sister Claire and to shore them up while they remained fresh. He could not bear her being gone and her violent departure was still so obscenely current that he found himself having to check that reality had really got it right. So here he was, looking for her in places where she most conspicuously wasn't, in the hope that their very emptiness might still define her shape somehow. The sense of loss increased as he entered the streets she had known best, but this was welcome. His grief seemed to operate on the assumption that greater pain would bring swifter solace. In his current state, even contemplating an end to his suffering seemed disgraceful.

He wondered whether it was possible to grieve for a whole life. Perhaps he ought to try. The idea of devoting himself to her memory appealed to him since it gave him purpose. He would spend his time imagining what she might have said, doing what she might have done, going where she might have chanced to visit. Thus she would continue to live for him, hidden away inside his head. Which was better than nothing. Yes, he thought, he would stick around this town for a while, to be where she wasn't, where she was. He stopped and looked around at the surrounding townhouses, whose beauty had formerly left him cold. He would learn to love these grey stones in the same way she had.

This gave him heart. He enjoyed resolutions. Making the rucksack more comfortable on his shoulders, he began to savour the lessening noise of traffic. The car-breeze had dissipated, now that there was only an occasional vehicle crossing over the road on the way to or from Broughton Street. As he approached the first invisible side of the triangle he felt, through the numbness, the light hairs on his forearms rise up. This was accompanied by a light tap-tapping that gathered momentum as it passed up his ribs. It was a peculiar but not unpleasant sensation; he ignored it.

Without a specific plan Magnus was heading for Bellevue, a flat once rented by Claire and now – so he understood – owned by her old flatmate and close friend Isabel. Despite his best intentions the thought of seeing Isabel again, and all the intensity it would require, resumed downward pressure on his morale. The choice was that or the ordeal of his parents: a difficult call. So he decided to prolong his walk and kept going, following a path that he felt would have appealed to Claire in her old city, trying to work out the routes that she must have taken when she lived here. He was guided by half-remembered addresses and street names, the locations of her favourite bars and cafés, the patterns of her work and study. In his mind he visualised the city layout and saw the route-lines burst out from the three points of the triangle, zigzagging, doubling back and taking sudden exits off the map towards unmarked destinations. It started to block his mind. The amount of information contained in a life: just the routes! He felt dizzy. The human brain wasn't designed for two.

Magnus turned into a small cobbled lane that would provide a short cut towards Northumberland Street and the west side of town. He breathed deeply and heard the echoes of footsteps under the arch: his own, of course. Soon he had passed into the silence of the little mews. It was a peculiar place, tucked away behind the high townhouses, wide streets and tree-locked gardens circled by railings. Here, in this odd city spot, surprisingly intimate like the back of a knee, he found himself having a communion. It felt, for a moment, similar to homecoming. His spirits rose again. Flexing his shoulders under the weight of his rucksack he imagined how these familiar windows and pavements and rooftops would have given Claire a glow of good times past. As he walked he gave up trying to figure out routes and instead just allowed himself to wander, although it felt like he was being led. The roads and houses were magnetised, pushing him one way, pulling him another. It was as if Claire was close by, waiting round a corner or walking down a parallel street; he half expected to see her face in the window of a street-front café or hear her laugh in the echo of a tenement stairwell. He realised that in former visits he had stuck to a narrowly defined set of pathways to which he had paid little attention. This walk was opening his eyes to a different place altogether.

He came to a square called Drummond Place and lingered outside a large townhouse that looked uninhabited. It puzzled him. He had never been here before and its mild dilapidation suggested that it could not have been of relevance to Claire. He passed on until, some time later, he stopped at the top of a downward-sloping street with a dead-end. India Street. Again he felt this was familiar and he walked all the way to the bottom. Outside the last tenement, number fifty-eight, he wondered if one of these flats had been occupied by friends of Claire. He was tempted to press a buzzer at random, and see whether a familiar voice would answer. But the chances were that many of her contemporaries would have moved on by now, surfing the property boom out into the suburbs or countryside. He could see that money had changed the city in the last few years. Flats that were once student accommodation had now been transformed, each black door adorned with brassy nameplates, grand as headstones.

After well over an hour of walking, he was tired. He stepped over to some high iron railings and looked down thirty feet or so, on to Stockbridge. His forehead pressed against the rough metal of the bars. On the other side, below, was busy everyday life. There were shoppers swarming between delicatessens, a few office workers nipping out for coffee. He sighed. More than ever he felt disconnected, deadened, unaligned. Behind a line of smart cars and white vans, a bus came rolling down the hill, its tyres sending a loud rubbery rumble up from the cobbles. Glassily, Magnus watched as it stopped directly below him. Some passengers got off, and another one – Claire – got on.

Hold on. His knuckles went white against the black railings. *Hold on.* Claire? His dead sister? He strained to get a clearer look: her green beret; her brown handbag; her matching green overcoat with the hem that finished half-way down her calves. But the angle was too tight, and the bus doors shut. He stood back and told himself he was mistaken: Claire was a taxi addict, she never took the bus. Then, realising the absurdity of his last thought, he almost laughed. What, in fact, had he seen? A green beret of the same make. A coincidentally similar handbag. Another girl with her hairstyle from years back. His eyes scanned the dirty windows of the bus as it edged forwards into the traffic. Yes, it was ridiculous, but he wanted a second look all the same. He caught a glimpse of green in one of the near windows. She had sat down half-way along the aisle. Her face was obscured by a film of grime on the glass, but he saw a hand rise to her throat and pluck the skin absentmindedly as she flicked through a magazine with the other.

Claire. Unmistakably, incontrovertibly Claire. The bus began to move. He screamed her name. He saw the fingers halt, saw the head turn. He ran for the steps. He fell down them. The backpack broke the fall. He got up and continued to jump down the steps. He reached the pavement below and charged through the slow-moving crowd, the backpack yanking him left and right, bouncing, barging through the people, whose protests and curses fluttered and petered out behind him. His feet were thumping over the paving slabs, his breath sawed against his throat, and the bus kept going, pulling further away until it was soaked up by the curve. He cut across the road, causing a van to slither messily to a halt. A horn-blast followed, but he kept going, fuelled by adrenaline and a delirious sense of hope. When the bus did stop, too briefly, he was close enough to see that she had not alighted. Those passengers who did glanced at him with aversion and cleared a path as he pounded past. He didn't have the breath to shout again. It was all he could do to keep the bus in sight.

At the next stop, thank God, she did get off. Nimbly, she hopped down with one hand held up to the side of her face, talking into a mobile perhaps. The movements were Claire's exactly. He shouted her name again but he was too distant and too breathless. Hurriedly she disappeared into a roadside door. A shop, perhaps? He had her now, he thought triumphantly. His pace slowed to a jog, and he tried to swallow away a thick metallic taste that had formed in his mouth. Soon he drew up outside the door, and paused to catch his breath.

It was a French café with a sunny yellow exterior and a sunflower logo. Through the shifting reflections of traffic against the window, he saw a cake counter, the backs of wicker chairs, a serving hatch. He paused a moment longer to compose himself. As he straightened his clothes he considered again that light step of hers as she hit the pavement. Had Claire in fact ever been that nimble on her feet? Perhaps not. But the plucking of the neck outweighed his doubt. He even felt the beginnings of indignation. If he found Claire in there, calmly drinking cappuccino through a mouthful of chocolate brownie, he was going to kill her. He freed an arm from his backpack, saw that the veins of his hand were purple with pumping blood, and pushed open the door. Perversely wanting to extend the uncertainty, he delayed a close look at the clientele until he had closed it. Even then he did not turn round immediately, willing his name to be called from a table, to hear the vaguely mocking, affectionate voice that had featured, as memory testified, in so many important stages of his life. Unsurprisingly, it didn't come.

Feeling the exhilaration drift away, he cast an eye over the room. It was entirely full of women, mostly prosperous ones, who inspected him with unanimous aversion: the rucksack, sweaty back and roaming eye. It all added up to someone who might want to read out their travel diary. But Claire? A second sweep of the room confirmed, to his disappointment, that the undead were not taking coffee this morning. Unless, of course, she was hiding. The toilet.

He turned to a waitress who was making coffee at the espresso machine. 'Excuse me, did you see my sister come in here a second ago? Green beret, brown handbag.'

One of the customers at the cake counter glanced at him with distaste, then edged away. The waitress paused in her task, her face uncooperative. He sensed the whole room tuning in.

'No, I didn't see anyone. Sorry.'

The room seemed heavy with female hostility, unless he was imagining it. The waitress turned back to the coffee machine. But he wasn't going to leave before he had seen who was in the ladies' cloakroom. Defying the vibe, he took a seat at the only empty table, which was between the kitchen door and the coat-rack, where some shopping-bags had been left. How convenient: he could stash his rucksack there. But then he noticed that conversation had died: the clientele were nervous that he might steal something. Considerately, he moved one seat away from the bags, but two women at the next-door table were still staring at something. He followed the direction of their gazes. The soiled rucksack, a cherished relic from his year off ten years before, had fallen against and was slowly flattening a costly looking shopping-bag with string handles. The other bags gave the impression of pretending not to notice. Sighing, Magnus got up, dragged his offending possession upright again, and winked in the direction of the women, whose chairlegs clucked in disapproval. The waitress had arrived. 'What do you want?' she asked impatiently.

Magnus could not help but notice that he failed to inspire respect in serving staff, these days. She had a pretty downward-turning mouth and fascinating nostrils, although that might have been because her nose was stuck in the air. Magnus cleared his throat, aware of not having used his vocal cords more than once since Jan Smuts airport. 'I'd like a coffee, please.'

She didn't write anything on her pad. 'What kind of coffee?'

'Um. White?'

She responded to his smile by giving the polite impression that he had mistaken her for someone else, someone known to interact with eighties hairstyles. Nevertheless his request was accepted and she went off in the direction of the coffee machine. Magnus reclined in the creaking chair and winced. His back hurt. The rucksack was partly responsible, but the throbbing seemed more diffuse. He rubbed his lower spine and watched the waitress serve another customer a carry-out coffee. Then he coughed, causing one of the two women at the nearby table to glance at him in irritation, as if he was somehow spoiling their conversation about a coming bank holiday in the country. He glanced once more towards the ladies' toilet, whose door was firmly shut.

The waitress returned with his order but without eye-contact. When had he ever inspired such high levels of dislike? Perhaps they could sniff the grief on his breath. Maybe he had given away his suspicion that they weren't quite operating in his dimension. They probably thought he was mad. Magnus smiled softly to himself and lifted the hot cup of coffee. The numbness meant that he had to be careful not to scald himself or pour the beverage down his chin, so he sipped it gingerly, as if he was fresh from the dentist's chair. Despite these precautions, however, the coffee splashed and he put a hand to his mouth with a gasp. He stayed that way for several seconds, eyes wide, face slightly flushed. Then his fingers moved. He patted his face, touched his ears, tugged his eyebrows. His eyes dropped to the cup, which he lifted slowly, dripping, to take another sip. The crockery was hot on his lower lip, the coffee smoky in its flavour, the milk, he could distinctly taste, full fat. He looked around him, at the ladies who, with their peripheral vision, were keeping him under close surveillance.

He grinned. He laughed out loud. He put down the cup once more and pinched his own cheeks, overcome with the joy of reunion. His face had come back to him. He could taste, he could feel! But when had this happened? Had it been the jolt of seeing Claire again? What the hell? He was himself again. Relief and pleasure flowed through him and he was overwhelmed by an urge to share his good fortune. If only these people knew how precious were the small physical things. He longed to tell them that his numbness had gone, that he had edged that precious half-inch to the right, back into alignment with the rest of the world. With his sense of taste restored, he realised that he was starving. Scones all round!

But no, he mustn't scare anyone. Nor must he assume that his recovery was permanent. Perception played funny tricks. What if, for instance, they had all moved to the left? That would mean he had not returned to normal at all. Instead the whole world might have abandoned the rules of normal existence, and the dead were rising up and using the buses. For reassurance, he dipped a finger in the coffee and burned himself.

Then he heard the soft click of the toilet door. A tremor passed through him. He gripped the side of the table and turned to stare. It swung open. A woman stepped out, dark-haired, middle-aged, in a suit. Obviously she wasn't

Claire, or even a lookalike. Which left the question unre-solved. Either he had hallucinated Claire, or Claire was actually alive, or she had somehow escaped through a back exit. Either way it was too late. She was gone. The woman returned to her table on the far side of the room, where her business colleague was waiting with agenda and pen.

He started to cry. For the first time since the news, the reality of his loss struck home with full force. His numbness had been a protection as well as a curse. Pain pressed cruelly against his temples and drove sour tears from his eyes. He was alive and Claire was dead. It seemed very unfair.

'Excuse me,' someone said.

Having hidden his face with a hand he did not notice immediately that the waitress had arrived at his table. He glanced up, hand still shielding his eyes, as if against the sun. She was standing calmly in front of him.

'Excuse me, but you have to leave.'

He wiped his eyes and saw the wetness of the tears in his hands. They seemed shameful and dirty in this puritanically genteel place, worse than snot. He looked up at the waitress. 'Sorry. Someone died recently. I thought I was okay.'

She raised a sceptical eyebrow and glanced in the direction of the two women nearby. It was a shock. He had not expected her to care particularly, but he did assume someone might believe him.

'You've got to go.'

He blinked and looked round for his rucksack. 'Okay. Just give me a minute.'

She did not move initially. 'Right. One minute from now.' Then she returned to the counter and exchanged a couple of words with her colleague. Both of them looked in his direction and went back to work.

Magnus decided to leave the rest of his coffee and reached for his rucksack.

From the corner of his eye a girl passed by the café window and entered, panting slightly. She wore simple functional clothes: jeans, a top. She had small Saxon lips and wide-set brown eyes, which she used to smile at him, before turning towards the counter. He knew it was meaningless but nevertheless it had arrived at a vulnerable moment, and he felt immensely grateful. Her hair was straight and quite short, tucked thoughtlessly behind her ears. With that hale figure and fresh open face he could imagine her Digging for Victory and travelling by bicycle. She looked so wholesome. He wondered what she was doing in twenty-first-century Edinburgh when she ought to have been organising a picnic in rural surroundings. But for all her old-fashioned prettiness he admired the quickness of her glance, her busyness, particularly in this conceited coffee enclave. She ordered a cappuccino to take away. Mid-twenties, he guessed. A trainee vet?

His dazed admiration of the young woman was cut short when the colours in the room suddenly intensified and he felt a tension in his stomach. He thought he might faint. Numbness had given way to hypersensitivity, panic even. It triggered a hypochondriac chain reaction that, in the space of less than a second, linked this latest symptom with his earlier back pain and from there to a range of potentially fatal African ailments whose highlights were cerebral malaria and one of the flesh-eating diseases. However, without either a temperature or holes appearing in his body, he had to consider the possibility that he was merely exhausted. His heartbeat settled down and his gaze returned to the woman who was now paying at the till. Or could it perhaps have been an emotion? He had heard of love at first sight but he had no idea whether it was normal to suffer such extreme symptoms.

He halted his feverish train of thought. His emotions were all over the place. It wasn't love. He might still have a girlfriend, if Felicity changed her mind. Plus his hands were shaking and the blood seemed to have drained from his face. Physically it felt more like anger. He hazarded that it might be delayed indignation at the way he had been spoken to by the waitress. Either way it seemed that his claims to normality were still a little premature. He reminded himself to try Felicity again or, failing that, one of their friends.

However, he had to acknowledge that the Land Girl's sympathetic smile made him feel better. Was there any reason, he asked himself, why he shouldn't simply go up there and start a conversation? His minute was nearly up after all. Once again his heart began to gallop and a flush returned to his cheeks. Unclear whether this was a good or bad sign, he grabbed his rucksack, rose and prepared a set of friendly wrinkles on his brow. Unfortunately his foot had become twined in the seat leg and he found himself hauling the chair around the table while frantically hopping. By the time he had unknotted himself the girl had shot out of the door. Maybe that was fate telling him she was not for him. Fate, or something like it. The two women at the near table had looks of open contempt on their faces. Disappointed, he went over to the till and set about convincing himself that this missed opportunity would all turn out for the best. He was in mourning, after all, and in no fit state to make new friends.

Isabel's was the only place he had to go. She would understand. But first he would have to buy some clean clothes. He looked at his trousers. Now, those might explain the reception he had been given. They were wrinkled, travel-stained, sweaty. Having once declared that clothes didn't matter, he now suspected otherwise. If only he had been born with the sixth sense, dress. Realising that the waitress was itching to get him out of the door, he paid and she dropped the change into his palm at arm's length.

Magnus came out of the café, the rucksack growing heavier by the minute, and located the nearest clothes shop, which he entered, nervously fingering his sheafless wallet. A man who disliked shopping in all its forms, but particularly clothes shopping, he was determined to minimise the trauma of this transaction. Speed was key. He shut the door with a ding and sensed, to his right, the presence of an assistant. He also sensed, to his dismay, the presence of designer clothing. Normally at this point Magnus would slowly reverse out of the establishment, but this time he held firm. By now the shop assistant had unfurled from behind the cash till, and Magnus was already striding smartly along the racks. Imperiously, he pulled out a garment for closer inspection, feeling, however, like an illiterate pretending to browse in a bookshop. Despite his best efforts the assistant's approach filled him with panic. He hated being watched as he went through the highly private process of gauging the absurdity of his appearance in a mirror. He also suspected that all shop assistants had a structural contempt for their customers and were constantly casting judgement on their vanity and ugliness. While pretending to inspect a pair of trousers whose colour he barely registered, he felt a growing conviction that he was not worthy of such clothes. He imagined that other pedestrians would stop and tut disapprovingly to see an expensive pair of trousers gone to waste on someone like him.

'Can I help at all?' asked the assistant.

Magnus jumped, even though the question could not be considered particularly surprising. Her smile was unpushy and friendly, but to him it seemed a mere veil for mockery. He defied her. 'Yes, actually you could. I was looking for trousers.'

She glanced at the pair in his hand then back to him. A playful smile appeared on her lips. 'How's your sister?'

Taken by surprise, he merely stared back at her. Not having met this woman in his life, he didn't want to break the news.

'She . . . she's fine,' he replied, and immediately regretted it. It seemed irresponsible, even dangerous, to deny Claire's death and encourage his paranoid delusion. No doubt he needed to face facts, stop chasing buses, and repress the urge to stake out ladies' toilets in coffee shops.

She cocked her head to the side and squinted strangely at him. 'C. Calder?'

He guessed that Claire must have done some of her clothes shopping here. He nodded. The assistant laughed and clapped her hands. 'I was right! Sorry, but you do look a bit alike. I wasn't sure till you picked out the trousers. Pelucci must run in the family.'

He swallowed and looked down at the label on the trousers in his hand. Pelucci. He'd never heard of it. The girl took them from him and glanced at the label. 'I think you're more like a thirty-four.' She went back to the rack and flicked through the hangers. 'I remember the name from the credit card. Your sister used to come here quite often. We chatted a bit, although she hasn't been in recently.'

He cleared his throat. 'That's because she moved to Africa.'

The girl returned with another pair of the trousers. 'Really? Try these on. I thought I saw her go past the window the other day. Back on a visit, perhaps.'

'I don't think so.' He took them.

Her own brow furrowed briefly. 'No? Well, then, maybe not. There's a cubicle behind you if you'd like to try them on.'

He turned woodenly towards the saloon-bar swinging doors. Was this possible? Of course it was, he told himself, as he entered the small, discreetly perfumed changing room: someone in this town has bought the same beret as Claire. And if this same person tried to shake off a lunatic running behind their bus, it hardly counted as suspicious behaviour. He pulled off his trousers, and stepped into the new ones, not convinced. He noticed irritably that the shop assistant was hovering beyond the door because he could see her shadow through the slats.

'Are they all right?' she asked. 'Don't worry if they're a little tight, there's quite a bit of give.'

It was like sitting in a public toilet and being asked by the attendant how everything was moving along. 'Fine,' he replied tolerantly.

'Shall I pick out a few shirts?'

He hadn't asked for shirts but he said yes to get her away, and the shadow between the slats disappeared. He zipped and buttoned the trousers. They fitted remarkably well. She must be good, he thought. A shirt flopped over the top of the door, making him jump. He hadn't noticed her return.

'The trousers fit fine,' he said, pulling the shirt down from the door. He looked at it and grimaced slightly: it had high collars and was patterned, just the kind of shirt that Claire had tried to persuade him to buy the last time she dragged him out on a shopping expedition. The kind of shirt that he would have instantly dismissed as loud or too trendy. He tried it on. The shadow was on the slats again but the girl had not said anything. 'Do you have any jackets?' he asked, as he buttoned the shirt.

A jacket flipped over immediately, again without a word. He pulled this down too. It was made of soft leather. How funny, he thought. Leather jackets were another thing Claire had failed to persuade him to buy. Too expensive, he had always said, too Hell's Angels. He shrugged it on and looked once more at the shadow on the door. Then the smile fell from his face. Suddenly he had lost confidence that it was the girl who had handed him these clothes.

'Are you there?' he asked, softly. Again, no answer. His right arm reached out and slowly pushed open the door. He peered out. The girl was there but with her back turned. She turned round and smiled.

'So, how are they?'

He breathed a sigh of relief and leant against the wall.

'Are you okay? You look a bit pale.'

He felt weak. 'It doesn't matter. The clothes are fine. I'll wear them to go.'

A transformed Magnus stepped out of the shop promising to pass on a hello to Claire when he next spoke to her. He did this with a pained grin. The lie felt so awkward, and he was also having to deal with the hit to his credit card. He turned left and walked rapidly up the hill, feeling jumpy, still disturbed by the fright he had given himself in the shop. Then he caught sight of himself in a shop window. It caused him to stop and stare. For once, a pleasant surprise. Internally he might be a mess, but outwardly he was a man of style and taste, relatively. The clothes were so well chosen that they almost gave credibility to his foul hairstyle. The only downside was that the rucksack now looked positively toxic. He held it away from his body, and turned to see himself in profile. Claire would have approved; in fact, she could almost have dressed him herself.

Seeing a telephone box up ahead, he decided to give Isabel a call.

Two

Magnus paid the taxi driver and emerged from the cab. It had dropped him at the mouth of Bellevue Terrace so that it could turn round, which left him a walk of fifty yards to Isabel's door. It seemed like a long way. Hoisting the rucksack, he walked the pavement, bent over like an old man. The straps of his bag impeded the flow of blood to his hands, which clapped numbly against his labouring thighs like table-tennis bats in a long and interminable rally. A breeze from the Forth caused his crippled hairstyle to flap damply. It was time to get off the street, but there was no guarantee that she would be in. His phone call had got the answering-machine.

From behind him came a high-pitched hoot and a motorbike pulled up sharply at the kerb beside him. The rider yanked up the visor of his helmet and grinned. 'Magnus! Is that you? Remember me?'

The man pulled his helmet off to reveal a completely shaven head and a duck-like top lip that warped into a friendly smile.

'Gav? It's good to see you again. You were at university with Claire, weren't you? Studying anthropology.'

They had met before a few times and got on well. Gav turned the engine off, then kicked down the bike stand with his boot. 'So how is it going?' he asked.

Gav became serious. 'I couldn't believe it when I heard the news. I am so sorry. Have you just come back?'

'Yes. Thanks.'

'Where are you off to?'

'A friend's. Isabel. You?'

'Home and then the Basement bar. Why not come along later – if you feel up to it, that is?'

Magnus scratched his head. 'Maybe. I don't want to depress anyone.'

Gav waved his hand dismissively. 'Don't be ridiculous.' Then he looked at Magnus with concern. 'It must be strange being back here, though, in her old haunts.'

'To put it mildly. It feels like she's still here, in my head at least.'

Gav nodded thoughtfully. 'I felt the same way when my dad died. But you know it was Claire who helped me out when I was down?'

Magnus's curiosity was pricked. 'Oh, yes?'

'She was writing her thesis at the time, on African ritual and stuff, and she told me about something she'd read, a tribal belief. Have you heard all this before?'

'I'm not sure. Go on.'

He laughed, mildly embarrassed. 'It sounds a bit nutty, but okay. There's this tribe in Madagascar or somewhere that believes in reincarnation. The way it works is, when a loved one dies the spirit migrates to their closest relative. Then, after a while, when it's got over having lost its body, it's ready to be reborn, and that's when someone else in the tribe or village gets pregnant.'

Magnus became curious. Claire's work had never interested him in the slightest when she was alive, and their communication had broken down somewhat in the last few months, out of laziness as much as anything. Now, these things seemed to have a fresh significance.

'But the interesting thing for me was how they think of grief. They don't see it like we do, as the pain of separation or loss. It's more like the shock of another spirit coming on board the same body. It's like you're bearing the weight of the spirit's anxiety somehow.'

Magnus considered that, and approved. 'I like that. It makes you feel you're being useful in some way, doesn't it?'

'That's what I thought. Didn't she ever tell you all this stuff?'

'I'm not sure I listened at the time. Although I remember her Buddhist phase quite vividly.'

They both smiled. It was true. How could he forget the day she'd come home from school with her hair shaved off and a commitment to veganism? 'You've gone mad,' he remembered Mother screaming, to which Claire had replied, with insouciance, that she ought to be grateful, adding, 'You're lucky the barber refused to shave my eyebrows.'

All the razors in the house were subsequently locked away and threats of solitary confinement were issued in the event that the eyebrows went. Claire had to content herself with converting Magnus to her nascent cult, which, since he was at the malleable age of thirteen, met with partial success. For a start, she looked quite good with short hair, like a streetwise Sinead O'Connor. Pep-talked and cajoled in the sisterly bedroom, befuddled by the fumes of joss, Magnus eventually visited the same barber's shop and had the initiate's grade-one cut. But if he hoped to emulate the shock effect of his sister when he got home, he was disappointed: everyone laughed at him at dinner. No, they roared – even Claire from behind her plate of rice and beans. He could still recall how his ears, always slightly prominent, had burned red with shame. Why did he always have to look the fool? Why did she always come out looking so good?

Gav appeared to sense Magnus drawing in on himself. 'Anyway, sorry to ramble, you're probably dying to put your feet up and relax a bit.'

'Okay. Oh, by the way, do you know where that thesis is by chance? I'd be curious to read it.'

'It must have got lost years ago. She threw most of that stuff away when she switched to teacher training. I'm off, then. See you later, maybe, or just drop by whenever you want. I'm in the bar most days.'

'See you.'

Gav turned the ignition on his bike and drove back on to the main road, leaving Magnus to complete the last few steps to Isabel's doorstep alone.

Standing in front of number fifteen, Bellevue Terrace, he realised that it was years since he had last visited, back in the era when Isabel and Claire had been renting together. It seemed a long time ago: he had been pale, poor, uneasily single and doing supply teaching to pay the rent while he continued to nurture, with increasing hopelessness, an ultra-low-budget film project. So what had changed? Well, he had a slight suntan. And he was determined never to return to teaching in London. Unless it was absolutely necessary, of course. Which gave him about two weeks in Edinburgh, unless he found money from somewhere. He wished he didn't have to worry about these things right now. It would be so much easier to have ready access to family money, like Isabel, for instance, instead of having to beg. Although he had to admit that life had never been easy for Isabel in other ways. Friends, self-esteem, academic success and a clear complexion had eluded her from an early age, apparently, until she came before Claire, one transforming day, during auditions for a university theatre production. How many times had he heard Isabel recall the great casting episode? The nerves, the stuttered lines, the flushing, and then the terrified euphoria when she received the note. Claire took a characteristic directorial risk and cast her in the lead female role of Lady Macbeth, in which Isabel would later be considered a modest success by the college rag. For Isabel, however, it was the crowning triumph of her life, for which she would pay Claire eternal gratitude.

All well and good if the experience had actually given her confidence and ambition, thought Magnus, but it had previously struck him that she had never quite recovered from the part. So far as he knew, since university she had gained little experience of acting work or, indeed, anything else. Claire's advice and encouragement was always listened to reverently, but Isabel had a chronic lack of initiative. When Claire left town to follow her own ambitions, she seemed to withdraw and immerse herself in nostalgia for those glorious student days. He shuddered to think how Isabel, always highly strung, would have taken the news. He had better prepare himself.

The door buzzer was quickly answered by a soft click and hiss from the grille. 'Yes?'

He reared back. The intercom alarmingly amplified Isabel's voice. Waiting a moment, he then leant in cautiously and put a smile on his face. He believed in giving good intercom, whatever the circumstances. 'Hello, Isabel, it's Magnus here.'

'Magnus!' Her exclamation had not given him time to retreat a safe distance and the distressed intercom responded by whistling something vaguely Hawaiian-sounding. Her disembodied voice floated over the inter-ference: 'Come in, come up. I will be with you in a moment.'

The door sprang open and he barged his way in with the rucksack, pleased that she didn't sound too depressed, but a little surprised too. He arrived on the second floor, panting, and found the door. He knocked and waited. Some hurried activity could be heard behind it – last-minute tidying presumably – while further down the corridor her neighbour was playing the Monkees. The inappropriately cheerful music jarred his delicate nerves. He wished she would hurry up and let him in.

Until Isabel opened the door Magnus would never have believed that beauty could arise out of suffering. His experience so far had taught him that grief was messy, ugly and corrosive. When she appeared, however, he had to concede that grief had performed expert flattery. The pale complexion and sharp cheekbones were lovingly enhanced. Her blonde, slightly curly hair was cut short, while her body remained slim and upright. When she saw him, her upper lip arched and showed her teeth, which were prettily set apart. Where he was puffed-up and blotchy, she was alabaster; while grief had crumpled him physically and shoved him out of alignment, the same emotion had given her the discreet glow of a modern martyr. As ever, her sad blue eyes were rimmed with anguish, although this time the motives were noble, rather than vaguely hopeless.

They both stood there, neither quite knowing what to do. In the past they had always met in Claire's presence. In normal circumstances the two women would hug and kiss and he would drift in on the back of his sister's charismatic wave. Now the rules had changed. Everything had. Amid this uncertainty his sister's absence now seemed more palpable than ever. For a start he and Isabel had never been at all physical with one another. Considering herself Claire's best friend, Isabel's observation of distance could have signified either lack of attraction, or its opposite. Until now he had never given it much thought. But her acquisition of beauty – which he couldn't help feeling was somehow disgraceful – now made it an issue.

She had been caught unprepared. Her hair was ruffled

and she looked as if she had only recently dressed or got out of bed. Now that he looked closer her face glowed not with spiritual radiance but with freshly applied moisturiser or some other unguent. A slight flush of excitement appeared on her cheeks and when she smiled her welcome he also noticed a dab of lipstick on one of her front teeth, presumably left over from the night before. He had never seen her wear makeup before and had never imagined her spending evenings out in company. But perhaps that was his problem, not hers. Besides, he was also being assessed in these first busy seconds of reunion. He smiled ruefully, dropped his rucksack to the floor and pushed his smudged glasses back up the bridge of his nose. The new clothes helped, he hoped.

She opened her mouth to speak but was interrupted by a boom of music. The neighbouring door had opened and two wealthy-looking male students emerged, laughing raucously. They glanced at Magnus without curiosity, then clattered down the stairs. The door was shut again from within, muffling the Monkees so that the song's ecstatic refrain sounded, to Magnus at least, like 'I'm a bereaver'. A manic laugh swelled in his chest but he kept it there. Now was not the time for black comedy. He returned his attention to Isabel, waiting for her to complete her sentence.

'Magnus,' she said, in a soft resonant voice, 'she has shed her body but her spirit is still with us. With you especially.'

Isabel dramatised even when the subject-matter was quite dramatic enough. As a result the moment felt awkward. The nice thing was she made him feel relatively sane. He took a moment to formulate an appropriate reply. 'Thanks, Isabel.'

Leaning forwards, he put a hand on her shoulder and pecked her on the cheek, to which she didn't respond one way or the other. Her eyes were distant, her half-smile stayed where it was; she didn't even invite him in. He gauged the situation carefully. 'Can I ask you a small favour, Isabel, please?'

She became grave and gripped his hands tightly. He was suddenly the focus of all her attention. 'Ask me whatever you want, even if it sounds mad. If there is anything I can do. Anything.'

He took another uneasy moment. 'Great. Thanks. But you might find it a bit tricky.'

'Tell me, Magnus. What is it?'

He cleared his throat. 'Can we act normally, please?'

He saw the first glimmer of uncertainty in Isabel's face. 'I . . . don't understand.'

'I mean, can we pretend that none of this has happened for a few minutes? I'm totally jet-lagged, stressed-out, smelly. I can't think straight, I've had a very weird time. I need a shower and a cup of tea, and then I want to talk about something trivial. Anything. Anything but – that. For the time being.' He looked at her straight. 'Can you do that for me?'

She seemed to shrink slightly. She bit her lip. Then she let go of his hands and stepped aside to let him in. 'Of course I can. I'm sorry. I should have thought of that myself. Please come in.'

'Not at all.'

Cheered, he stepped inside and shrugged off the rucksack with a groan of relief. He glanced around him at the flat, which he had not seen in ages. Everything was new. No way could her alleged acting career have paid for this. He knew from Claire that the family was rich; apparently they earned their money from sports equipment, and were based somewhere insidious like Loughborough. 'Wow, this is an improvement. It looks lovely.'

Isabel, it seemed, was having problems adjusting to the disciplines of small-talk, but she made the effort. 'Yes, thank you. I had it decorated not long ago, after I'd bought it.'

'Really nice. Can I go through?'

'Yes. Of course. Can I offer you—' She interrupted herself. 'But you already said. Tea.'

'Thanks. One sugar.'

'Yes. Right.'

Isabel had followed him into the sitting room but then exited left and went into the kitchen to put on the kettle. He cast his eye over the heavy tablecloths that hung down to the floorboards, the covered lamps and framed prints of eighteenth-century rural life. Heavy brass fire irons were ranged in front of a fake coal fireplace beside a large CD collection of classical music. The overall impression was half Victorian boudoir, half country house. It was old-fashioned and slightly exotic: not an entirely accurate reflection of Isabel, but not far off either. On the wall, holding pride of place, was a framed poster advertising the legendary student production of *Macbeth*, with Isabel's face peering over the shoulder of the male lead. At the bottom was written: 'directed by Claire Calder', followed by several other credits. Magnus realised that a decade had passed since then. A lifetime for his sister.

Isabel was saying something in the kitchen but he had not been listening. 'Sorry?' he called, but didn't receive an answer, so he continued to stare at the poster.

She came back into the room. Pulling out of his reverie, he asked the dreaded question, mainly to get it out of the way: 'How's the acting coming along, then?'

She looked distracted. 'Oh, some small parts at the Lyceum, a bit of TV work, you know, nothing very exciting right now.'

'Good. Oh, by the way, I ran into Gav when I was coming here. Do you know him? He remembered something quite sweet that Claire wrote in a thesis.'

'I thought we couldn't talk about Claire,' she snapped.

He conceded her point. 'You got me there. Of course we can, now. I just needed to get my bearings. I was wondering, do you remember what it was about? African religions or something, wasn't it?'

'No, I don't remember, not off the top of my head.'

'He said she threw a lot away.'

The kettle whistled and Isabel hurried back into the kitchen. He turned and looked out of the window: so much was lost and irretrievable. Perhaps one day he would even forget Claire's face. Inevitably, the full picture would fade, leaving just a few stubborn nodes of reference – the shape of her nose, the way she smiled – from which he would have to join the dots; dots, like constellations, that would become ever more distant, and difficult to read.

He turned towards the kitchen but stopped before the door. Once again he heard her talking softly as she located mugs and teaspoons, although it was difficult to pick up what she was saying. Music could still be heard through the walls from next door. Softly, he approached her from behind and listened as she chattered away on her own.

'Yes, he does look worn out, poor thing. Needs feeding up? Please! You're not his mother.' She poured hot water into the mugs, then she laughed to herself. 'But do you think he will stay? Wouldn't it be lovely if he did? Yes. Quite.'

Magnus was somewhat bemused. 'Talking to yourself?' he asked.

Isabel swung round and spilt hot water over her hand. She seemed disoriented as she groped for an answer. 'No. Listening.'

Magnus took a moment to realise that she had just made a joke. Listening to herself instead of talking to herself. Good. A bit weird, but good. He laughed with appreciation, but then noticed that her hand was red.

'You've scalded yourself. That's my fault for making you jump. Let me see.'

Unprotestingly she showed him her hand. He turned on the cold tap at the sink and put it under the stream of water. He held it there for a moment. She was looking at him curiously. He let go and stepped back.

'Thank you, Magnus, I'm fine now. I'll be through in a second.'

He returned to the sitting room, where he slumped on the sofa and wondered what was going on. Talking to yourself wasn't a crime, but it made him uneasy for some reason. Still, at least he knew he had a bed if he needed one. His eyes floated across the furnishings until they settled on an old ceramic cider butt, which contained a silver-topped walking stick and a green-patterned umbrella. He recognised the umbrella: it used to be Claire's. Stuck there carelessly like that, unfurled with a bent spoke, it was so easy to imagine that she had used it five minutes before.

Isabel entered the room with two steaming mugs and noticed what he had been looking at. She stopped in the middle of the room. He got up, took his tea, then nodded towards the umbrella with a small grimace. 'It's like she's just popped out of the room, isn't it?'

Pointedly she said nothing: he had asked to keep their talk small, and she was going to respect his wishes until he apologised. Sighing, he sat down again, took a slurp of tea, then looked up at her; she had not moved a muscle. He gave up. 'Isabel, I'm sorry for being so silly at the door. Only I had such a shock this morning. I'd just got off the coach, I was walking the streets, getting some fresh air, and then I could have sworn I saw Claire.'

He waited for her response. She frowned with sympathetic concern and came to sit next to him, ready to listen. Reassured, he continued: 'Honestly, my heart nearly stopped. I didn't see the face, but her clothes, the manner-isms, everything seemed to suggest it was her. Although obviously . . .' He faded out and laughed nervously.

Isabel put a hand on his knee and squeezed. 'Go on.'

'I actually ran after the bus and chased her down to a café. And when it turned out to be nobody I felt — desolate. Hurt. Like she had seen me but wanted to avoid me. Or didn't care.' His voice quivered. 'Or didn't even recognise me. I thought I was going mad.'

Isabel tutted. 'You're not going mad. No, no.'

'But it was even worse before that. For the past two weeks, I've just felt numb. Literally unable to feel myself. Like I'd been partially jolted out of my body. It was horrible.' He stared at her, searching for a sign that she thought he was strange. But all he saw was concern. His head went into his hands again. 'God, it's just self-pity, isn't it? Claire's dead, and here I am complaining about my paranoias.'

Isabel moved up close and took him in her arms. She held him as he struggled not to sob and she continued to hold him as he slowly took control once more. Eventually he gave her a little squeeze back and they parted.

'It's all normal, Magnus. Normal. I've had the same thing. I ended up cornering a foreign-exchange student who was wearing a similar hat.'

He laughed. 'Really?'

'I think I might have given her a fright.'

'I think I may have too. No wonder she legged it.'

She responded calmly. 'It feels so inexplicable and strange for everyone. But just remember, you're not alone.'

He smiled through watery eyes. 'Thanks for being here. It's a real help.'

'We're not alone.'

'No, we're not.'

'She's still with us. She really is.'

He wiped an eye. 'Yes, I suppose so.'

'In fact I was just talking to her.'

His hand fell slowly from his eyes to his lap. He nodded steadily and leant forwards. 'Talking.'

'Yes. I find it helps. And seeing you again is wonderful.' She raised a hand timidly to touch his cheek. 'The likeness. I can see her in you. It's a comfort.'

He hoped he didn't look disconcerted. How hypocritical he would feel, spewing out his exotic experiences only to shrink back from the confessions of the person who had listened to him so understandingly.

'Magnus, do you really believe it was her you saw?'

Her eyes searched his face. Her earnestness made him uncomfortable. If he said yes to her question he realised that she might actually take him seriously. He looked away, and his eye snagged on the umbrella again. A suspicion crept into his mind, then crept away again. He shrugged and fell back on rationalism. 'No. Obviously it can't have been. Though it did feel like it at the time. There must be someone who looks like her.'

She looked thoughtful. 'Unless . . .' But then she stopped herself. 'No.'

He sat up. 'What were you going to say?'

'Everyone experiences something strange in their life. Something they have to struggle to explain. I suppose that in the end it comes down to belief.'

Magnus scraped his chin, disconcerted by the mention

of religion. 'I don't really have any faith. I suppose I'm trying to understand it as . . .' He sought the correct word. 'Adjustment.'

It sounded hopelessly inadequate and he saw the dismay in her face, but it was rapidly smothered by loyalty and she nodded respectfully. He noticed that the music from next door had been shut down, thank God. The silence lengthened.

'Can I take that shower now? I need to pop round to my parents' after.'

'Of course. I'll show you where it is. I had a new one put in.'

They got up together and moved towards the hallway, but then she stopped and looked at him seriously. 'About the umbrella. Claire left it behind. No need for it in Africa, I suppose. I hope you don't mind that I use it.'

'Don't be silly.'

'I should probably have taken it round to your parents'. I did mean to. But, you know, it's just about the only thing of hers that I've got.'

'Isabel, please, keep it, it's yours.'

'You could take it with you if you wanted.'

He found his patience depleting. 'Isabel. I said keep it. So keep it.'

Satisfied, she led the way. 'All right, then, I will.'

Taking him down the corridor she pointed out the bathroom door and, opposite it, a guest room, which looked very comfortable indeed. 'You know you can stay here, if you want. As long as you like.'

'Yes, I do know. Isabel, that's really kind.'

'I mean it.'

'Thanks for the offer, but . . .'

She raised her hand to interrupt him. 'Is that a yes?'

'Not yet it isn't. I need to talk to my parents first. Plus I'm thinking of actually moving up here, starting a video business. I'll need to rent a place of my own.'

She seemed very pleased. 'Well, that's wonderful. But why not move in here? At least until you've found a place of your own.'

Ungratefully, perhaps, he wasn't at all sure. 'I'll just take that shower.'

Biting her lip, she stepped back to let him pass. He went into the bathroom and softly shut the door, just as she added, 'There's clean towels and . . .'

The click of the lock cut her off. He leant against the tiled wall and sighed with relief, then stripped off his clothes and turned on the shower. He put his hand under the head to test the temperature and realised, with a start of pleasure, that he no longer needed to worry about scalding his numb body. Pushing up the temperature a little further, he stepped in and gloried at the passage of every trickle of water over his skin. The heat seeped into his muscles and his shoulders flexed as the tension gave. Amid the wreaths of steam his hands joined over his belly and slowly, solemnly, he bowed his head under the jet of hot water, as if in front of a private Cenotaph. The seconds passed; his fringe became a spout. One minute became two. But he wasn't performing an act of remembrance; it was an act of forgetting.

Three

Magnus reached his parents' house at Inverleith Row by foot. It was a long street of solid Victorian dwellings and lay just beyond the New Town boundary, marked by a clock, which also served in his mind as the last outpost of Claire's territory. He felt nervous as he walked, and only slowed his pace when he was well beyond it. His sighting of Claire earlier that morning still preyed on him, despite the soothing possibility that she might have been a foreign student, as Isabel had suggested. What if it really had been Claire? Those fingers that he saw plucking at the throat through the departing bus window had been real; he was sure of it. He shuddered, then felt guilty: why, he asked himself, should a person's death cause them to become frightening? His earlier instinct to run after Claire had surely been worthier of her memory than this cowardly fear that he might see her again.

But he still couldn't understand why, if it was her, she had run from him. Was it because she wanted to spare him trauma or shock, or could it be that the dead were scared of the living? He paused at a side-street to let a car past and pondered this curious thought. Perhaps Claire needed time to reveal herself. Perhaps she was watching and waiting, shadowing him until the right moment came along. That would explain why he didn't feel alone. If so, it was fine by him. He was at her disposal. He would never run from her, not in any circumstances.

Magnus stopped outside a small front garden, which separated the busy road traffic from the tall bay windows of the house. It was a prosperous part of town and replica dwellings ran all the way up the gentle hill, occupied no doubt by bankers approaching retirement and the odd family hoisted up the property ladder by a move from London. From the back garden he knew that the spring leaves of the botanical gardens would be visible above the fence, touched a fetching shade of grey by the city pollution. There would be the disconsolate sound of ducks and perhaps the squawk of toddlers being led towards the aquarium. To be outside the New Town, even by half a kilometre, felt like returning to earth. Thanks to the tea and shower at Isabel's he felt better prepared for this parental encounter.

Lifting the rucksack Magnus opened the low metal gate and pressed the doorbell. Its tinny note echoed along the corridor within; he waited. On the whole Magnus regressed emotionally with his parents, reverting to a teenage state of confused resentment and unreasonable demands. But now, to his surprise, he anticipated the scales of power shifting. He had dealt more or less single-handedly with the situation in Africa and now his parents would be needing his support. The process of becoming an adult was sometimes terrifying but it could also provide a sharp thrill. He was about to see his parents as they really were: human beings stripped raw.

'Coming!'

Magnus heard the familiar voice, and some familiar footsteps come stamping down the corridor. There was a brief scuffle and scrape, then the door opened to reveal a plump man of middle age heaving golf clubs on to his shoulder. This was Father. He had become oval and smoothly bald in the last ten years, which nevertheless somehow suited his bumptious energy levels. He looked like he could be grabbed by his large ears and bounced around the garden. Impressively, he could also be quizzed on corporate-tax issues and get all the answers right – for a fee. In fact, Magnus's father could do many of the things that Magnus couldn't, golf being a pertinent example. But the jolly smile fell from the rotund face when he saw his son, and was replaced by undisguised horror. The Grim Reaper had appeared on his doormat, and was about to cancel the game.

Magnus was sufficiently shocked to play the part with gusto. Clearly Father had expected the doorbell to be golfing partners, ready to give them a lift to the course. With slow and damning judgement he looked down from the golf clubs to the outward-pointing brogues. The bottoms of the golfing trousers stopped a good inch above the shoes, tailored to what he claimed were Armed Forces Regulation Trouser Length. Magnus wondered how, if true, the British Army got taken at all seriously.

'Father,' Magnus said sombrely.

'My God,' Father replied. 'Magnus!' He looked over his son's shoulder, as if he was expecting a smirking television crew at the bottom of the drive (they had been bothered by local journalists when the news broke). 'What are you doing here?'

'I'm back from Namibia. I gave you the dates, remember?'

The answer was patently no, they had not remembered. So the two of them waited for Mother to approach. She would know what to do. Magnus was still standing outside when she appeared in the hallway. He noted bitterly that she was also wearing golf apparel and carrying clubs. Father stepped back so that she could see the disturbing development. She stopped in her tracks and put a leather golf-gloved hand to her mouth. 'Magnus.'

'Mother.'

'You're here!'

'Yes.'

Sensibly assessing what the situation required, she set down the clubs to embrace him, but was concerned that they might slip down and damage the wallpaper. Magnus watched her as, gingerly, she laid the golf-bag flat on the burgundy carpet. She took some time to arrange the woods so that the golf-club cosies nuzzled comfortably together. Then, satisfied, she straightened and smoothed the wrinkles in her trousers, which had gathered beneath her jutting belly. That small bulge, which had once contained Magnus and before him his sister, had since been bolstered by other items: individually wrapped mini

46

pork pies ingested every Saturday evening in front of the television; celery sticks and diet dips; flat white bread and cold-cuts shorn of their quivering fat. Magnus remembered that his stomach had felt empty on his walk from Isabel's. Now it was flooding with bile and his appetite was cured for ever. His new-found maturity went the same way, decimated by adolescent fury: he was outraged by his parents' apparent well-being, he was disgusted by Mother's golf-club cosies and he bitterly resented the way they were about to put up with his rage with such insufferable tolerance.

She stepped over the furry club-covers, indicated that her husband should stand back to give her more room, then held out her arms and showed that she was ready to perform the maternal embrace. She did this with short inward hand gestures that made Magnus think of the flippers of a pinball machine. But it worked. His anger swivelled violently into neediness, and he found himself stepping forwards to be firmly stifled in diamond-chequered yellow lambswool. He heard a heavy clunk; it must have been Father letting his golf-bag drop on to the scrubbed stone doorstep. Her body stiffened with irritation on hearing this, perhaps for fear of damage to the floorboards, but she was sufficiently moved by their reunion not to say anything.

'You forgot, didn't you?' Magnus whined, muffled slightly by Mother's breastmeat. He lifted his head up. 'How could you forget?'

There was a pause and Magnus was released. He cast an injured look of filial accusation from one parent to the other. They looked at one another gravely, a look Magnus instantly bridled at because it appeared to exclude him. The usual parental telepathy occurred, then they nodded agreement and stepped back to let him in. Magnus could hardly believe it: were they in some kind of mad denial? Had they completely flipped? He was tempted to force them into an open declaration of penance, but suddenly found that he couldn't be bothered. His petulance lapsed into exhaustion; it was an old trick of theirs.

The ritual of return began. With a glazed expression, he wiped his feet on the welcome mat using hygienic backward kicks as prescribed by Mother. Next he held out his filthy rucksack and dropped it into a plastic bin-liner that Mother had whisked from one of her hidden drawers. The bundle was then taken directly to the utility room, in preparation for disinfection and all the other necessary precautions.

Magnus then entered and turned left into the sitting room. Claire, of course, would have stomped straight through all these unwritten regulations just to be annoying (back in the days when she visited at all), even though she wouldn't have dreamt of soiling her own flat: cleanliness was in her genes. Magnus, on the other hand, was slovenly but ultimately obedient. When he was younger he hoped that his messiness was a symptom of latent creativity. Many drafts of a screenplay later, he was forced to entertain alternative explanations. He just didn't have the energy.

From the utility room he heard the washing-machine sucking in water, and Mother joined him a few seconds later, pulling down her sleeves. He heard a car pull up outside the house. She glanced out on to the street. 'Just you set yourself down there,' she said. 'Would you like a glass of shandy?'

He said he would. It was a beverage that he had always disliked and Mother had always stocked. She smiled as if she knew her son's ways and bustled into the kitchen.

Father joined him. 'You look as if you're bearing up,' he said gruffly.

Magnus was not inclined to respond. In the ensuing silence Father looked him up and down approvingly and tried to think of something to say while Magnus stared sullenly back. 'Smart,' he said at last. 'Good.'

'Jesus,' said Magnus under his breath.

Father frowned and looked at his watch. 'Darling, Gordon and Kitty are outside and we're due to tee off in under forty minutes.'

'Well, just you go out and tell them that I'm seeing to Magnus,' she called from the kitchen, 'I won't be long.'

Father seemed mildly displeased. 'See you in a bit, then.' He went out.

Magnus looked around the room, from the fancy wall clock to the vile Thai prints brought back from a holiday five years before. Something was missing, although he couldn't identify what it was.

Mother re-entered and rolled her eyes, seeking his indulgence for Father's brusqueness. She handed over the can with a colourful plastic beaker and laid two drink mats on the coffee-table; one for the can, one for the beaker.

'Your father's been very depressed,' she whispered, as she leant down. 'It will do him good to get out. And our friends have been so kind. We couldn't very well keep turning down their invitations. And how are you, dear? You must be exhausted.'

He shrugged.

'I'll just do the nine holes seeing as you're here, then we can hear all the news.'

He sighed. 'Mother, you don't have to cut short your fun for me.'

She straightened up. 'Oh, well, in that case we can wait for dinner this evening. You're not going anywhere just now, are you? There's sandwich material in the usual places. Tidy up after yourself, please. See you later this afternoon.' She air-kissed the tip of a leather-clad finger and dabbed his nose with it, then went out, shutting the door behind her.

The car drove off. He heard the refrigerator start up its electrical hum. He looked around the room again and only then noticed an empty silver picture frame. With a small cry of righteous indignation he jumped up and proceeded carefully to ransack the house, including every one of Mother's known drawers, until at last he unearthed what he was looking for: the photo albums.

He opened the first and flipped through it, tossed it away and started on the second, then the third. His jaw wagged soundlessly. Gone. Excised. Not a single picture of Claire remained. He sat back, disbelieving.

A moment later his eyes hardened and he searched in earnest, destructively, throwing stuff over his shoulder until he managed to locate, at the back of a linen drawer, one bent old passport photo. She must have been about fifteen, with straggly dark hair and an uncertain leer on her face. But it would have to do. Returning downstairs, he wiped the already spotless picture frame with his sleeve and placed the tiny image eloquently in the centre. It was then returned to its rightful place, below Father's line-up of antique pewter tankards.

He stepped back and grunted with a certain satisfaction. It was truly a dreadful picture. The light was so bad and the hair hung so limply that you couldn't even see her mole, and it was one of those details without which an entire face lost its charm. Positioned about a centimetre above her top lip on the right, it resembled a Regency beauty spot and gave her face a hint of decadence completely at odds with her personality. Without it her nose seemed a little too long, her mouth a little too wide, and her wit a little too sharp. With it, her brains and intensity became fascinating. The mole suggested she had a hidden side to her nature, which men probably hoped was a passionate interest in sex. They were close, but wrong. It was a passionate interest in death. He didn't know whether she was ever aware of her mole's power, or if she really considered it a minor defect as she tended to claim. Unfortunately it was too late to ask.

He adjusted the frame's position slightly. He knew that he was using her here as little more than a chess piece against his parents. But he didn't believe that she would mind. She might even have approved.

Wearily, Magnus stepped over the littered items and

climbed the stairs to his room. But hold on: did he just think of it as 'his' room? Perhaps he should have said the 'guest room', which was what his parents called it when he was supposed to be out of hearing. He was particularly sensitive to these things. It reminded him of the way they had sneakily sold the big family home in County Durham when he and Claire had been away at their respective universities, then timed their purchase of this Edinburgh house just as Claire left to take up a job in London. Coincidence? Maybe. His parents had always maintained a sneaky distance.

The first thing he did on entering the room was check the bedside drawer. Inside, to his immense relief, he found a sheaf of bound papers. It was the first draft of his screenplay, with '*The Existentialist* by Magnus Calder' printed on the title page. Pressing the dog-eared sheaf to his chest, he savoured a mix of dreaminess and acute self-consciousness. Magnus Calder. Its Scottishness sounded impressive, he thought, for which he and the family had to thank a stray Dundonian, apparently. In reality they were English, his parents having moved north purely for the purposes of golf and a less demanding job for Father. Magnus ruffled the manuscript's pages affectionately and put it back safely in the drawer.

He then noticed with alarm that his second most sentimentally precious item, an Airfix model of a Lancaster bomber, had been removed. In its place was a hand-painted stork with a baby in its beak, a shepherd lass with a basket of eggs; and two bottle-nosed dolphins smirking in the ceramic surf. Mother had to be responsible for those obscenities, although he was less certain about a strikingly ugly wooden carving in the corner. What was it? Some kind of monkey's head? A baboon? Magnus picked it up with distaste. About four inches high and quite heavy for its size, it seemed out of place next to Mother's other ornaments. The creature's mouth was wide open to show sharpened teeth, and its front paws were raised under the chin. Turning it over, he found a small ridge around the base, which suggested that the head connected to another piece. He put the carving back. Perhaps Father had brought it back from one of their (in his opinion rather extravagant) holidays, on which he was never invited. Eyeing the ceramics once more, he had a small, vicious urge to smash them. But instead he decided to take the moral high ground in preparation for the evening encounter. Besides, Mother would not have thrown away his Airfix model, surely.

She had not. He found it in the cupboard and a smile spread across his face as he held it up and flew it once around the room at arm's length. Then he flopped down on the bed and inspected the broken propeller on the port wing. Claire had been responsible for that. The incident was still fresh in his mind even though he had been seven years old when it happened. It was the day he learnt about life's great flaw. The past surged up once more.

Magnus had been administering a version of extreme unction to his fading hamster, Trumps. He was at an age when he already knew about heaven and the Holy Ghost, but watching death physically happen was a much more profound revelation. He positioned himself beside the sawdust-filled tank, misting the glass with his breath. Watching the rodent's laboured breathing, he was moved and appalled. Over the hours, as the movement of its furry belly became gradually less pronounced, his young mind began fully to grasp the tragic enormity of death. He had been in this elated, tearstained state of enlightenment when Claire had barged in and ruined it all.

'What's going on?' she demanded, and peered over his shoulder.

At this point Trumps was riding the last dip. His snout was pointing upwards, while his little chin of matted white fur trembled almost imperceptibly. Magnus took a while to respond. He wanted to encapsulate in a dignified phrase the sheer scale of what was happening, but it was impossible. 'Trumps,' he said eventually, 'is going to sleep.'

Claire looked closer, then screamed, 'No, he's not, he's dying! Quick, we've got to save him.' With that she reached into the tank, grabbed Trumps and took him to the nearest surface, which happened to be a draining-board. 'Stand back!' she ordered, when he tried to intervene. He was sent flying back against the wall and had to watch, sobbing uncontrollably, as she attempted cardiac massage with an index finger and mouth-to-mouth resuscitation, which could only be achieved by putting her whole mouth round poor Trumps's head and blowing. He was very soon dead and Claire left the room in a vile temper. 'You could have saved him, you evil little bugger, but you preferred to watch.'

Magnus managed to forgive her, mainly because she

took the loss much harder than he did. She was ill for several days and would not get out of bed until she had been inspected by a doctor, pronounced fit, then dragged from the sheets by Mother. Ordered to sit at the table and eat supper with her brother, she just scowled at her plate. He had watched her with curiosity: what on earth would deter anyone from eating egg-and-soldiers?

'I'm not going to die,' she said at last, with ferocious conviction. 'You lot can if you want to, but not me.' And at bedtime he discovered that she had stepped on his recently constructed Airfix model.

Magnus knew that most people would have found the tantrum of a ten-year-old girl something to laugh about and forget. Claire, after all, had grown into an outwardly sane young woman. It would have been natural to assume that she had a settled if neglectful relationship with her own mortality. For most young people, after all, death was something that happened to others. But Magnus sensed, partly from her silence on the subject ever after, that beneath her confident exterior, at her core, death was an implacable underlying daily terror.

He could hear the washing-machine churning downstairs. Sprawled on the bed, his eyelids fluttered for a second. He could definitely understand Claire's fear, but he didn't share it. The spin cycle began, causing a soft whine to reach his ears. Hardly a pleasant sound, it was nevertheless familiar and sent him to sleep.

His hands woke first. They jerked towards his face to pat and prod the skin, fearing that the numbness had returned. Fortunately, however, his cheeks felt the fingertips, and he sighed with relief. His heart stopped bouncing against his ribcage, and he turned on to his side, blinking in the gloom. It had been a deep, jet-lagged sleep. There was a noise on the landing: it had to be Mother, tidying up the chaos he had left behind after the search for Claire's pictures. Claire, who was dead. Claire, who might yet be alive. His heart was beating fast again and he sat up, attempting to divert his thoughts to less distressing topics. Mother tiptoed past his room. This reminded him of childhood fevers, where in his dreams the world had reverted to a gargantuan ocean and he was being tossed up against a sky, which was taut as a sheet, distorted by faces. He remembered how he used to wake up from these nocturnal drownings, gratefully panting in the dry air. Now, as an adult, the panic and relief were replaced by straight melancholy: there was no hell, but there was no heaven either, and the dead were left to roam.

He drew himself up and put his feet on the floor. A drawer clunked shut beyond the door. There was no doubt that other people were suffering in this house. Nobody brushed off the death of a daughter. He told himself he shouldn't be angry with his parents because they continued to play golf and cling to normality. If only they wouldn't shut him out when all he wanted to do was help. This was hard to forgive, because it confirmed his suspicion that he had always been shut out. Noises were emanating from the kitchen and so he began to look for his shoes: there were matters to be discussed.

His bad post-snooze mood had not improved when they sat down to dinner. Behind Father's head, he could see the large picture frame containing Claire's tiny face. She was still slightly askew. Leaving it be must have caused Mother's orderly mind a good deal of anguish. Clearly, then, something was afoot. But no mention had yet been made of the ransacked house they had come home to. She placed the grilled gammon steaks on the kitchen table and he eyed them warily. Each portion had a suspiciously identical shape; while this might have been a result of the pig's figure, to Magnus it was typical of this conformist little household. Buffalo scrotums arrived next, puffy, grey and wrinkled, although on closer inspection they proved to be overcooked jacket potatoes. He stabbed his with a fork. It sighed.

'So, Magnus,' said Mother as she sat down at the table, 'do tell us *all about it.*'

It sounded as if she asking about a safari trip he had taken rather than wanting to know the details surrounding her daughter's death. Father began calmly to eat.

'Are you sure you want to hear? I told you most of it on the phone.'

'Yes, Annie,' said Father. 'He's told us the substantive facts.'

'I know. But still.' Mother paused to cut her potato. She steadied it with a finger and struck home firmly with the fork. This produced a puff of superheated steam, but she didn't wince. Magnus watched, fascinated. Numbness must be her natural state. If she ever went down in a flaming jumbo he wouldn't be surprised if the rescuers found only a battered flight recorder and a full set of fingers in the economy section, wrapped around a carbonised handbag strap.

'It was in the *Scotsman* too,' said Father. 'Last thing you need, having the press on your tail at a time like that.'

'They didn't do a bad job of it, though, darling, did they? They used the nice photo.'

The potato was briskly disembowelled, its innards mashed and buttered. Magnus, who had immediately stiffened at the word 'photo', continued to watch. He was amazed by their insouciance. The picture frame on the shelf continued to go ignored, even though it blared for attention like an approaching lorry.

'I'll go through it again, if you want,' said Magnus, willing himself to be dispassionate. 'The car was driven by an American aid worker. Claire had got a lift from him to go into town, pick up her mail, do the shopping. They were on the road to Rundu when they most likely hit a sand spot. They rolled, it broke both their necks and the car was found burning.'

A pause was required. His chest felt tight, and he closed his eyes. For a split second Namibia came back to him. Red dustclouds rose in swirling Paisley patterns, like those that had lifted into the sky behind his car as he drove to Claire's school in the north. Women walked under mounds of firewood, improbably nonchalant. They passed by with the regularity of street-lamps while the dirt road was straight as a motorway, aiming towards a flat sky of blue. He could feel the miles per hour creep up, and how the threat of sand spots receded in the hot slipstream. He knew how the sky had rolled for her, blue twisting to red, over and over, until all momentum died and the horizon steadied once more, marred only by a black funnel of smoke. He saw the truck's underbelly glimmering in the sun as fire roared softly within.

A split second. He opened his eyes and forced himself to continue. 'It's how tourists die, apparently, although not always in flames. The fuel tank was ruptured. I signed the forms at Windhoek police station. She was cremated and I scattered her up near the school where she worked, as we agreed.'

He had succeeded in getting to the end. Then, for no sensible reason, he decided to be malicious. 'Of course, it might have helped if you'd come over too, but I understand completely.'

Father's knife paused in its sawing but he said nothing and his eyes didn't move from his plate. Magnus knew that he had overstepped the mark. Tears appeared in Mother's eyes and he felt bitter satisfaction. She was ashamed, and rightly too.

'We talked about that before you flew out to Namibia,' she said. 'You can't say that now, when we agreed everything before.'

Magnus cut up his gammon steak into a series of small triangles. The punctured buffalo scrotum remained uneaten. His appetite had disappeared again. 'I see you've cleared out the photos of her. What did you do? Burn them?'

Quite suddenly his father broke down. He jackknifed forwards and his mouth hung open. His face went red as if something was caught in his throat. But it wasn't that. His eyes were crunched up and a string of saliva extended

itself from a corner of his lip and gyrated dangerously as
his body vibrated with a long, deep, silent sob. Magnus
watched; his mouth hung open too. His wish had been
fulfilled: this was Father as never before, and it was
appalling.

Father twisted away from the table, wiped his mouth
with his hand, got up, and went over to a package that
Magnus had not noticed sitting on the sofa. He opened
it and from the top took a heavy envelope, which he
put to one side, causing several photographs to spill
out. The rest of the package was made up of video
cassettes. With a streak of spit still glistening on his
chin but otherwise recomposed, Father took one, put it
into the video machine under the television and pressed
play. He then returned to the table and sat down with
his back to the screen. Calmly wiping his chin with the
napkin, he finished his meal, while over his shoulder
almost every flattering picture of Claire that had ever
been taken appeared on the screen in sequence. It started
with the first shots of her as a baby in her mother's arms;
it progressed to Claire as a toddler and from there to a
skinny little girl with pigtails, holding baby Magnus in
her arms. Tears were filling his own eyes now.

Mother sighed. 'Your father spent hours putting this
together, Magnus. Collating, chronicling, sourcing pictures from all her friends. Then we took them to a shop
that puts them into remembrance packages like this. We
picked it up on the way back from the golf course. They
sometimes put these things to music, but we thought
better not. It might have been a bit over the top.'

'Has it turned out all right?' Father asked his wife, refusing to look at the work himself.

'Yes,' said Magnus fervently, and reached out a hand towards his father's hand, but both wrists were jerked away. 'Dad, I'm sorry.'

'Fuck off.' He kept his cutlery aloft until Magnus withdrew his hand, whereupon the knife and fork were returned to the plate, perfectly in line, side by side.

Mother seemed to judge that it was time to change the subject. 'Magnus, did you notice the carving in your room?'

He turned away from his father's plate, and blinked at her. It took a moment for him to register the question properly. 'The what? Oh. Yes. The monkey head.' Normally he would have remarked on how revolting it was, but he judged that it was better to keep his opinions to himself. His voice was timid. 'Where did you get it?'

'Actually it's Claire's,' she replied, lapsing thoughtlessly into the present tense. Magnus immediately felt a jolt of guilt for having considered it ugly. 'It was in three pieces, which fitted together: head, tummy and bottom. She must have sent it before the accident, but it reached us afterwards. You know what the post is like.'

'Where are the other bits, then?' he asked, trying to be conversational even as his eyes flicked from his father's unreadable face to the photos of Claire on the screen beyond. She was now approaching ten years old, and grinning toothily from a swimming-pool in Tenerife, with white water bubbling up around her. The foam had been caused by him, if memory served correctly; she had had his head trapped between her knees beneath the surface. Happy days.

'She asked me to send them on in the note. Each bit was meant as a gift for a different friend. You know what she was like, always posting stuff back home that I was expected to forward to someone or other. It was cheaper for her, I suppose, sending things all in one package, although it rather irritated me at the time.'

'Who were they for?' asked Magnus, feeling a pang of jealousy that Claire had never sent anything for him.

'People I don't know. Someone called Marjorie Owen at Ashton School, an old colleague I suppose. And Rosie someone. It seemed a shame to divvy the bits up like that, rather queer, in fact, but she did say. The head is for Isabel. I thought you might want to give it to her yourself.'

'Oh, yes, I remember Isabel,' said Father. '*Very* nice girl.'

So he was speaking again at last: Magnus was highly relieved.

'She's doing rather well treading the boards, isn't she?' said Mother. 'Bought her own flat and everything.'

'I saw her earlier on today, in fact,' said Magnus.

'Oh?' Mother smiled hopefully. Since he had never mentioned Felicity he wondered if she was looking out for a wife on his behalf. How exquisite that they thought Isabel might do the job. If only they knew her better.

Mother folded her napkin and opted not to probe. 'Truth be told, I'll be glad to see the back of that carving. Not my cup of tea at all.'

She collected the plates. Father sat back. 'Kitty likes African tribal art, doesn't she? Brought some back from their safari in Botswana. Very colourful.'

Mother swung the conversation round to Magnus. 'So, what are your plans, dear? You've given up your rooms in London, haven't you? Presumably the school didn't offer you a full-time position.'

'I didn't want a full-time position. As you know.'

Mother glanced at her husband cautiously. 'Perhaps your father might help you find some work at Ashton. Claire had a successful year there, didn't she, before she decided on Africa? You might ask the headmaster, darling, at the next old-boys meeting.' She turned back to her son. 'Magnus, did you know they made your dad chairman of the Old Ashtonian Association?'

'Really? Congratulations. However, I don't need Father to pull any strings for me, thank you all the same.' He cleared his throat. 'By the way, I've decided to relocate. Here.'

There was a pause after his declaration. Father made a small inquisitive noise that implied alarm. Mother took the plates to the sink, seemingly unperturbed. 'But your teaching qualifications are English. You'll have to retrain if you want to work in a Scottish school.'

'I know that,' he replied, with laudable calm. 'Don't worry, I won't foist myself on you any longer than necessary.'

'Oh. Well. You can stay as long as you like, dear. We don't mind.'

If there was enthusiasm in her response Magnus didn't detect it. They didn't want him here. The evidence was overwhelming. He remembered Father's look of horror on the doorstep; he remembered the eighteen holes they went through despite his arrival; and, most of all, he recalled the platoon of dolphins shoving his childhood off the end of the shelf.

Magnus stood up. 'I'll call for a taxi.'

They looked slightly surprised by his declaration but were not obviously disappointed. 'Are you staying with . . .' she hesitated delicately, drying her hands on a tea-towel, '. . . a friend?'

'Yes,' he replied, then realised that he had better ask for some money before he went: his credit card wasn't going to get him very far. Inwardly he cursed a life that had never allowed him the least bit of personal dignity. He coughed delicately and sat down again.

'So, what are you going to do if you're not going to teach?'

'I intend to set up a film company.'

With great effort Father nodded, sending his chin deep into neckfat. 'I seem to remember you wrote a play or something.'

Magnus had prepared himself for the pitch, sort of, although he had expected a more receptive audience. 'Yes, there's that, but also I intend to do some commercial stuff. Professional videos, weddings, corporate commissions, you know.' He looked for a sign that this half-truth had found its mark. It was difficult to tell. Father's expression was still politely interested. 'Well, look, you just spent money on a video, didn't you?'

'Darling,' interrupted Mother, 'the school play! Didn't you say they were looking for someone to film it for the parents?'

Magnus nearly lost his temper. 'I do *not* need you to find me work.' He took a moment to control himself, then continued. This was the crucial part. 'However, I could do with another form of assistance.'

Meeting more silence, he plunged ahead. 'Father, I'm going to need some start-up money to buy some proper equipment, print cards, cover initial overheads. What I mean is . . . five thousand. I'll pay you back.'

He bit his lip and glanced over at the progression of photographs on the TV screen. Claire had reached university. The crop-haired vegetarian Buddhist had given way to a surly radical in a vast Oxfam overcoat. That last photo must have come from Gav. He turned back to Father, who had raised one of his amazingly elastic eyebrows and put a big smile on his face. This was not a good sign. He was about to perform the Famous Music-hall Scottish Accent. 'A wee dram afore ye go?'

Magnus stiffened. Despite all provocation he would not lose his temper. Besides, this might be the prelude to a serious discussion. 'Yes, that would be nice.'

Discreetly, Mother went next door. Father rose up and took a bottle of whisky from a kitchen cupboard along with two glasses. He poured while Magnus prepared to receive a considered, man-to-man response.

'Have you thought of joining the club?' Father asked, in a roundabout but shrewd way.

'The golf club? No, I haven't given it any thought at all.'

'Well, perhaps you should.' Father sipped his drink appreciatively.

Magnus waited and wondered what he was getting at. 'For work, you mean?'

Father raised a connoisseur's eyebrow and dandled whisky on his tongue. 'No,' he replied. 'For golf.'

Four

Magnus made his way out of the door into the dusk. The rucksack
was warm on his shoulder from the laundered clothes that
Mother had just put in there, fresh from the dryer. He
would have much preferred a cheque.

'Wait a minute!' she called from the stairwell, and
came down bearing the monkey head. 'You nearly forgot.'
She gave it to him and watched as he weighed it in his hand
and stuffed it into his pocket.

Father came up behind her and smiled. 'I'll see about
the Ashton job. Say hello to Isabel from us, won't you?'

'I will,' he replied, consigning the request to the
low priority section of his memory, where it instantly
evaporated. ''Bye.'

He walked down the path and closed the small garden
gate behind him. His parents were watching him go: they
were side by side in the doorway, the light from the
corridor spilling out over the lawn. Father raised his
hand. 'Let us know how everything goes.'

Magnus noted how relieved they looked to be left

alone, and began his walk back to the New Town. Swine, he thought. Surely he wasn't such bad company as all that. Then he recalled the way his father's hairy wrist had leapt away from his touch. He tried to think about something else. The monkey head was knocking against his hip. Mother was right, it was a strange gift, but Claire had always enjoyed baffling her friends by sending them exotic items from abroad that had no obvious purpose. Be it penis sheath or nose trumpet, the item would only be fully explained when she had returned and been given supper. This one probably had a function too, other than decoration. A Third World domestic appliance, perhaps? Since Claire wasn't coming back he presumed they would never know.

Magnus passed the street clock on his way back into the New Town and felt, for the second time, a light tapping sensation along his ribs, but he was too busy thinking of that last photo of Claire the student radical to pay it any mind. He remembered her vividly during that phase, always lambasting him and others for not displaying sufficient commitment to her various causes. Most of all, he remembered her convincing him, over the phone from the Edinburgh students' union, to join her in an NUS rally against student loans in London. Never a political animal, Magnus had nonetheless given in as usual and asked the relevant student activists at his Durham college how they were getting down there. The time of departure was punishingly early and he had struggled to make it, hopping on board with only seconds to spare.

They were already on the motorway by the time

he realised that the signs were pointing to the West Midlands, and he was on his way not to London but to Manchester where his fellow passengers were meeting other pro-lifers to shout at doctors and staff outside a clinic. Later that day, having made his excuses to Claire for not appearing at their rendezvous, he heard from an excited friend that he had been spotted on the television news. A sweaty phone call rapidly followed. He had been a non-participating observer, he explained to Claire. The symbolic candle in his hands was not a sign that he denied a woman's right to abortion: he was merely holding it for a pretty demonstrator while she hitched up her leg-warmers. It had all been a dreadful mistake. His claims were met with silence. Weeks passed before she spoke to him again.

He continued to walk. The wide street was lit by lamps. Always withdrawn, the New Town tenements on either side of him now seemed to pull back further from the road as he passed. From the corner of his eye, in a strange optical effect, they warped out of shape, as if viewed through a bubble, before reverting to their original lines. He was dog-tired still; his back ached; he was lonely, accompanied only by the sound of his footsteps on the pavement. They seemed to form an echo that did not, however, quite synchronise. He looked behind him but there was nobody there.

Was there, in fact, anyone? Felicity wasn't talking to him. His colleagues were not the type he wanted to open his heart to and his friends – all of them in London – had been neglected over the past few years. Now that he was abandoning both the metropolis and his career, the effort to reconnect seemed futile. But then he thought of Piers, his best friend from university, whom he had seen more of recently, with Felicity. Yes, he would put in a call.

Stopping at a phone box, he dialled the number and got straight through. A playful female voice answered. 'Hello, Piers's personal assistant speaking?'

It sounded remarkably like Felicity.

'Hello? Who's that? Felicity?'

No response. He waited, a long time, for Piers to arrive.

'Magnus?'

He read it all from the tone in his friend's voice.

'Piers?'

'Yes. Look, I'm so sorry about the news. Really sorry. So's Felicity.'

He felt the betrayal in his gut. Silence lengthened. 'You and her?'

Piers cleared his throat. 'Yes. But, Magnus, please—'

That was as far as he got. Magnus reeled out of the booth. How could this happen now? Why? He looked around at a grey stone world, which he had thought was already completely bled of colour and happiness. In fact, there had been a little left: he watched it drain away. The wind ruffled his hair. There was nothing else to do, no one else to turn to, but Isabel.

She stood back to let him in and smiled, obviously pleased to see him. Despite his black depression he couldn't help but notice that she looked healthier, as if some life had been restored to her. Surely that wasn't down to him? That would mean someone appreciated him.

'How did it go?' she asked.

'Oh, they're bearing up, as Father would put it.'

They walked into the sitting room and he turned to face her. 'You wouldn't believe what I just found out. My girlfriend. My best friend.'

Her blue eyes opened wide, processing the information in his face. She held his hand. 'You need a drink.'

She was about to fetch a glass but he stopped her. 'Listen, Isabel, if the offer is still open I'd love to stay here for a while, until I'm sorted.'

She looked back sombrely and seemed to think about it. 'Oh, all right, then.' She looked so pleased and grateful, it almost thawed the coldness inside him.

He glanced into the corner and saw a bottle of his favourite whisky. 'Lagavulin? I don't remember you drinking whisky,' he said.

'I don't.'

'You didn't buy it for me?'

'No. Yes.' She laughed and put a hand over her mouth. 'You don't mind, do you?'

'I'll forgive you, in the circumstances. But I should have brought something myself.' Then he remembered the carving. 'Having said that . . .' He reached into his pocket and brought out the carved head of the monkey. He held it up in his fingers, then twisted it so that it faced her. She stared at it and the bow of her upper lip, which she had consciously closed as she waited to be shown, rose up in surprise. She looked very pretty when startled. 'It's not from me. It's from Claire.'

Reverently, Isabel took it from him.

'She posted it just before the accident. To be honest, I'm not sure what it is.'

'It's a baboon,' she replied.

'Really? How can you tell?'

She glanced up at him quickly, then down again. 'I don't know. It just looks like one.'

Magnus nodded: fair enough. Holding the carving tight, Isabel sat down, deep in communion with Claire. She hardly noticed when he sat next to her and, to his surprise, he felt a shameful twinge of jealousy. He must have been enjoying her attention more than he knew. In profile he noticed how her nose was girlishly upturned. It made her look vulnerable and passionate at the same time.

As if divining his feelings, Isabel's eyes lifted and moved softly over him.

He swallowed. Was it normal for such ambiguous messages to be passing between them at a time like this? Was this a vicious, immediate rebound from Felicity? No. He felt that the nature of the bond between him and Isabel – this grief – would prevent anything developing, and he was glad of it. If only everything didn't have to happen at the same time.

'Do you want to talk about it?' she asked.

'What? Felicity and Piers? God, no, not now. I just want to forget them. Let's talk about something else. Anything but those bastards. Isabel didn't seem to have a problem with that. Maybe she had grasped his tendency to try to block out the issues that gnawed at him the worst. She joined her knees together and pressed the carving into her lap. 'All right, so tell me about your journey back from Africa. It must have been exhausting, after all you'd been through.'

Piers, he was thinking. Piers and Felicity. It made sense in retrospect. But fuck them. They were worthless human beings. Forget them. Think about more important things. Talk about your journey.

So he sat back and rolled out a string of transport anecdotes; of Levi Hakusembi to Rundu, Rundu to Windhoek and the flight thereafter to Johannesburg, Heathrow and Edinburgh. His mouth made various shapes of O as he looked her over. She was hunched up as if concentrating very hard, but he guessed that she wasn't listening to a word. She seemed to be preoccupied by, or trying to ignore, something else. What did she really want to know, he wondered. He shifted uncomfortably on the couch and looked up at the bookshelf against the far wall: plays, acting texts, a fat biography of Schubert. He turned his attention back to her. Her fingers were investigating all the grooves in the dark wood of the carving. Her thumb moved over the creature's high-calibre dentistry, then down to its lower jaw, which rested agape between its raised paws. It resembled a dog begging for a piece of meat.

Magnus found that he felt strange. His pulse was skipping erratically and sweat had broken out on his forehead. Red sand moved kaleidoscopically in his vision. He raised a hand to his head and it seemed to take an age to arrive. He felt dizzy. She looked strange too. She was chewing her lip, gripping the carving, the blood draining from her face. He found that he had stopped talking. The conversation had just faded away and neither of them had noticed. His vision returned to normal. He took a deep breath, exhaled, and sat back.

'Did you hear me, Magnus?' she asked.

'Sorry, I'm jet-lagged. And still a bit shocked. What was it you said?'

'Where are the other two bits of the carving?'

How did she know there were two more bits? Or had he told her already? Or was it obvious? He tried to order his befuddled mind and wade back to normality. 'My mother said she posted them on to friends of Claire's. Personally I would have kept them together. I mean, who wants a carving of a baboon's bottom?'

Isabel's tone was impatient. 'Which friends?'

He struggled to remember. There was too much sand swirling in his mind. But a moment later it cleared. 'There was someone at her old school but I can't remember the name, Marjorie someone. And another called Rosie, here in Edinburgh. Any idea who she might be?'

Isabel frowned and looked away. 'No, I don't think so.'

Magnus had a feeling that she was withholding something. 'How are you feeling, Isabel? You seem a bit pale.'

She straightened suddenly and her blue eyes flicked away, left and right. 'Do I?' She got up and placed the carving thoughtfully on the mantelpiece, then returned to the sofa. 'I bet you look worse than me.'

Her hand went to his forehead and pressed. It felt cool. He enjoyed the moment. Felicity and Piers melted away: two trivial people, gone for ever. Was it possible to get over a six-month relationship and a ten-year friendship so fast? But next to death, it all seemed too silly. Being here with Isabel wasn't so bad, he decided.

She straightened up. 'You might have a slight temperature. I hope you remembered to take your malaria tablets. Why don't you go and lie down?'

When she talked in that sure voice he found it soothing, even though he knew that there was nothing sure about her. At least she cared. At least she was there for him. Groggily, he levered himself up from the sofa. 'If you don't mind.'

She led the way to the spare room, which he remembered, having glanced into it on his way to the shower earlier in the day. His eyes were already drooping, but he woke up when she opened the door.

In the space of an afternoon she had completely reorganised it. There was a large writing desk, seemingly brand new, with pens and paper and a modern desk-lamp aiming down on it. She had put up shelves and plugged in a telephone. A computer sat in the corner, not brand new but obviously there for him to use if his work demanded it. And the bed that had been there before. Surely she couldn't have done all this for him. It would have meant rushing out and spending all afternoon shopping.

'You've built yourself a little studio,' he said.

'Do you like it? Move right in.'

It was for him. He laughed nervously. She smiled as

if she didn't quite understand the joke. He scratched the back of his head and frowned.

'Really, Isabel, I don't know.'

'I don't need help with the mortgage so don't worry about rent.'

'It's not that.'

She waited for him to explain. He didn't know how.

'I mean, I did say I wasn't sure about staying here before I went.'

She nodded. 'And then you came back and said . . .'

'Yes, but going out to buy all this stuff beforehand. Isn't it a bit, well . . . ?'

'Presumptuous?'

He did not want to offend her. 'Not exactly, but . . .'

'Pushy?'

'No!' He groped to express himself correctly. 'I suppose I feel a bit – obvious. As if you knew my decision in advance.'

'Let's just call it female intuition.' Her playful expression then turned serious. 'Magnus, I think that we need . . .' She attempted to rephrase. 'That we can *help* each other. Am I wrong?'

He looked at her levelly. 'I'm never going to replace Claire.'

Isabel met his gaze without flinching. 'How do you know?'

There was a long silence; a decision to make. Her eyes hung upon it, and filled with tears as if attempting to weigh the balance in her favour even as it tilted, slowly but inevitably, in the opposite direction. He shook his head sadly. This had been Claire's flat once, and now it was Isabel's, but it could never be his. There was no future in this place for him, only the past.

'Sorry, Isabel, I'm going to have to say . . .'

But he didn't manage to finish because she fell on to her knees, then slumped against the wall, hands to her face, weeping bitterly. He stood there uselessly, wondering why he had chosen isolation, why he didn't have the strength to help. Time passed in sobs. The raw noise of recrimination and pain and abandonment filled the narrow corridor until, eventually, she spoke: 'I wake up and I think she's still alive. And then I realise. It's like an amputation. It's sending me mad.'

He groaned with recognition. They shared this illness, even though their symptoms weren't all the same. 'I know. Isabel, it's been the same for me.'

'Your sister meant everything. I can't stand her being gone.' Magnus put a hand on her shoulder but she violently shook it off. 'No! I won't accept it.'

He watched as her body choked and gagged on the dregs of loss. He slid down the other wall and rested on his haunches, respecting the distance that he had just imposed between them. He hated himself, but it was for her protection as much as his own. Did grief really bring people together, like Gav had suggested, or did it banish individuals to distant worlds, forcing them to struggle in isolation for their own survival? He spoke to her from a thousand miles away. 'I'll still be close by. It's just there are too many memories in this flat. We'll still come through it together. I promise.'

Snot and tears shone on the fingers through which she spoke. 'I don't want to come through it. I'm not leaving her behind.'

He held out a hand; it snaked across a continent. 'Come on. Get up.'

'I mean it.'

He waited. She did get up eventually, but not at his behest, and he followed her back into the sitting room, where she immediately went over to the mantelpiece and clutched the carving to her chest. She had her face turned away from him. 'Go on, go, then.'

But he stayed a moment longer. He had to ask. 'What is it you know about that carving?'

'I don't know anything. Go.' Still he waited. Where should he go, exactly? She swung round to face him, her eyes wet and furious. 'I said get out!'

Five

Only when he had stepped out into the evening air did Magnus realise that he had forgotten his rucksack. But the tenement door boomed shut behind him and he knew there was no way he could buzz again and retrieve it. Not tonight, anyway. In the meantime he had to find somewhere to stay, or face the humiliating prospect of crawling back to explain that the reasons for his earlier refusal of Isabel's hospitality had been cancelled by the brutal fact of homelessness. It was that or stay with his parents. What a choice.

Then he remembered Gav. He would be in that bar up the road. He might even have a spare bed. At the very least he could have a beer and think things through.

Pacing towards Broughton Street against the wind, he brooded over what had just happened. He knew why he had turned her down. Two depressed people shouldn't move in together, particularly if one of them was so manifestly desperate. But he had also been upset by her theatrics, by which she seemed to claim Claire for

79

herself, as if she was the chief mourner, not him. Perhaps she thought she was hurting more. The thought made Magnus grit his teeth with anger. It offended a strand of arrogance in his suffering.

But why, he asked himself, had it had been so important for Isabel that he stay? One disturbing clue arose from a distant evening at the pub when he had come up to visit Claire: she had joked that he and Isabel would make a hilarious couple (whatever that meant). It had been a mildly embarrassing moment for both of them; at the time he sensed neither of them found the idea at all appetising. But now Isabel was trying to draw him close. It seemed unhealthy that grief should transform her feelings towards him so suddenly. At this stage in life, moving in with a woman, even as a flatmate, had certain implications. Accepting Isabel's invitation would have put him in debt to her, which his instincts told him was not a good idea.

The walk began to cool him down and his temper abated. Slowly but steadily guilt soaked through his shoes, and he considered turning back. He remembered the sound of Isabel crying in the corridor, and her face covered by shiny fingers. He had been cruel: he was too protective of his sister's memory. Up ahead the pedestrian crossing turned red and he stopped to let traffic pass. On the other side people thronged the street and laughter rolled down towards him with the taxicabs. Death was merely a distant concept for them: what was the point of trying to join them? The light turned green but he did not cross. He waited; the light went red. He ran.

One drink.

Magnus pattered briskly down a set of pocked stone steps and pushed his way into the Basement bar. He still felt sad but his head was clear. Furthermore his walk up the street had passed without incident or paranoia: this was progress. The room was full and damp shirtcuffs rose and fell on all sides. He knew immediately that he didn't fit into this place, any more than he did in the sophisticated coffee shop on the other side of town. The crowd seemed to sense his otherness and drew itself together against him. But he needed to find a friendly face, and Gav had invited him. He tried to insinuate his way between their bodies, and got rejected. He asked to get through but was ignored and forced back all the way to the entrance. So he waited and watched for an opening.

He was both fascinated and repelled by the way that in physically crushing people together their wills and individualities could be subsumed. In his mind the crowd was becoming an amoeba, feeding itself up with alcohol. The more the alcohol levels rose, the more strongly the amoeba was dominated by its own animal objectives. Sweat broke out over Magnus's face once more; he felt faint. Then an opening presented itself as a queasy young drinker with cropped hair lunged for the exit. Magnus shoved his way in, and magically the panic subsided.

The tobacco smoke seemed to clear and he could now make out individual faces in the crowd, shifting like particles in ooze. Names and possible identities slowly formed around some of them. Friends of Claire were in there with him, he felt sure of it. He also felt, obscurely, that one or two of these faces belonged to people whom she might not have wanted him to meet. The sensation was particularly distinct when he noticed a girl three layers of bodies out from the bar, expertly riding undulations caused by the toilet traffic. She rolled forwards then leant back, balancing a glass of something carbonated. Although she had not engaged anyone directly in conversation she was smiling without any apparent effort. Then he registered the wide-set brown eyes and recognised her as the Land Girl he had noticed earlier in the café. Seeing her there, confident and alone, made the amoeba seem less fearful, possibly even benign. In his present state of mind this seemed a far-fetched but attractive idea. If she could enjoy it then why couldn't he?

Perhaps, he thought, she was on drugs. He looked closer but could see none of the signs. Certainly she appeared to be taking an uncomplicated pleasure in the present, but she wasn't glazed. He continued to observe. She was not unsteady on her feet, she seemed spatially aware. Very cautiously, and against his most sceptical instincts, he speculated that she might, in fact, be happy.

Curious. Magnus had never quite grasped happiness. It seemed to him a complicated goal to set oneself in life. He recalled this opinion to reassure himself against the dangerous idea that it might be possible to feel consistently good about yourself. In the meantime he was being moved by osmosis towards the bar, but his gaze returned to this fascinating woman, who seemed to have kept up a settled state of well-being for over a minute now. It was gripping to watch: would she suddenly implode or just gently deflate? More seconds passed, another minute, and he had to concede that she showed no signs of suffering some kind of euphoric fit. He was impressed, almost inspired. On this evidence the world had to be a better place than he previously imagined. An outer coat of grief peeled back. He fantasised about making a flamboyant and reckless sacrifice on this woman's behalf, because she had given him hope. He wanted to meet her. This time she would not get away. Optimism surged through him and he decided to get a drink. With a sunny smile he uncharacteristically won the attention of the harassed barman. 'Hello! Can I have an Irish coffee, please?'

'Fuck off to a Starbucks if you want hot drinks.'

'Well, in that case I'll have a pint of beer.'

Since the bar space had become fiercely contested he began to move back in her direction. But the amoeba reacted violently against this idea, sending him in a wide involuntary arc towards a shining bald head that bobbed into sight. It was Gav, dipping a duck-like lip into his beer and listening carefully while his companion talked. The grave expression, heavy grey eyelids and freshly donned tropical shirt made Magnus think of an undertaker on holiday. Two chilly pints in someone's hands splashed Magnus's shoulder-blades and this in turn caused him to wet Gav. The flexing of the crowd packed them in on all sides and the girl was out of sight. Magnus apologised for the spillage and was welcomed with enthusiasm into the small group, which had taken refuge behind a pillar. He wondered whether Gav had primed them to be extra friendly.

'So you're staying up in Edinburgh for a while,' said Gav. 'It will be good to be close to your parents, I suppose.'

'Hm? Oh, yes, there's that.'

This, in fact, was the only major disincentive for relocating. Magnus was discovering that the etiquette of bereavement required much minor dishonesty. Wanting to change the subject, he considered asking for a place to sleep, but opted to delay. He took a sip of his drink and glanced around the room. The pillar was an excellent vantage-point with views of both the door and the dancier end of the bar where some music decks were being set up. The happy girl with the brown eyes seemed to have disappeared. Then he noticed that she had resurfaced at the far corner of the bar. 'Do you know who she is?' he asked, pointing at her.

It took a while for Gav to identify whom he meant, as the amoeba did all it could to keep her out of sight.

'That one,' said Magnus. 'The one wearing the teal wrap-top and the black sno-pants.'

'The what?'

'The one with the tits in the tight green top.' Having hastily translated his description for male consumption, Magnus blushed hotly. Where on earth had he learnt the words 'teal' and 'sno-pants', and how could they possibly have emerged from his mouth in a bar?

'Oh, her. That's Rosie. She goes out with Colin.'

Magnus was interested enough by this information to stop worrying about how he had acquired the vocabulary of female tailoring. Colin was the name of Claire's old boyfriend. The unopened letter in his rucksack — which he had picked up at the Rundu post office along with other unclaimed mail for Claire — might have been sent by him, if he had identified the jerky handwriting correctly. Not that he actually remembered seeing Colin's handwriting before. It just seemed likely. 'Claire's Colin?' he asked.

Gav's confirmation was given somewhat reluctantly. His attention was wandering back to his friends' conversation.

'Rosie knew Claire, then, did she?' Magnus persisted.

'Claire and Rosie weren't on the best of terms by the end,' replied Gav. Magnus took this in. He looked over at her again and recalled the strange physical sensations — the rush of blood, the shaking hands — he had experienced the first time he saw her in the café. It must have been intuition, he concluded, or a particularly strong coincidence. This did not set his mind at rest.

'I think Claire may have blamed Rosie for the breakup with Colin,' Gav continued. 'Things sort of came to a head when she was out in Namibia.'

Magnus drew from this that Colin had started an affair with Rosie when Claire was away, or possibly even before. At the time Magnus had not considered the end of Claire's relationship a terrible tragedy, partly because he and Colin had not got on well during their brief encounters. He was reminded once more how, for all their closeness in the past, there were whole swathes of his sister's life about which he knew nothing.

His curiosity to meet Rosie was now sharpened further, even though he was sure that Claire would have hated him to fraternise with the enemy: she had always valued loyalty in these matters. But, then, she was dead, and he could see no harm in it. He decided on an excuse to make his sortie. 'I've just spotted someone I know. See you in a bit.'

Gav smiled discreetly and looked away, while Magnus attempted to make his way across the room towards Rosie. He found himself caught among an adhesive circle of young women.

'Hello,' said one, who was wearing a nicely fitting white shirt, probably from Monsoon.

He was shocked. He had not encouraged this stranger to approach him. This never happened to him. A DJ started up behind them and conversation became impossible in that part of the bar. One of her friends was shoved forwards and fell into his arms, laughing. Magnus steadied her but she didn't seem to be in a hurry to leave. Had his personality magnet switched poles and suddenly become attractive? Glimpsing his reflection on some polished metal he decided that it couldn't be his physique, which was battered and aching, or his hair, which despite the shower had reassumed its just-out-of-a-hedge look. Must be the clothes. Pushing his slightly steamed spectacles back up the sharp ridge of his nose he affected casual indifference and tried to locate the whereabouts of Rosie, while the girl in the white shirt shouted conversation at him. Soon the female circle grew an outer crust of males and Magnus remained trapped within. He began to resent the amoeba on a personal level, as if it was obstructing him on Claire's orders, although he knew this was absurd. Then suddenly he sighted his target through an archway of sweaty backs. She was sitting in an alcove talking to someone he could not see. Was it Colin?

He started forwards, but a violent outbreak of dancing cut off the far side of the bar completely. She disappeared from sight again. Angrily he drained his glass and was donated another. He was drinking alcohol on an empty stomach and the result was rather pleasant: a kind of spangled jet-lag. He considered abandoning the mission, or at least delaying it, but decided to try once more and forcefully apologised his way through the crowd. Every metre was a stiffer maul. High-backed iron chairs were shoved in his way, immovable walls of shoulders had to be surmounted, there was even a skirmish that caused him to take refuge against the wall as drunken lateral punches flew and the bouncers came in to make their own, more considered, acts of violence. The bar excreted people via the exit.

Obliged to retreat in the direction of the bar he once again encountered the strangely friendly girl with the white shirt, whose name sounded different every time he asked. She was drunk and wanted to know more about his impressions of Africa. Her grasp on his elbow was like a baby's: surprisingly strong and not fully under her control. So for a second Magnus bent all his attention on her and launched into an anecdote that required a vigorous arm gesture. This persuaded her to let go of his elbow and he immediately broke off mid-sentence, burrowed through her companions and committed himself to a frontal assault on the dance-floor. After strong initial resistance he was moving fast, too fast – in fact, he was being propelled out of control in the direction of the far wall. The damp slap of his palm against sweat-drenched brick saved his nose. A frustrated shove of bodies from behind flattened him against the wall. The crowd withdrew.

Panting, Magnus looked around him, into the relative gloom of the corner seating. He apologised to the couple whose feet he had stepped upon. Rosie had disappeared. He received a tap on the shoulder, turned round, and there she was. 'Are you okay?' she asked. 'I actually heard you hit the wall.'

'Nothing serious, thank you.'

She did not seem to notice his likeness to Claire, which was a relief. He quickly followed up. 'You're Rosie, aren't you? I'm Magnus, a friend of Gav's. He's over there.'

She looked vaguely across the room, then back to Magnus. Even with a name-prompt, she was making no connection with Claire. He felt compelled to spell out who he was, but when she smiled he decided that instead he might enjoy a short holiday from being Claire's brother. 'I've just moved here to live. He's about the only person I know.'

The man Rosie had been talking to was not Colin. He forced his way along the edge of the crowd, taking a sliproad to the urinal. She glanced at Magnus's faint suntan and then his hair. 'So where have you been?' she asked. 'The 1980s?'

When asked, Magnus talked about himself in a vague and fraudulently optimistic way. He was, for the record, a young filmmaker who had travelled to Africa, partly for inspiration. As he spoke, he became aware that Rosie was inspecting him, less his face than his body, and more with curiosity than admiration.

'All right,' he said at last. 'What is it? What are you looking at?'

She put a hand to her mouth, then laughed. 'Sorry, it's your back I'm interested in. I mean, your conversation too, of course, but . . .' Her face acquired a professional mien. 'Have you always had that stoop?'

'That's putting it a little strongly, don't you think?' he replied, slightly offended. But it was true that he had been suffering increasing pain across his back and neck pretty much since the numbness had lifted. Shoulder pain had been in the ascendant more recently, but now it was giving way to the lower back.

'I'm a physio,' she replied, with authority.

'I have been getting twinges, as it happens.'

'Where does it hurt?'

'Lower back, but higher up too.'

'Chin down, straighten your neck,' she said. 'Shoulders back, tail in.' He obeyed and immediately felt a soft click in his lower back plus some mild muscular relief. She pressed a hand against his chest and another at the base of his spine. It felt even better. He was standing to attention in front of her. 'I could try to fix it for you if you like.'

'How much do you cost?'

'I do a charity case at least once a month. If now suits you, that is?'

It seemed a little abrupt, but then he thought of Felicity and said yes.

Six

Rosie led Magnus along Heriot Row and on to India Street, whose paving slabs took on a dull glow from the white lamps above. In darkness the whole area looked beautiful to him; rich and out of reach. If only he could afford a place of his own here. He cursed himself for having chosen a socially useful career rather than one that pillaged Latin America and earned him a respectable amount of money. Why had it seemed so inevitable? He supposed it was his character. From a young age he had commanded no respect from his peers. Mysteriously this had led to his dressing in corduroy and wanting to do good. Therefore he had become a teacher. Simple. But far more important, he now realised, was following Claire's example. It was stupid, really: matching up to her was always going to be an unreachable ambition. She was a force of nature in the classroom. She turned her pupils into disciples. Magnus only ever inspired pity in some of them, while the rest tore him to pieces. But he had stuck with it – until now. With Claire gone there was no longer any point.

He remembered this street from his walk earlier in the day, and the feeling he'd got outside that house at the bottom. He looked up at the street numbers, which continued to grow steadily, irreversibly, like their proprietors' capital. It occurred to him that he should have tried harder to smooth things over with Isabel. His guilt, carefully repressed, had found a way through at last. Isabel: the woman who had offered him free accommodation; Isabel, the woman to whom he had entrusted his rucksack before he disappeared to the pub, which he had now left in the company of another woman. Yes. Isabel. Perhaps he should give her a call. He checked his watch but it was after eleven: too late, unfortunately. Hmm. A massage was no guarantee of a berth for the night, and Gav had disappeared by the time they left the bar.

Clearly, the practicalities of life demanded his attention. He would take matters in hand tomorrow, he thought, and squarely address the problem of finances. He would follow through his strategic investment in clothing with a haircut and a shave. He would set up his own business and become a success in his own right, following his own ideas. Satisfied with this glib life-plan, for now, he relaxed some more. He glanced over at Rosie's shining profile and admired the way that she didn't bother to keep up polite conversation. The house numbers kept ticking: forty-two, forty-four, forty-six. The place he had noted earlier in the day was fifty-eight. 'So it's your flat we're going to, is it?' he asked.

'Mine? No, his. Or, rather, ours. At least it soon will

be – I hope.' She looked at his mystified expression, then laughed at herself. 'It's my fiancé's.'

'Oh.'

'He's been staying up near Inverness recently, for work. We're number fifty-eight, nearly there.'

Number fifty-eight. Magnus's premonition had therefore proved disturbingly correct. This was one of the dots on Claire's map. He saw the dead-end approach. She must have walked the same route a hundred times and even considered this place her home. He knew that they had co-habited for a while. A knot of nervous expectation tightened within him. Suddenly he felt as if she was there with him, drawn by a masochistic curiosity to see the flat in which Rosie had taken her place. He attempted to master his paranoia: his mind and body were playing up in the aftershock of Claire's death, that was all. Shame didn't come into it, and if he did occasionally think of Claire in the present tense it was just mental shorthand. In fact, maybe all this was actually healthy for him. By tying up the loose ends of his sister's life, he could then proceed with his own. Magnus wove this limp thread of modern psychology because it avoided a simpler and less appealing explanation; that he found Rosie attractive when he ought to hate her. But why ought he to hate her? All he had was a vague suspicion that she helped cause a split between Claire and Colin. She had been perfectly pleasant to him so far. Was it possible, he speculated, that Claire knew something he didn't, and had somehow prompted him?

He was walking too fast. He slowed down and gave her a small smile of apology. She returned a look he could not fully decipher. Was she judging how he had handled the news that she had a fiancé? Together they passed under the last of the white street-lamps, which cast a weak, disordered shadow, and reached the bottom of the street. Stockbridge spread out below, quiet now except for the burble of a bar further down the road. A couple were using the cashpoint and a single woman hovered on the kerb, waiting for a taxi. Rosie climbed the steps to number fifty-eight. Magnus was going to follow but he took another look at the woman below. She had a hand to the side of her face, as if suffering from a headache. Rosie groped for her keys in her handbag. He climbed the steps and she opened the glossy black door. About to follow her in, he took a last glance at the street below, vaguely curious to know whether the woman had found a cab. Claire was staring directly up at him. Or someone like her. Her face was obscured by a scarf and there was a blankness to her expression. But the bearing, the clothes were identical.

On impulse Magnus ducked out of sight and the door slammed shut behind him, sending a grandiose echo up the tenement steps. His heart hopped in his chest: *Did she see me? Did she see who I was?*

Rosie was already climbing. 'I'm right at the top, I'm afraid,' she said, panting slightly as she went.

He should have confronted the woman and put his mind at rest, but instead he hurried after Rosie. In truth he was scared. It can't have been her, he told himself, with each heavy step. It can't. It can't. And yet the laborious beat of his feet and their corresponding echo up the stairwell

seemed to invoke the opposite conviction. Fate was going
to punish him for this doomed connection he had made
with Rosie, despite all the efforts of the amoeba.

Rosie reached the top ahead of him and stopped in front
of the first door on the left. She bent down to put a key in
the bottom lock as Claire must have done many times. It
was too late to back off now, he told himself. Or was it?
As she fumbled with the second lock he knew he could
still run back to Isabel and she would take him in. But
then he would have to face the pale-lit streets alone.
He quivered with indecision. Rosie opened the door and
looked at him with her broad brown eyes. Tamely, he
followed her in.

Entering Colin's flat, he felt a jolt inside. He made
an educated guess that the sitting room's appearance
had changed radically since Claire's time, and that the
changes would not have met with her approval. For a
start it contained living pot plants. For all her success in
nurturing pupils, his sister had had the opposite effect on
vegetation. And just as she would have resented Rosie's
success with ferns, she would have been equally appalled
by the surrounding untidiness: there was orange peel in
the fireplace, cup-stains on the glass tabletop, and a teabag
in the ashtray on the window-ledge.

Magnus, on the other hand, liked it. He felt calmer
now that he was inside, and went through to the kitchen
where Rosie was clearing the large wooden kitchen table.
She gave it a quick wipe.

'There's a fresh tablecloth and towels in that drawer if
you could lay them out. Towels then the cloth on top.'

Magnus followed her instructions. A moment later the unfolded cloth floated over the table on which he was about to be served. Slightly confused about what to do next, he glanced over. Her straightforward sober smile did not suggest anything out of the ordinary. She threw him a smaller white towel. 'Go on, then, undress as far as your boxers.'

She opened a cupboard and started to assemble bottles of various sizes. He looked at the towel in vague despair, then his eye caught on a piece of paper beside the telephone. The scribbled dates and times were irrelevant; it was the handwriting, which was identical to that on the letter. His guess about Colin's authorship had been right. Somehow his intuition had become infallible. Preoccupied, he took off his clothes, and waited in his boxer shorts with the towel draped over his lap. The pain in his back had miraculously disappeared prior to treatment. He cleared his throat, in need of small-talk. 'Does it take a lot of training, being a physio?'

'It's the same training as a doctor, more or less, except we skip the internal organs.' She returned to the table, stroked flat the tablecloth and patted it. 'Right, hop up.'

He lay on the table, face down. She spread oil over his back as her fingers started to work their way along his muscles, gently at first, then gradually deeper. He felt like a map. She asked him to roll on to his side, drew his knee up and pushed. After some other minor contortions, she went to work in earnest. It was not painful to begin with, but where she pressed he found routes of tension shooting out in unexpected directions all over his body. He had half hoped the session would be at least mildly sensual, but it developed into a strenuous physical test. Her strong fingers dug into his shoulder and white street-lamps lit up along his arm. That hurt. 'Can you feel that knot, right under the shoulder-blade?'

He could. He also felt the second one under his other shoulder-blade and a third concentration of tension in his lower back. Together they formed a diagram of pain that flared and glowed as Rosie worked. India, Bellevue, Drummond. Her fingers were starting to make terrible incursions now, each one aimed precisely at the most sensitive points. Her knowledge made it so easy to hurt or heal. He tried conversation to send his mind elsewhere.

'So when did you qualify?' he asked, his voice sounding thick and close.

'Oh, I'm not qualified yet,' she replied lightly. 'Why did you think this was free?' Magnus decided not to ask any more questions. 'Do you have a family history of back problems?'

'Uh.' His father had slipped a disc a few years back, but Claire had always had problems with her spine. It then occurred to him that Rosie might have given a similar massage to Claire. How would it have felt, he wondered, to have your hands on the naked body of your rival? Did she imagine how her lover Colin's hands had moved over Claire, which routes they took, inciting pleasure or pain? Distinctions were blurring. Was it his pain he felt, or Claire's pain, or the whole family's pain? Was the pain in his body or his mind? Rosie's fingers seemed to be untwining all these aching confusions. He utterly submitted. Seeing that his body was making its confession, his mind moved tactfully away. The pain that, during long nights, had denied him sleep now let him float free, moored only by the faintest umbilical link. He thought how easy it would be to sever. Who was it lying on the table below? Time went by and his questions lost their urgency, submitted, went silent.

Once again he saw the red dust of Namibia spewing off a road and a low sun made green by the tinted windscreen of a four-by-four. The green sun blinked between the mountains, straight into his eyes. It wasn't a dream, nor was it a memory of his own. He had imagined himself into the last calm sight of Claire's life: a dawn that had failed to bring the day.

After who knew how long he felt her hands palpate him slowly towards consciousness. Magnus, in response, was orienting himself again; aware of the table he was laid upon, the herbal fragrances of the oil, and a not unpleasant tingling in his fingertips. He opened his eyes and was surprised to find that Rosie had brought her ear close to his mouth.

'What did you say?' she asked.

'Did I say something?' he replied. 'I don't know.'

'You mumbled something about a letter, and Colin.'

'A letter? No. I don't know. I was dreaming.' He felt uncertain and exposed, as if he had given something away that he wasn't aware of.

Rosie took her hands off him and resumed her professional mien. 'Now turn over, Magnus, on to your back.'

He did this with some difficulty, blinked, smiled through the ache. He felt that he should say something but then she climbed up on to the table. He closed his eyes again, wondering what to expect. Rosie put a knee on either side of his chest, lifted one of his arms up and joined her fingers behind his neck. His skeleton made a cracking noise. She climbed down again, then walked to the kitchen sink and washed her hands.

The next thing he knew he had fallen asleep again and woken up to find Rosie digging her fingernails into his eyebrows. The pain was sharp, awakening. Then she let go and he was able to sit up.

'Thanks,' he said, with the shaky gratitude of someone disembarking from a rollercoaster. He searched for a suitable question to break the silence. 'It was kind of you to pick out a stranger in a pub. Brave, even.'

She smiled. 'You looked sufficiently docile. I felt like I knew you already.'

She seemed to be waiting for him to say something. He looked for his clothes, which he found, in defiance of a lifetime's habit, in a neat, folded pile. While Rosie cleared the table he put on his trousers. He had accepted her generosity under false pretences; he shouldn't be here. 'I'd better be off,' he said, as he put on his shirt.

'Where to?'

'That's a good question.'

She looked at him. 'If you need somewhere to crash, you can stay here for a while.'

Magnus couldn't believe it. Was it normal in Edinburgh

for a female, engaged to be married, to offer floor space to the vaguest friend of a friend? 'Never make open-ended invitations to strangers. They don't always leave so easily.'

She shrugged and ran a hand through her soft brown hair. 'You're not a stranger. We're moving out soon in any case, to another place across town. If you wanted to stay for a while it would actually suit us. We're looking for a short-term tenant, you see, before we sell.'

He thought about it. Despite the impossibility of accepting (although, he asked himself, why was it so impossible, exactly?), it was an extraordinary offer. Where else was he going to find at short notice? Maybe the time had come for him to assert his own interests over those of Claire. 'It's very tempting,' he said doubtfully.

'You'd have to pay rent. Not much, though.'

He took a deep breath. His two-minute holiday from being Claire's brother, which had extended itself into several hours, must now come to a close. He had to tell Rosie who he was. This would clarify the situation and no doubt dissolve the offer. The temptation would be thereby neutralised.

'Rosie, this is all unbelievably kind of you, but there's something about me you don't know. My surname.'

She rolled up the cloth he had lain upon and stuffed it into the washing-machine. 'Let me guess,' she replied, turning to him. 'Calder?' She smiled at the look of surprise on his face. 'Actually, no, I'm not in the habit of hanging around in bars and inviting strange men home. Colin had just left when you came in. He's away to a shoot in the north. You know he's a film producer, don't you?'

'You recognised me? Why didn't you say?'

'Because you didn't.'

He went and sat down, confused. 'But if you know who I am, why all this?'

'That's the question I should be asking you. Assuming you know the history of me and Claire and Colin.'

He looked at her sharply. 'You know she's dead.'

She didn't flinch. 'Yes, I heard.'

He looked away. 'I don't know why I came to find you across the bar. Curiosity, perhaps.'

Although he knew there was something more: namely, the indefinable emotion that had passed through him when he saw Rosie earlier in the day.

She smiled faintly and leant against the kitchen work surface, one hand on her hip. He liked the way she held herself: it suggested an old-fashioned female ability to deal with things; fortitude, even. 'For me too, I think.'

He drew in his breath. 'This is a weird situation, even by my standards.'

To his surprise she became angry. She stood straight. Her brown eyes became sharp-angled, her complexion darkened. 'Why? Because you're supposed to hate me? Because I'm supposed to leave the room if you enter it?'

'No, it's not that. It's . . .' His voice faded away because she was right. That *was* how it was supposed to be. Although he couldn't quite justify it.

Her anger fell back. She pursed her lips and crossed her arms. 'My being friendly, it's not guilt, if that's what you're thinking. Claire and I were good friends once. Remembering that is important for me.' When she saw the uncertainty on his face she turned away and flapped a hand towards the door. 'Please do whatever you like, if you're not comfortable with this. I won't be offended in the slightest.'

He really ought to walk out now, an instinct told him to do just that. But his decision failed to connect with action. He realised that he wanted to stay here, despite the taboos of death that rippled between them. There was something to be learnt here, or gained.

'What about Colin? It's his place, after all.'

She was wiping a surface now, with her back to him, as if he was already dismissed. 'I could always have talked to him.'

He took a step towards the door, but lingered. 'Well, then. If that's the case . . . Can I?'

She stopped wiping and turned. Friendliness rushed back into her face and her smile was generous and congratulatory, as if he had done something courageous and right. 'So you'll stay?'

Magnus was still unsure, but exhaustion decided. 'For tonight, if that's okay. I still think it's better that you sleep on it.'

'Sure. There's a sleeping-bag and a pillow in that cupboard, and the sofa's comfortable. You look like you're about to collapse.'

He smiled ruefully as he got up. 'Jet-lag.'

'Help yourself to anything you need,' she said, and turned towards the stairs. But then she halted. 'Oh, by the way, was Colin still in contact with Claire out in Africa?'

A warning to be cautious flickered in his weary mind, even though he was on the point of shutdown. He thought of Colin's unopened letter, which lay in his rucksack at Isabel's. 'No,' he replied. 'Not that I know of.'

She was watching him closely through the half-shut door. Then she said goodnight, the door closed and Magnus was left in the silent living room.

A minute later he lay down on the large sofa and pulled the sleeping-bag up to his chin, proud to have staved off his jet-lag to the point where he could now slot back into a normal sleep pattern. What a situation, he thought, as his eyelids drooped. He was glad that he hadn't told Rosie about the letter: it wouldn't have achieved anything except complication. In the morning he expected that everything would be clearer. He turned over on to his side and curled up. The city glow beyond the shutters infiltrated the room but it was welcome, as were the snorts of traffic from the road below. In Namibia he had lurched about for hours on various badly sprung hotel beds, encased in numbness, seeking either escape from reality or escape from sleep, while mosquitoes whined beyond the net. Here the tainted darkness offered a milder oblivion. Within seconds he had taken it.

Seven

The reek of petrol and the howl of an engine at the reddest extreme of its rev-count did not, surprisingly, wake Magnus immediately. It was a process of disentanglement that went on for some time, partly because he was so completely disoriented. He reached out and patted floorboards: that's right, he was on a sofa, in a flat. But that noise – how could it be so deafeningly close? After several babyish blinks he looked at his watch: 3:14. In the afternoon or morning? Through cracks in the shutters he saw street-lamps burning below. He hopped across the room in his sleeping-bag, opened the shutters and looked down at the street to see if there had been a crash, but it was empty, uninhabited. The noise was incredible: it seemed to be coming from within the flat rather than outside it, while the petrol fumes suggested an immediate danger that the whole place might explode. He began to think a little straighter. Where was Rosie? Couldn't she hear it, or was she overwhelmed by the fumes, wherever they were coming from? He let the sleeping-bag drop to the floor and ran into the kitchen, looking left and right for the source of the noise. He opened a cupboard but found only a vacuum-cleaner. How could this be? Helpless, panicked, he ran back to the sitting room and noticed, as he passed the door on to the corridor, that the volume and also the smell increased. He returned to the door and hesitated. The extremity of the engine's suffering warned him away but it also begged to be turned off. He could feel the floorboards vibrating under his bare soles: he had to act. He thought again of Rosie and his hand went to the door-handle.

The corridor was dark. There was no car but this seemed to be the epicentre of the sensory assault. The walls were shaking, about to blow. He saw petrol streaming down the stairs and at the top the woman had her back to him. Even in the gloom he knew that it wasn't Rosie. She was wearing an overcoat or dressing gown and her short hair was pasted to her skull, an indeterminate colour. She had crouched down and appeared to be picking fluff from the corner of a carpeted step, her hand and feet causing the petrol-flow to rise in gleaming crests. She did not seem aware of the impending catastrophe. The petrol streamed down over his own toes; it was hot and stung his skin. He screamed to catch her attention but he couldn't be heard as she continued with her insane domestic concern. He wanted to climb the steps but he lacked the courage. He screamed again, despairingly, but then his cry died in his throat.

Claire?

Unhurried, the figure straightened up and turned. It

took a moment for him to recognise Isabel because a large area of her face, from her nostrils all the way down to her chin, had been cut away. The remaining flap of skin on her cheekbones seemed to hang from her eyes like a veil. Beneath it were her exposed gums, through which the full length of her tooth-roots could be seen. They were brown. She had wooden fangs, like the vile baboon. Her flayed chin dropped. He saw her tongue lift and flop within, grotesquely fleshy. His stomach turned to water and his breath came out short and halting. She looked down at him. He saw black eyelashes touch briefly against the skin flap – she had blinked. She appeared less in pain than confused. Her hands hung loosely at her sides, oblivious to the racket. Magnus, fighting for breath against the acrid stench of the fuel, found his voice again at last. 'Get out get out get out!'

His fingers dug into his temples as he backed against the wall. Cramps gripped him. He closed his eyes but he still saw her blue eyes, which seemed to contain an accusation. In contrast to the horrific wound below their beauty was weirdly heightened, like a collage. 'Leave me alone,' he whispered. 'Get out!'

Isabel came splashing down the stairs towards him and with each step her veil of skin swung in a way that made her look revoltingly seductive. She walked calmly down the corridor, opened the front door and left. The engine died. The sting of fuel over his ankles lessened, then stopped.

Rosie had appeared on the landing, in a nightie. Her bedroom light was on and she held an electric plug in her hand, attached to a flex, which led all the way down towards him.

'Good morning,' she said, squinting down at him with a pained expression.

Magnus looked from her down to a vacuum-cleaner that stood beside him. He was shivering, his body covered in sweat. He smelt the warm electric motor and the plump dust-bag. The floor was dry. There was no noise apart from his own panting.

Rosie nodded towards the vacuum-cleaner. 'I've been meaning to get that fixed. Whatever controls the rev-count doesn't work. Lucky I pulled the plug before it went bang.' Then she noticed how shaken he looked. 'Are you all right?'

He ran a hand through the damp roots of his hair and checked that he hadn't wet himself. Thankfully not. 'No.' His voice was raspy. He slumped down on the bottom step and put a hand to his heart, which was still beating furiously. He looked up. 'Did you hear anyone on the stairs?'

She looked worried. 'I'm not sure. Maybe I did, but that must have been you, plugging in the machine. Wasn't it?'

'I don't know.'

'Did you see someone? I always double-lock the door.'

He got up and tested the door. She was right: it was locked firm. He must have dreamt it. He came back. 'I'm sorry to have scared you. It was just an incredibly vivid nightmare.'

'Do you want me to come down? Herbal tea?'

'No. No, thanks, I'm fine now.'

'You don't look fine.'

'Really.' He attempted to smile.

She cocked her head and lowered her eyelids. 'Vacuum-cleaning in your sleep. It's a new one for me. How do you do it?'

'You can go back to bed if you want.'

'If you're sure.'

'Sorry to have woken you up.'

She shut the bedroom door softly behind her.

He went back to the sitting room but remained avidly awake. The weekly malaria pills would go in the bin tomorrow. His doctor had warned him that the drug could cause side-effects in some people, including nightmares and impaired vision. That was most likely the explanation. Every few seconds his nostrils twitched, scenting petrol once more. And Isabel's wooden mouth. He shuddered and crept back to the sofa, where the sleeping-bag lay, even though the prospect of sleep terrified him. What he needed was a twenty-four-hour news channel whose reports of stock markets, drought and civil warfare might provide him with security and orientation, but he didn't want to risk disturbing Rosie again. A soothing book seemed safer. He found a P.G. Wodehouse on the bookshelf and started to read.

In the morning Magnus woke up to the sofa closing in on him. He was surrounded on all sides by hostile synthetic material, apart from a narrow slit through which he could see elaborate cornicing and a cylindrical light-shade in navy blue. He had his doubts about whether its modernist feel gelled with the classical tones of the rest of the flat. Then, failing to wriggle out of the rut between the seat cushions and the back of the sofa, he asked himself why he was taking an interest in interior decoration, became anxious and promptly fell back to sleep.

Some time later he woke up again, still on the sofa, and found that his jet-lag had evolved from surreal thoughts to straight exhaustion. He could not muster the energy to move, but initiated the mental steps that brought him to full consciousness.

The first thing to deal with was the headline news, broadcast directly to his brain every morning: Claire Dead. The news never changed but, half asleep and with defences down, he felt it like nausea. There would follow a period of disbelief and confusion until, after some time, he forced himself on to the second step, reorientation. His world had to accommodate this event and attempt to make sense of it. He quite often skipped the second step. The third step was to decide to enter the world once more. By this he meant simply opening his eyes and getting up. It was usually very difficult. Today was even more so.

He fought his way out of the sofa. He was not assisted by the sleeping-bag or a right arm whose circulation had been cut off by his sleeping position. Eventually he swung his feet on to the bare knotty floorboards and kicked aside the book he had been reading. He felt like shit. Disliking himself in a general way he went to the bathroom, clamped his buttocks to the cold toilet seat and put his head into his hands. In comparison to reality his nightmare had not been so bad. However, as he recalled the waving skin flap, his scalp prickled with sweat once more. He must check on Isabel, pick up his rucksack and make his excuses. He would also have to tell her who his new landlord and -lady were. Claire's betrayer and Claire's other betrayer.

Emerging sorrowfully from the toilet, he headed into the kitchen and made himself a cup of tea. He had just flicked the wet teabag towards the steel sink with a stray fork when he heard Rosie's footsteps descending the stairs. The teabag, which had clung briefly to the side of the sink, fell with a damp plop. He added milk and went to sit down. Traffic rolled over the cobbles in the street far below, and the rumble seemed to make his eyeballs vibrate. Rosie might throw him out on the strength of the vacuum-cleaner episode.

She appeared in a dove-grey dressing-gown and leather slippers. Her eyes were slightly puffy. Without acknowledging his presence she refilled the kettle by the sink. Behind her the large window was completely filled by Portland stone, although on closer inspection at least a third of the view was made up of thick, undifferentiated cloud. None of it moved. Grey begat grey; Edinburgh's weather made tenements of the sky.

The kettle's low rumble became gradually louder, merging with the slow noise of traffic from the road below. Rosie seemed, from his brief acquaintance with her personality, uncharacteristically sullen. He thought he should say something. 'Rosie,' he blurted, 'I'm so sorry for last night. It won't happen again, I promise.'

She scratched her hair and searched for a teaspoon. Clearly she was not a morning person. 'That's okay.'

'Are you going to speak to Colin and tell him I'm moving in?' He knew he sounded too hungry, pushy even, but he found it almost impossible to disguise his craving for somewhere to live.

'I will do, don't worry. I'll show you the room, if you want. You could have used it last night only it's full of junk. I'll have it cleared today.'

She took her cup of tea and he followed her upstairs. The room was small but it would do. 'This is fine,' he said.

'So, then, bring your stuff whenever you're ready.'

Rosie took her tea into the refuge of her room. When the door closed he asked himself what stuff he had up here, apart from the clothes on his back or in his bag, a damaged Airfix model and a battered copy of a screenplay. There were his things in London, but their net worth was pitiful and he had no strong sentimental attachments to any of them, not even the obsolete electric typewriter or the heap of decaying paperbacks. Indeed, leaving them behind suddenly appealed: they were no more than the tawdry relics of a misspent youth. He asked himself how many of the past eight years in London he could remember clearly. The answer was depressing: all of it. There were no black holes caused by glamorous bingeing; no broken hearts or bastard children. Even his debts were embarrassingly tiny by most standards. The tragedy was that his twenties had been dedicated to sober, earnest failure; a long and honest plod in the elfin footsteps of his sister whose tracks had now vanished, leaving him duped and hopelessly lost.

Inescapably, Claire was on his mind as he stepped out timidly on to the street and looked sharply both ways. Thankfully, there were no lone female figures to ignite his fears, and he headed swiftly down the steps in the direction of Isabel's place. The Saturday-morning streets were fairly busy and he sought cover in numbers as if he were under some kind of surveillance. It helped. Among the zestful shoppers he relaxed a little. He flexed his shoulders and was pleasantly surprised to discover that the massage had done its work. This cheered him. But his sense of well-being was short-lived.

The closer he got to Bellevue Terrace the more he felt that Isabel was going to find it difficult to forgive him for what he had done. He rehearsed his justifications: it might be unorthodox renting a room from Rosie, perhaps even vaguely indecent, so soon after Claire's death, but wasn't it also an act of reconciliation? And, more to the point, wasn't it his life? Reflexively, he checked there was no one behind him and pressed the door buzzer to the flat.

She was waiting for him at the top of the stairs and he was shocked: she looked exhausted. Unironed, unmatched, her clothes looked as if they had been put on as a detestable chore. She blinked continually to ease her sore, bloodshot eyes, and the curls of her unwashed hair formed lifeless hooks, flung carelessly over her skull. She showed him into the sitting room without comment, and his glance immediately latched on to the mantelpiece where the baboon's head presided above the fake coals, from which gas flames fluttered against the springtime chill. How innocuous it looked, how homely. But he didn't feel warm.

'Are you tired?' he asked, as he turned towards her.

'I stayed up late, reading.' Her voice was soft but raw. She flicked her head to move a pale lock of hair from her eye. It rested on the corner of her eyebrow.

'Oh, yes? Something interesting?'

She stared at him. 'I was expecting you to come back last night.'

'I didn't get that impression when you threw me out.'

'You were leaving anyway.'

Not wanting an argument, he started again. 'Can we talk, please?'

She motioned him towards the sofa, but remained standing herself. He cleared his throat. He cleared it again. Damn, his mind had gone blank.

Seeing that he was tongue-tied, she sighed. 'So how was the pub?'

He laughed, embarrassed. She seemed to have grasped his need for small-talk. Hopefully it would lead towards what he wanted to say. 'Fine. Although I made an odd discovery: female fashion. I've never previously taken the slightest interest, and yet now I find I can talk about sno-pants and use words like "teal".'

Expecting her to laugh or look bewildered, he was surprised that her expression did not even flicker. Perhaps, he speculated, fatigue had dulled the impact of this extraordinary development, so he continued with growing enthusiasm. 'It's odder than it sounds. I mean, I know that it's possible to acquire knowledge unconsciously, we do it all the time, or forget that we read something or other. That would explain, for instance, why I know that your shirt comes from Kookaï. I could have seen it in a shop window or in an advert. At a stretch it might also explain how I can now judge that it doesn't match your trousers. But . . .' here he raised a teacherly finger '. . . it doesn't explain why I *take an interest* in your shirt. It doesn't tell me why I notice these things when, in the past, I wouldn't even have registered the colour of your wallpaper.'

She looked irritated. Perhaps it was the hair in her eye. She turned away and walked across to the mantelpiece where she rested an elbow. Her thumb stroked the baboon's skull. 'So, let's hear your theory.'

He felt on the spot, but couldn't pull back now. 'Well, it could be a psychological reaction. Claire liked clothes. I could be trying to take her on in some way. Gav said something to me that stuck in my mind. An African belief about spirits residing in their relatives? Maybe that planted a seed in my mind. In the same way that I keep seeing Claire on the street, out of the corner of my eye.'

This caught her attention. She was immediately rapt. 'It happened again? How did you feel seeing her?'

He pretended not to hear the last question. 'And that's not all. I had this appalling dream. Christ, it was horrible, so real. You were in it.'

She looked disconcerted but with an effort she smiled, showing her square, evenly spaced teeth. They were quite unlike the fangs of his dream. 'Lead role in your nightmare. I'm flattered. Did I have any good lines?'

'Actually you didn't say anything.' He wondered whether he should go on, but it all came out. First he told her about the sound of the broken engine howling out of control, and the stream of petrol. 'And then I saw you. At first I thought it was Claire because you were picking at fluff on the stairs carpet, which is a Claire thing to do. But when you turned . . .' he gulped at the memory '. . . you were mutilated. Your lower face had been cut away. Not from an accident. More like amateur surgery.'

Isabel, who had listened calmly enough to the first part of his dream, blanched. Her lip arched and her blue eyes glittered, as if she was about to cry. But there were no tears. Realising she was upset, he decided not to mention how her wooden fangs shone with blood and instead tried hastily to explain it all away. 'Of course, I can see how all these things got mixed up. The petrol and the whine of the engine, I suppose that relates to Claire's accident, helped along by the absurd vacuum-cleaner. And the rest . . .' His explanation lost impetus.

Her hand gripped the mantelpiece, but her tone was casual. 'So, according to you, this is all the power of suggestion, is it?'

Magnus scratched his neck. 'I suppose so, yes. What else could it be?'

She just stared at the baboon's dark head. God, she looked wrecked: worse than him.

'What were you reading last night, Isabel?'

Her eyes flared. 'Something of Claire's, as a matter of fact.'

'What?'

'Her thesis.'

'But you said you didn't have anything of hers, apart from the umbrella.'

'I found it at the bottom of a drawer.'

He was not sure that he believed her. 'May I read it?'

She replied quickly. 'Yes. Of course. Once I've finished.'

'Well, what does it say?'

'I can't explain until I've got to the end. Besides, you don't want any more nightmares, do you?'

He smiled. 'Her stuff was never bedside reading exactly. So what's it about? Human sacrifice? Cannibalism? Cult suicide?'

Her lip twitched. 'Yes, something like that. But tell me your plans.'

The topic of conversation had been neatly cut short, but perhaps this was his opportunity to come clean. 'Ah. Yes. I had a stroke of luck last night. I met someone with a room to rent.'

She didn't seem surprised. 'Oh? That's wonderful. Have you come to collect your things?'

Pleased that she had accepted it with such good heart, he relaxed a little. 'Yes, actually I am going to do that. But also I wanted to see that you were okay.'

She shrugged. 'Well, here I am.'

'I feel a bit ungrateful, not staying here. It's just . . . I need a space of my own.'

'Do you have the money to pay your rent? I expect your father didn't cough up.'

There was no point in denying it. 'No, but I'm working on it.'

'I'll lend you some, if you like.'

'No. Thanks, but really—'

She interrupted him. Her voice was suddenly sharp and clear. 'You need to eat as well. Will two thousand do for now?'

'I . . .'

'Of course you can pay me back. Have you thought about how to earn some money?'

'Well, yes. Did I mention that idea of mine to make videos of events and stuff? But that means buying equipment and I'm hopeless with the banks.'

'Do you need more? I can take out a loan.'

Magnus could hardly believe it. He had been caught unprepared. 'But I haven't fully thought it through yet. I need to organise a business plan. You should know a bit more before—'

'Your mother gave me an idea on the phone last night.'

He blinked. 'You called them?'

'I thought you might be there. Anyway, I could research a bit and drum up some work for you, just while you get started. I want to see my investment paid off, you know.'

He smiled slackly. A loan from Isabel? He was uneasy about such a simple solution to his money problems, as well as the way she had liaised with Mother, but her businesslike tone was reassuring. It seemed to put them on a more sensible footing. Furthermore, a debt would provide him with much-needed motivation to forge ahead with the business. This was an offer he could not afford to turn down.

'If you're really sure. But it sounds like I won't have much time to concentrate on my screenplay.' She made a swatting gesture, which slightly offended him. However, he let it pass, all things considered. 'What can I say? Thanks, Isabel. I just wish there was something I could do in return.'

She nodded in a way that made him instantly and ungallantly regret the comment. 'There is. Remember those two other parts of the baboon carving? I want you to get them for me.'

He was caught off-balance. 'But why?'

Her bloodshot eyes were now steadily fixed on him. 'It seems a shame not to have them together. Besides, I'd like a proper memento.'

It seemed like a rather complicated favour to perform. 'I'm not sure if I can.'

'You said you knew where they were sent. There was the lady at the school. And then the other one.' Her prompt hovered.

'Oh. Yes. Rosie.'

'Yes.'

Again she waited. Embarrassed, Magnus decided to complete his confession. 'Actually, I might be able to help you there. You see, Rosie is going to be my landlady. You might not have heard, she's getting married to Colin. Colin as in Claire.'

He feared Isabel's reaction, but none came. Her voice strengthened, the politeness in her tone reflecting determination. 'No, I didn't know. But in that case you could ask her about it today.' She walked over to the book shelf and picked up a cheque-book and pen. She spoke as she wrote. 'You can start to think about the equipment you need to buy. It's the only thing I'll ever ask from you.' She turned, tore the cheque from the book and held it out. 'Will you do it for me? Please?'

He stared at it. His hand reached out and took it. 'Right,' he said.

She flushed. Her shoulders relaxed and he could see relief spreading through her, but she turned as if she wanted to hide her pleasure. 'Wait here. I'll dig out your bag for you. I put it in another room.'

But he didn't wait. He followed her as far as the entrance to the corridor, just in time to see her slip into the guest room. From inside he heard a whispered dialogue. Was someone else in there, or was she talking to herself again? He crept forwards and tried to hear what was being said, but only caught the back end of it: 'There, you see, he's agreed. You can't say I haven't done my bit . . . What?'

He slowly pushed open the door and Isabel immediately stopped talking. There was no one else in the room. She hauled the rucksack towards him. 'Here you go.'

He took it from her. 'Who were you talking to?'

'Nobody, of course. Now, I've got things to do.' She motioned him back along the corridor. He lifted the rucksack and she followed him to the door, which she opened for him.

'It was Claire, wasn't it?' Her body stiffened but she didn't answer. He felt blood rush to his face. 'I want you to stop playing these games, Isabel. It's not healthy, in fact it's upsetting. Can't you understand that? She's my sister.'

She was humbled. 'I didn't mean to upset you. I'm sorry.'

'You were talking about me, weren't you? What were you saying?'

'That's private.'

'You were talking out loud. I'm entitled to know——'

She cut him short. 'No, you're not. Not when you're about to walk off and move in with . . .' She struggled briefly with her temper, mastered it, and finished her sentence more calmly. 'With somebody else.' He was shoved out of the flat. 'Don't forget your promise,' she said, then closed the door in his face.

He stood there for a moment, glowering. Claire's thesis held a clue to what was going on in Isabel's mind, and why she had decided to strike this extraordinary bargain for the remaining parts of the baboon. Making the rucksack more comfortable on his back, he went down the stairs and out on to the street. There, he groped in his pocket for the last of his change. It was just enough. He hurried to the corner, promptly caught a taxi and was driven off towards a bank to deposit the cheque. Rumbling over the cobbles in the badly sprung cab, however, he had a sudden thought and rummaged through the contents of his rucksack. He was relieved to find that Colin's letter addressed to Claire was still there, firmly glued shut. A little too glued? He inspected it in the light but could not be sure whether it had been steamed open. Perhaps his suspicion that Isabel had pried was a symptom of his own curiosity. Spontaneously, and with a certain amount of shock at his own behaviour, he tore it open and began to read.

Eight

In his newly arranged room at India Street, Magnus swivelled his chair and cast a cool eye over his purchases. From various Leith Walk second-hand stores he had sourced a computer with psychological problems, a convalescent video duplicator that shut down on him without provocation, and a printer that burped fruitily as it delivered smeared copy. Behind his bed there was a roll-down white screen (with romantic-looking stains) and in the other corner a film projector of Eastern European provenance that resembled a heavy machine-gun, on a tripod. The only whiff of genuinely recent technology lay beside the cheap video machine. It was a digital camera — Leith-bought again and, no doubt, freshly burgled.

Proudly he hefted the camera in his hands despite a lingering sense of disloyalty to his father's sole donation: an old Super 8, which lay obsolete in a drawer. He hoped that these investments, made with Isabel's money over the past few days, would shore up his shaky credibility as a professional video-maker. Video-maker. The title felt clumsy; the camera did not.

Magnus could take no pride as yet in having set up his own business, although he had surprised himself. Somehow, over the course of a week and despite the daze of grief, he had organised himself in a way that had successfully eluded him for over a decade. Yes, it was true that he was only broaching the outer margins of the film world, but it was better than supply-teaching in London, where Felicity and Piers were no doubt working off their guilty consciences every night in his sour-smelling bedroom. The thought made him groan, but thankfully he didn't have the time or inclination to dwell on it. This morning he was set to perform his first ever commission, that of filming Rosie's wedding. Positive thinking was required; focus absolutely essential (he had been reading about these things). Anxiously, he twiddled a knob on the camera. It was the sort of camera on which twiddling knobs felt especially good.

Indulging in positivity was a mistake, however. His ability to keep going made him feel guilty, just as his parents' equal success made him angry. There was not much difference between them. Mother and Father clung to the outward appearance of nothing having changed while he, on the other hand, sought outwardly to change everything. He had not experienced another nightmare since the one that had featured Isabel's mutilation. Nor had there been another sighting of Claire in the street. She was fading from his life, and his despicably healthy survival instinct was encouraging it to happen.

The suspicion gnawed at him that Claire's death, even at this early stage, had raised the value he put on his own life. Had he not taken an illicit pleasure in all sorts of daily activity? For instance, he had spent a scandalously large part of Isabel's business loan — which he was not even sure she could afford — on garments. Of course, while handing over the credit card he had justified the Kenzo suit as a legitimate expense: he couldn't very well film a wedding in a pair of jeans, even if they were prestigiously labelled (a pair of Armani jeans were hanging in his cupboard, in fact). A flush of shame spread across his face. Would such considerations even have crossed his mind before Claire's death? The answer was no. Taking an illicit pleasure in life again was a damning sign that he was steering away from death and, with it, memory.

Inescapably, it seemed, things were looking up. Physically he felt improved — Rosie's massage had helped — and outwardly he was active. Perhaps this meant that he secretly nursed a sibling rivalry. Was Claire's destruction the fulfilment of a secret desire? He recoiled from the thought but that only seemed to persuade him it might be true.

However improved he looked on the outside, confusion still reigned within. Last week he had used his new computer to visit various American grief websites where he discovered that his nuttier experiences — his sightings of the dead, his bizarre physical symptoms of numbness and dislocation — were by no means exclusive to him. He had stopped short of participating in a discussion group, however. He did not want to talk with other people who saw the dead on buses. It was as simple as that.

Magnus brooded some more. Maybe his sibling-rivalry theory was right. Maybe he didn't want her back. If only he could be more like Isabel. However weird, her heart was in the right place. She longed for Claire to return. That was why she talked to her all the time.

As if on cue, the phone rang. Guessing that it was her, he let the answering-machine take it, deciding that he was too busy. Setting aside the camera he began to fold some home-printed flyers which he would send to schools, institutes and anywhere else that might conceivably want a 'professional' film record of an event (inverted commas were circling his new career like vultures).

'Please leave a message for Magnus Calder of Trenchant Films,' went the machine and Magnus whimpered with self-consciousness.

Then there was a beep and his mother's voice came on the line. It sounded hesitant and self-conscious; she was still suspicious of modern advances in telephony. 'Yes. Hello, Magnus, this is your mother . . .'

He picked up and adopted a hurried, officious tone. 'Yes, Mother, what is it?'

'Hello, dear, so you're there.'

'I'm about to go out. I'm filming a wedding in an hour.'

'Oh, really? That is nice. Anyone I know?'

He considered telling her the truth, but it would be complicated to explain that her once prospective son-in-law Colin was tying the knot with his flatmate.

So he lied instead: 'No, not really. Mother, I have to work.'

'That's why I was calling. Do you remember that your father mentioned Ashton was putting on a school play? Well, they want to make a video record for the pupils and parents.'

How many more times did he have to tell them? 'Mother, I do not need Father to fix a job for me. Is that clear?'

'But he won't be fixing anything. It's just to tell you there's an opportunity. I've got a phone number if you'd like to ring yourself.'

'I've got to go, Mother. Now.'

She sighed. 'Well, all right, then, I won't keep you. Good luck. Remember to clean your shoes.'

He hung up, and almost immediately the phone rang again. Rolling his eyes, he waited. This time it really was Isabel. Her voice came on the line, sounding strained, listless but persistent. 'Hello, Magnus, this is Isabel again. Could you pick up, please? All right, if you're not there then please call me back, as soon as you get this message.'

He raised his eyebrows and licked an envelope. He was glad that she did not have the number of his mobile phone. There were various reasons why he did not want to see or speak to Isabel, but guilt was the guiding theme. He would not be able to repay her loan for a very long time, however well his business performed. Furthermore, he had as yet made no effort to track down the other two pieces of the baboon carving. He could not identify why he felt so much resistance to the sole favour she had asked of him, but he suspected that it related to the last and most significant reason for his wanting to avoid her: namely the scale of her continuing grief, which now threatened to dwarf his own and which, as a consequence, caused him to feel a certain resentment. The constancy, even heightening, of her suffering made him uncomfortably aware that his own appeared to be reducing incrementally as time went by. He couldn't help this. Claire's death, while a daily part of his existence, no longer exerted its grip with quite such relentless cruelty. He had read on a grief website that such things were all part of a natural process. Natural processes, however, did not seem to apply to Isabel.

He turned his attention to the work diary. A couple of requests for his services had already come in from old friends of Claire. One of her address books had proved a useful mailing list: not only had her network of contacts been substantial, but quite a few were getting married, or having babies, and were demonstrating a willingness to assist the bereaved younger brother as he tried to make his way in the world. Being considered a charity case wasn't so bad so long as there was rent to pay and an ambition to reach the bottom rung of the property ladder. The implication of the desire for property, he knew, was that one day he might want someone to share it with, but he swiftly halted that line of thinking. Relationships could be considered at a future date. In the meantime he resolved simply to stand with the camera pressed to his eye, still as a rock, while christenings, nuptials and anniversaries broke on either side of him. He wouldn't try any fancy film work. He would be competent, get paid, and everything would work out in the long run. That was his new philosophy.

Glancing at the bedside clock, he saw that time was running short. Nervous flutters filled his belly. This job was his chance to establish a reputation: it was crucial that he chose the right shirt to wear. The choice had been narrowed down to a Reporter number of ivory hue and a more provocative Sorbino in dark green when he heard the front door open downstairs. Rosie had already decamped to a friend's house in preparation for the ceremony so this must be Colin, fresh (or more likely stale) from his long shoot in the north. Manly footsteps ascended the stairs, two or three at a time. Rosie had already made an ironic comment about how pleased she was that her fiancé had managed to fit their wedding into his hectic work schedule, so no surprise that he and Magnus had yet to speak to each other. That moment was now approaching. He pulled open his desk drawer and checked that Colin's letter addressed to Claire was still where he had put it. His ears burned as he thought about its contents and he remembered the cramps that had immobilised him when he first read it in the cab – severe enough for the driver to suggest dropping him at the Royal Infirmary instead of the bank. He straightened the papers on his desk, hastily twiddled the camera settings back into place and set it down carefully, out of harm's way, in the corner.

He heard a knock on his bedroom door. Then it opened and Colin stepped in. He had barely changed:

still young-looking, with upright wavy brown hair, long skinny legs and a high narrow chest, which he revealed as he rapidly unbuttoned his shirt. It was completely smooth. 'Magnus, hi. I seem to be running late.'

When Magnus had moved in, he had promised himself not to dwell on Claire and what she would have thought of the circumstances in which he found himself. He had a theory that they were linked to his paranoias and funny turns. But when he saw Colin pull off his shirt and put on a fresh white one something hormonal dashed through his system. While he could see how Claire had found Colin's matador body attractive, he had not been expecting to respond to this hasty strip show with a girlishly fluttering heart. And, despite the veil of hurried informality, Magnus could tell that Colin was not pleased to see him again. After all, who would want to see the brother of a dead ex-girlfriend set up shop in their flat, even if they were desperate for rent? But as they pumped hands Magnus was relieved to sense that all he had to deal with from his landlord was strong aversion, not full-blown hostility. Presumably Rosie had not mentioned the massage. Suppressing a certain sly satisfaction, he assumed the mien of a perfect lodger and smiled. 'Colin,' he said, 'how are you? Looking forward to the big event?'

The faint lines on Colin's high forehead crinkled in his attempt to maintain his own smile, but his wide handsome mouth twitched at the edges.

'A bit tired, to tell the truth,' he replied. 'I'm just back from a shoot.' Then he looked around the room.

He whistled softly. 'You've done quite a job on this room. I don't think I've ever seen it so clean.'

It was true. Magnus had cleaned and disinfected with almost manic intensity. The skylight window had been freshly buffed while the small patch of carpet was certified fluff-free. His hand crept up to his neck, where he began to pluck the skin. Colin watched him.

'Anyway,' Colin resumed, 'how's everything going? I hear we're in the same business.' He aimed a jocular punch into his tenant's shoulder.

Magnus did not welcome the false professional camaraderie. Rosie had already informed him that Colin was a success story, producing high-budget television advertising and developing a slate of low-budget feature films. Now he would have to say something humble. 'I'm just starting out. It was good of you to choose me for the wedding.'

'It was all Rosie,' replied Colin, without hesitation.

Magnus was mildly embarrassed. The honesty was no more called-for than the filmmakers-in-arms stuff.

'Is there something wrong with your neck?' asked Colin.

Magnus blinked and let his hand drop from the now red skin beneath his Adam's apple. 'No. Why?'

'Claire used to do the same thing when she was nervous. It must be a family trait.'

There was a further moment of uncertainty. Magnus wanted to put Colin on the defensive and there was only one way to do it. His old friend and enemy, guilt. 'Well, you've certainly moved on, haven't you? Life's looking up.' He made sure that his cheerful tone contained a suitable measure of accusation.

Colin stopped buttoning the fresh shirt and his gaze fell to his feet. He had probably been expecting this. 'Yes and no. I was very sorry to hear about what happened to Claire. I don't know what to say except . . . Well, you know the circumstances. We had broken up. But she was a lovely girl.'

Magnus let Colin's last comment flutter, broken-winged, to the ground. 'Yes. Thanks for saying that. I wasn't going to mention it right before your wedding.'

'Rosie said you had to go out to Africa to deal with all the paperwork. How was it?'

'The worst time of my life.'

He nodded stoically. 'Of course.'

'Do you still think about her?'

'Yes, of course I do.'

'You didn't have to say that.'

'You didn't have to ask. But since you did, I told the truth.'

Magnus smiled. 'Perhaps it would be easier for you and Rosie if it wasn't true.'

'Neither of us wants to forget Claire, Magnus. You wouldn't be here if that was the case.' Colin looked down. 'I was devastated when I heard.'

'Not even a little relieved?'

Colin went pale and stared back. 'What do you mean by that?'

Magnus watched Colin's discomfort with only mild pleasure. Amazingly he felt pity for him. 'Colin, she was on her way to Rundu to pick up the mail when the accident happened. She never got there. She never read your letter.'

Colin flushed now. His hand went up to his wrinkled brow. It looked like a confused salute. 'But you did?'

The question didn't require an answer. 'It's a good thing she didn't get it, don't you think?'

Colin let his hand drop and stared directly at Magnus. 'Me and Rosie had argued. I was letting off steam when I wrote it. I wish to God I hadn't sent it.'

He hit home. 'Why? Because it was all lies? You didn't still love Claire? Rosie wasn't "a stupid mistake that's gathered momentum"?'

The barefaced quotation sent ripples of indignation and, finally, shame over Colin's face. 'I was angry. I might have meant it at the time.'

That was enough for now. Magnus took a deep breath. 'However, don't think I'm here to cause trouble. If you feel uncomfortable about me renting here, Colin, I'll find somewhere else to stay. I don't want to upset anyone.'

Colin was being cautious. The letter was playing its part. His voice was soft and very restrained. 'Not at all. We'll be moving out soon anyway. You can have the place to yourself until we sell.'

Satisfied, Magnus clapped his hands together. 'So what's the address of your new place?'

'Twelve Drummond Place. Why? . . . What is it?'

Magnus had made a noise of recognition. It was the unoccupied property that had made an inexplicable impression on him when he took his first walk around the city. He made an intuitive guess. 'Was it a house you looked at once with Claire?'

Colin eyed him uneasily, presuming perhaps that Claire had mentioned this to him. 'Well, yes, we did look at it, a long time ago. Just speculation, though, for fun.' He glanced at his watch and changed the subject. 'Look, let me or the ushers know if there's anything you need. The best man's a professional cameraman if you want some advice. He works with me.'

Magnus acknowledged receipt of the put-down with a faint smile. 'Anyway, best of luck.'

Colin's eyes weighed him up. 'Are you going to mention any of this to Rosie?'

'No. I like Rosie. I just hope you make her happy.'

'I'd like the letter back.'

'You'll get it. I only read it because there wasn't a sender's address on the envelope.' Colin nodded, although it was unlikely he believed the lie.

Magnus glanced at Colin's watch. 'You'd better hurry along.'

There was a silence. Colin seemed partially reassured and went into Rosie's room to finish changing. Magnus dressed himself (Sorbino won the day), gathered his equipment together and was on his way downstairs to call for a taxi when he saw through the bedroom door, from the corner of his eye, Colin struggling with a cufflink. He hesitated on the landing, seized by a small but irresistible impulse. Succumbing to it, he tapped on the door and came in.

'Let me do that.' At first Colin continued to struggle

but then, with a soft swearword, let Magnus slip the cufflink through. It was mother-of-pearl. Magnus sensed that they had been given to him by Claire, a suspicion backed up by Colin's flustered embarrassment as he inspected them.

'There we go,' said Magnus, and stepped back to look at the groom, who stood in front of him, besuited and slightly awkward, like a boy preparing for his first day at school.

'Well?' asked Colin, nervously.

Magnus assessed the suit. Conservative in cut and extremely well tailored, it betrayed no sign of Rosie's influence in its choice. For some reason this was a good thing. Magnus narrowed his eyes, then stepped forwards again, straightened the knot in Colin's soft silk tie, brushed a hair off the jacket and spotted a fleck of shaving foam on the groom's right earlobe. Bizarrely tempted to remove it himself with a thumb, he nevertheless suppressed the urge. 'Shaving foam, right earlobe. Otherwise perfect.'

Colin wiped it off and checked himself in the mirror, then glanced at Magnus's reflection. 'I hope you don't mind me saying this, but you remind me of her. Quite strongly, in fact.'

Magnus felt a jolt of pride. 'That's okay. Unless you're uncomfortable with it.'

Colin ran fingers through his hair. 'Strangely enough, I'm not now.'

Magnus smiled briskly, and went down the stairs. 'I'm calling a taxi if you want a ride?' he called, over his shoulder.

'I'm being picked up. But thanks. See you there.'

Magnus noted that Colin's voice sounded more relaxed than before. He felt satisfied by this, and there seemed no reason to ask himself why as his mind filled with thoughts of work.

Dumpy grey clouds had settled above St Mary's Cathedral, where some of the guests were smoking a last cigarette and talking hats, slander and previous weddings. Magnus wafted among them with his camera, locking faces in the frame, trying to loosen the starched jocularity that a lens inspires in the British on formal occasions. Perhaps this was how the Queen saw the world, Magnus speculated: an array of overdressed people with fixed grins, trying to say the right thing, while others smirked from the sidelines. Undeterred, he kept up the search for someone who was glib or stupid enough to say the wrong thing and raise a laugh; this, he assumed, would sell a few more copies of the finished video. Children were his last resort: they would perform for him readily enough, but wouldn't leave him alone for the rest of the day.

Colin was weaving through the crowd, accompanied by someone with an usher's carnation in his buttonhole. Magnus intercepted them at the mouth of the cathedral and took initial aim at the professional cameraman. 'So, what's your job, then?'

The usher smiled tightly. 'I'm the best man.'

'Still single?'

'Yes.' The usher chuckled at his own response as if he had said something witty.

Not a natural performer, Magnus concluded. He turned the camera on Colin. 'And you, sir? Are you married yourself?'

'Me?' He smiled slowly. 'Not yet.'

'Seen anyone you fancy?'

'She ought to be arriving soon.'

'Ah, so you're the groom.'

Colin kept smiling. 'I think you knew that, Magnus.'

The two men barged past. Magnus swung back to the congregation, who were now filing into the church. He saw Gav, who looked more like an undertaker than ever with his dark suit and grave expression. 'Hello again, Magnus,' he said, and looked into the camera with complete indifference. 'I see you've found your feet already.'

'Yes, thank you,' Magnus replied, lowering the camera and making sure that it was turned off. He had already discovered that it was easy to leave it running by mistake and he didn't want to waste battery power. 'I'm a little surprised to see you here, to be honest.'

'Likewise. But I remain neutral in matters relating to other people's love lives. I'm glad you're of the same mind. We've not seen each other since that night at the Basement, have we?'

Behind them another usher ran up with a mobile phone to his ear. 'The bride's about to turn the corner.'

Gav slipped away into the church with the tail-end stragglers. Magnus jogged towards the road and started filming just as the limousine came into sight. It drew up, and Rosie's father, silver-haired and upright, stepped out smartly. He walked round to the near side of the vehicle and opened the door. Rosie emerged with a winning smile for the camera and an affectionate one for her father when he offered her a hand. But what Magnus noticed first was her dress. It was a simple cream sixties-style strapless number with an empire-line bust and a straight full-length skirt. She had kept the headdress simple too – an unfussy veil pinned neatly to the crown of her head with a few pale roses, so that the material fell away cleanly down her back. A surprisingly un-meringue choice, he thought. It was fashionable but understated – although she might have made a better choice with a neck that was slightly less than swanlike, and, actually, didn't the creamy shade of the fabric verge towards custard in the wrong light? It clashed with her hair.

'Stop!' Magnus said, from the pavement where he was sprawling. Rosie gasped, laughed and went over to help him up.

Her father failed to display similar concern. 'Bloody fool,' he shouted. 'You tripped up on the bloody kerb.'

As Rosie brushed him down, his first thoughts were for his beloved camera. Fortunately it was undamaged, his protective instincts having caused him to put his skull between it and the paving slab. 'Are you okay?' she asked. 'My God, this reminds me of when you ran into the wall at the pub. Are you accident prone?'

He got to his feet and straightened his spectacles. He was thinking like a female: what was so fascinating about empire-line busts anyway, apart from what lay beneath them? 'I'm sorry about that. Can we do it again?' He glanced over at the mouth of the cathedral and saw the minister there, looking very impatient. 'Don't worry, I've got the approach of the limousine. Let's just do the bride's exit from the car once more.'

'Of course,' replied Rosie, then spent a moment calming her father. 'Come on, Dad, take two. And remember to smile.'

Her father returned to the car and banged the door shut behind him. Magnus positioned himself more carefully this time, and readied the camera. Rosie was going to climb back into the limousine but then she stopped and returned once more.

She approached. 'Are you all right there, Magnus?'

The camera came down. He was on the verge of tears. 'I can't go through with this,' he said, despairing. 'I've got it all wrong. Colin said that his best man's a professional. Get him to do it.'

Rosie touched his arm and squeezed. 'What are you talking about? I want you to do this. You'll be fine.'

'But I don't even know where to stand.'

'Nonsense. You made exactly the right decision. Stand just where you were a moment ago.'

'I still think you should get a professional to do this. Oh, God, look, everyone's waiting.'

'Don't worry about them,' she replied firmly. 'You are a professional. But this is your first job. You'll remember this for the rest of your life. Just enjoy it. Have fun. Do whatever you like. Okay?' Magnus sniffed, then nodded. 'How about a smile?' She wiped away a stray eyelash that she had spotted on his cheek. Effortfully he obeyed and she gave him a kiss on the cheek. Fortified, he placed the camera to his eye once more. The best man had appeared beside the minister at the door to see what was the matter. Rosie gave him a thumbs-up and jumped back into the car.

'Okay, let's roll.'

A few minutes later Magnus was filming Rosie's entrance on the arm of her father. Everything seemed to be going less disastrously now, although his arm was still shaking a little. He couldn't really understand why Rosie had taken the risk to employ him for her wedding day, and why Colin had agreed. Unless his presence here in front of the Edinburgh community, even in a filming capacity, was meant to be a tacit blessing of the union, which might neutralise gossip regarding her alleged theft of Colin. Or perhaps it had been simpler and less calculating than that.

But how did he feel about it himself, knowing what he did about the letter, and imagining how appalled Claire would have been? Might it have been better to show it to Rosie? No, in the end that was Colin's decision. The fact was, he genuinely wanted to do this favour for Rosie, as a thank-you for helping him find his feet. A million other women in her position would have given him as wide a berth as possible. Magnus definitely felt better now. Perhaps he was wrong about Claire: perhaps she would have accepted the outcome with good grace. He smiled at the generous thought. This was meant to be a happy day. Perhaps it was only his imagination that suggested Rosie was riddled with doubt.

Magnus tracked her up the aisle and a few moments later she arrived at the altar to join her gently sweating groom. He heard someone hiss behind him. Then he was prodded sharply in the calf. A relative was gesturing that he should move out of the way. He fixed the camera to the tripod, checked that everything was in order and, with the gravitas of a butler, withdrew behind a pillar. The service commenced. Everything was okay. The best man had not even looked in his direction, let alone cast judgement on his working methods. He took a deep breath and felt the tension float away. He was actually beginning to enjoy himself.

A few minutes later, his self-confidence renewed, Magnus judged that the footage might have become a little too static. Ignoring the irritable scuffle of the relative he stepped forward and carefully took the camera in his hands again. Moving to the back of the minister who, he could tell, loathed his presence at the altar, Magnus filmed the couple's faces over his shoulder in anticipation of zooming in when it was time for the vows. However, the service was taking longer than he expected, and while waiting for the vows he thought he might turn the camera's attention to the doting congregation once more, just for a bit of colour. At which point he saw, beside a pillar, someone wave at him. It was Claire.

She was wearing the same beret that she had had on when she passed by in the bus, except now she was wearing large Jackie Onassis glasses and a long white mackintosh. He let the camera drop, shocked but also embarrassed. Even from a distance he could see the mole above her lip. Seeing that she had caught his attention, she stopped waving and stood staring at him with her hands on her hips, mouth turned down. He wondered what on earth she wanted. Then she extended her middle finger. Slowly but with great feeling she rotated her hand and stuck it up. Her lips moved once more, but this time unambiguously: Fuck. You. Only then did he realise that he was missing the vows.

'Shit,' he gasped, and jerked the camera up.

'I will,' said Rosie.

He was still fumbling to get the camera back into position as the couple exchanged a kiss. When he had a chance to look up again, she was gone.

Nine

The wedding guests had moved into an old Victorian hall on the west side of the city for the wedding dinner/disco. Any function split by a forward slash had the power to knock all the festive feeling out of Magnus, and he was already shaken by what he had witnessed at the cathedral. Ghosts weren't supposed to be rude, especially in a church, although it was typical of Claire to be vulgar in church services. And the mackintosh: even taking into account the possibility that Claire was pioneering a new tramp chic, he felt certain that she would not be seen dead in one as grotty as that. She believed that transgressive behaviour in particular had to be well presented. People were watching, after all. Unless, of course, she was invisible to everyone else. That would be intensely frustrating for someone like Claire. While by no means a formal extrovert, she needed to be noticed. However, now that he thought about it, she had been hiding behind a pillar. Why would she hide if she was invisible? Magnus chewed his lip, touched his spectacles, and patted his carefully gelled-down hair. He was making the mistake of trying to apply rational thought to a hallucination, which was probably an expression of his guilty hang-ups. She was hiding because he was hiding something from himself. But do hang-ups stick up a middle finger at you? He had to consider the possibility that what he had seen was a living, breathing reality: Isabel's foreign-exchange student on a mission of retaliation, perhaps. Maybe someone else in the congregation had noticed her come in. Gav, for instance. He had been sitting at the back and, not being the romantic type, might not have had his eyes glued on the couple at the altar.

The guests were sitting down to eat and Magnus was thinking about where he should position the camera for the speeches when he noticed that Gav was saying goodbye to the newly-weds and preparing to slip away. He caught him as he stepped out on to the garden path. 'Where are you off to?'

'Work. I couldn't find anyone to take my shift.'

'Do you have time for a quick cigarette before you go?' Gav checked his watch and agreed. They lit up.

'Did you see someone come in after the ceremony started, wearing a white mackintosh, big sunglasses, a beret?'

Gav frowned and took a long drag. 'Maybe I did. Although I wasn't paying any attention. Someone who went off to the right, beyond the pillars?'

Magnus was excited. 'Yes, yes, that's right! Did you see her face?'

'Sorry. It was just out of the corner of my eye. Why do you ask?'

Magnus controlled his excitement, although just the possibility that someone else had seen the figure came as a huge relief. 'She distracted me when I was filming. I wanted to know who she was.'

Gav looked at him shrewdly. 'A beret, did you say?'

Magnus blushed. 'Yes.'

'Did she remind you of someone by any chance?'

He just looked at his feet. Gav put a hand on his shoulder; he was smiling. 'Can I ask you a personal question? When you went out to Africa, did you actually see her? I mean, did you see her body?'

Magnus took a step back. He laughed; it was a high-pitched noise. 'Are you suggesting she might still be alive?'

Gav's serious brown eyes didn't swerve. 'No. I'm asking you if you saw her body.'

He felt his fists clench. 'No. All right? No, I didn't. Does that make me a coward, then, according to you? If you must know, they told me she was burned to a crisp. They had to get dental records for identification. Satisfied?'

Gav raised his hands. 'Whoa, slow down. I'm just suggesting a possible explanation for why you keep seeing her. Some people say it's very important to see the body, to accept the person's gone. It was for me when my father died.'

Magnus stared at him hard, but realised his reaction had been out of line. 'Sorry, I know you're trying to help. It's just all a bit raw still.'

'That's okay, I understand. But I've got to go now.'

He began to walk away, but Magnus stopped him. 'One last thing. Claire's thesis. You studied with her. Do you remember anything she was working on that involved monkeys?'

Gav looked mystified. 'Monkeys? Wouldn't that be primatology?'

'No. Claire sent a monkey carving back. You know how she used to post things and make you guess what they were. But this one's got us truly stumped.'

Gav ran a hand over his bald head and rubbed his grey chin, which made a rasping sound. 'Now I think about it, she did mention a funny cult of some sort, but I think it was to do with baboons, not monkeys.'

'That could be it. Do you remember anything more?'

'It may have had something to do with *muti*. You know what Claire was like, the more obscure the better.'

'But what is *muti*, exactly?'

'I don't think there is anything exact about it. Some kind of African magic involving human flesh. There was an article about it in the newspapers not long ago. A murder in the African immigrant community down in London, a torso found in the Thames. But that's all I remember. Look, Magnus, I've got to go. You should try and dig up her thesis, if you can. That might tell you more. 'Bye.'

Gav went down through the gate and found himself a taxi. Magnus turned back towards the hall just as the door swung open and the best man came outside. He lit a cigarette and took a serious drag. 'Are you all right?' asked Magnus. 'Worried about your speech?'

The best man looked up at him and exhaled heavily into the cool air. 'Worried? I've just finished it, thank God. Colin's up at the stand now.'

Magnus stared at him, horrified. The film.

The best man glanced back with a pitying grin. 'Don't worry, you didn't miss anything. I was crap.'

But Magnus was already running indoors.

Night had fallen, the ceilidh had started, and people were dancing, drinking and doing foolish things that should have been filmed for posterity. Magnus, however, was sitting beside the exit with the camera in his lap and yet another cigarette dangling from his mouth. He was contemplating the bollocking he would get when the happy couple saw the huge omissions in their wedding video. He had not yet broken the news to either of them, but Colin must have noticed his absence for the first half of the speeches. A catastrophic technical hitch would have to be invented.

He pushed up his spectacles with the knuckle of his thumb and took another pull on the cigarette. Gazing across the dark garden, he tried to send his mind somewhere innocuous, but it was difficult with the 'Dashing White Sergeant' booming over his shoulders, especially now that it was being accompanied by the whoops of a lavishly drunk uncle. He could feel the vibrations running through the floorboards. He rose to his feet and stepped out into the garden, where he threw away the stub and looked up at the sky. It offered little in the way of interest. He sighed.

The tune came to an end, followed by laughter and

clapping. A moment later the inner door of the hall flapped open and a couple emerged, whom he vaguely recognised. They saw him but ignored him and trotted down the path in the direction of a nearby pub. It was not the first time that he had been blanked by guests who, in all likelihood, had been on chatting terms with Claire at the very least. In fact, those who had greeted him were in a small minority. Perhaps his presence at this happy event made her friends feel uneasy. He had seen their uncertain expressions in the camera frame, as if they suspected he was collecting film evidence of their disloyal attendance to use against them. This explained why those more independent-minded, or loyal, or simply two-faced people who had come up to him and expressed their condolences did it so furtively. Even if nobody else had seen Claire in the church, at least some had acted as if they had sensed it somehow.

The street-lamps shone white through the branches of the trees. A car passed by and then the road was quiet. He started to feel chilly. It was in that moment of relative silence that Magnus thought he heard something or someone move behind him. He turned and took a couple of steps with the camera under his arm. Another couple possibly? He glanced around the damp garden but could see nothing in the gloom except for the outline of a dustbin and some more trees. Another dance was launched inside – was it 'Strip the Willow'? Magnus felt the dampness in the air. Shivering, he thought that he ought to go back in for some jolly crowd coverage before the guests became too drunk and sweaty-looking.

As he reached the first step, he heard a woman's voice. 'Magnus?'

He stiffened. 'Yes?'

There was no answer. He recognised the voice but could not place it because it seemed to come from a distance. Curious, he followed a secondary path that circled the building. At the corner he hesitated. There was no light at all here, only two knobbly old trees, a potting shed and a high stone wall dividing the property from another garden. More tenements rose beyond, adding mass to the darkness. He could not see anyone. He didn't feel entirely safe.

'Hello?'

Nothing. He took a couple of steps forward. Everything was quiet but he felt quite sure that someone was standing nearby. Holding out his hand, he retreated to the side of the hall. This cut him off from even the faintest illumination. He hoped that it would prevent him being seen, although he did not know why he wanted to hide. He had been called but his caller had not shown herself.

Then he seemed to hear an intake of breath. He was a little scared, but still half expected this to be a joke, or perhaps something more interesting. He stayed absolutely still, pressed to the wall, listening for any sign. The darkness was heavy as soil. As the seconds passed, his uncertain smile fell away and tendrils of panic crawled over his skin. He couldn't move from the wall. Someone was close.

A sniff gave away her position. He strained his eyes. Protruding from behind the big old tree to the left he saw the hem of a light-coloured coat. Claire? His stomach muscles went tight and his throat dried out. Then he heard another sniff. He would have to step closer to see; he had promised himself that he would not run. With effort, he left the wall and tottered forwards, craning his neck. It wasn't the mackintosh. Relief streamed through him; then a second lurch of fear. His memory of the dream painted the darkness with a woman's white face, livid with a wound.

'Isabel?' he said. His query was cringing, as if it might provoke some unimaginable violence. 'Is that you?'

She didn't answer. He stepped out fully from the cover of the wall and looked behind him, still irrationally suspicious that they were not alone. Apart from the distant bloom of white light beyond the gate there was nothing, so he turned back towards the tree. He approached steadily to see if it really was Isabel. Reaching the base of the tree, he put his hand on the cold wet trunk and leant round.

There was barely any room where she was perched on a root, beside the high garden wall. Her forehead was resting on her forearms. He imagined the flapping veil of skin and the great wooden teeth below. His hand shook as he reached down to touch her shoulder. 'Isabel,' he said again, 'what are you doing here?'

She lifted her head. Her face was puffy, and the reproach in her eyes was accentuated by her smeared eyeliner. But she was unharmed. 'What do you want?'

Magnus squatted down beside her. 'You called me.'

'No, I didn't.' Then she raised her head, eyes shining with hope in the darkness. 'Maybe she did.'

He sighed: she was becoming increasingly difficult to deal with. 'No. It was you.'

'Claire?' she called, looking over his shoulder, searching the mossy darkness. 'Claire?'

'Stop it,' he ordered. 'Now!'

It had taken a force of will not to turn round and check whether his sister was behind him. His neck muscles were frozen. His voice was tight, constrained by the effort to be rational. 'Claire isn't here.'

She looked at him pityingly. 'She's in you, only you won't admit to it. If you opened up you'd see.'

'What is it you're doing here, Isabel?'

She leant forwards and took his hand. Her fingers were cold. 'We've got to help her.'

He pulled away his hand and stood up: he'd had enough. 'She's past helping.'

'Don't you want her back?'

'What do you mean by that? It's impossible.'

She just stared. A small smile twisted her lips. How could he have found that mouth pretty once? He turned away. 'Go home,' he said. 'You'll freeze.'

'Seeing her in the street was impossible too.'

Claire's appearance in the church flashed through his mind. He stopped.

Isabel became alert. 'There's something, isn't there? Something's happened. What is it?'

'I'm surprised you don't know.'

'I don't understand.'

'Since you're in regular contact with her.'

She clambered to her feet, and came close to him. She

put a hand on his shoulder and he shut his eyes, holding down the urge to sob. 'I'm scared,' he said eventually. 'I've no control. I don't understand what's going on in my head. I don't even know if it's *in* my head.'

'I know,' she said softly. 'But that's good. You've just got to listen to the voice inside you. What's it telling you? Is it telling you to do something? To keep a promise?'

'There isn't a voice.'

In the silence they heard a distant female voice. It came from the front door of the hall. 'Colin! Colin, come back!'

Magnus tensed, then smiled wistfully: it was Rosie's voice.

When he turned back to look at Isabel she was smirking at him bitterly. 'Have you asked your flatmate about that piece of the carving yet?'

'I mean to.'

Suddenly she turned fierce. She grabbed his elbow with a cold, tight grip. 'Do it. Get them. You took the money. I will never forgive you if you don't. Nor will she. Never.'

She? The intensity of her gaze frightened him. 'Of course I will. I said so, didn't I?'

Her grip loosened and fell away. 'Good.'

Rosie's silhouette emerged from the corner of the building and hesitated before approaching. He looked from Rosie back to Isabel again. He hoped that Isabel would go without waiting for an introduction but she didn't seem to be in a hurry. Instead she watched Rosie's unsteady approach in her dress and heels with seeming fascination. Her arm was outstretched, her fingers brushing against the wall to guide her in the dark.

'Is someone there?' Rosie called tremulously. 'Colin?'

Isabel's eyes moved to Magnus and he sensed sour amusement at his discomfiture. He raised his voice. 'Rosie, it's me, Magnus.' He hoped that the first person singular would be understood by Isabel as a hint to go.

Reassured, Rosie came towards him only to hesitate once more when she saw that he was not alone. 'Oh, hello.' This was directed to him, but she peered at Isabel, unsure of her identity. 'Who else is there?'

Magnus was about to make the introduction, but Isabel chose the moment to walk away, shoving Rosie as she went. They watched in silence as her figure floated across the patch of light at the front door and through the garden gate. There was a soft gust of wind and a clatter of wings in the upper branches of the tree.

'Who was that?' asked Rosie. 'Not a guest?'

'No,' Magnus replied. 'A friend of mine. She was just passing by and saw me. What are you up to?'

'Colin's in a mood about something. I just said I was looking forward to getting inside the new house and he muttered something about getting it exorcised first. What do you think that was supposed to mean?'

'I have no idea. Perhaps he's a little stressed.'

'Still, it would be nice if he could wind down now and then. You know, just for special occasions like his wedding.'

She chewed her lip in thoughtful irritation. Magnus led

her back towards the front door and they sat down on the step together. He fiddled with the camera on his lap, wondering whether he had the right to pry. Eventually he asked, 'What's really bothering you?'

'We've been having more arguments, that's all. Probably quite normal in the run-up to a wedding, I suppose, with everything to organise and him not being here. But he wants me to give up my physio training.'

Magnus was surprised. 'Really?'

'Yes. He thinks one of us needs to be around the house. He's right, of course, doing it up will be a full-time job and he's not going to have time. But still. It makes me wonder if I've done the right thing. I think there's jealousy in there too.'

'Christ, Rosie, don't say that now. It's a busy time for you both. Give it a year or so, things will look up.'

Rosie looked at him and smiled wearily. 'I've got the wrong man.'

'Post-nuptial depression. It's a passing phase.'

'I've fucked up, Magnus. What do I do?'

He didn't have an answer to that. She was tired, that was all. Then the hall door opened and the two of them were hauled back in to join the party.

Ten

Chopped garlic struck oil and hissed against the grooved metal of the wok. Chilli followed, swept imperiously off the wooden chopping-board with a knife that, in Magnus's hands, had already been busy preparing the ingredients for a curry, which had been Claire's speciality. Although he had never taken a strong interest in cooking himself, he found that he not only remembered how all the ingredients went together but had also discovered in himself a certain dexterity at the stove. This was the day after the wedding. The happy couple had given themselves a day to recover before the honeymoon and Magnus had promised to send them off with a meal. Despite a moment's hesitation – they needed time to pack – there was no convenient excuse to turn down the offer, even if Colin had wanted to.

'Is that chilli?' asked Rosie, looking over Magnus's shoulder. 'Great for me, but I'm not sure Colin will eat it. He has a problem with spice.'

Colin, who had been next door locating a bottle of

wine, came through at this point. Magnus reached for the ginger root. 'He'll like this one,' he replied, raising his voice so that Colin could hear. 'Stir-fried chicken, *à la* Calder?'

Colin paused, the corkscrew poised over the bottle. Rosie smiled. 'Don't worry, he can fix himself something else.'

'Not at all, I'll give it a whirl,' said Colin.

Magnus reached for the pieces of chicken and caught a glimpse of Rosie's expression, which was irked. Nevertheless she accepted a glass of wine. 'You've never given my curries a whirl,' she muttered.

Colin gave her a look that implied he was only doing this to be polite. Magnus knew better. Although he couldn't remember where he had got the information, he knew that Colin ate this kind of dish. He had grown more comfortable with knowledge of uncertain provenance, including fashion vocabulary. It didn't seem to do any harm.

A glass of wine was put down beside him, and he nodded thanks to Colin, whose meaningful glance, if he read it correctly, contained both a veiled warning and a query. Magnus merely smiled and flipped the contents of the pan to sear the chicken on both sides, an action that he had seen Claire do many times, but which he had never tried to emulate until now. There was no spillage; he did it once more and set the pan down, aware that Colin was watching him closely even as he chatted to his wife about how his pissed uncle had been dancing a little too close to one of the younger female guests. Strange how Magnus had always ignored or attempted the exact opposite of Claire's cooking advice when she was alive while now he adhered to it exactly. As he splashed in a mix of fish sauce, soy, orange juice and cumin seeds, the wok sent up a fragrance that set his mouth watering. If Claire was shaping his actions, the results were not all bad.

However, he was aware that her presence, manifest in this meal, might not be entirely comforting for his companions. Their chat continued merrily enough but he sensed that Rosie was suspicious of the curry's conception while Colin, judging by his gaze, was made uneasy by the cook's uncannily Claire-like actions, which Magnus, for whatever reason, found himself accentuating. He found this impulse difficult to explain. Not for the first time, he felt that his actions and gestures were not entirely his own. When had he ever offered to cook a meal for anyone before? How could he account for this nonchalant ability with the pan?

He had become aware of another small change too, whenever he looked in the mirror. As a child and all the way up to Claire's death, he had traditionally failed to see any likeness between the two of them. Now he could spend time staring at himself, searching for a suggestion of her in his own smile or sideways glance. Just this morning he had dabbed his lip with a black marker pen, curious to see if a mole would have the same transforming effect on him as he'd thought it had on her. Unfortunately it did not and he scrubbed it off, vaguely ashamed. He knew that emotionally he remained disjointed. Maybe he was healing wrong. Reaching for the salt, the soft white skin of his forearm brushed the hot pan. He yelped and jumped back.

'Are you okay?' asked Rosie, as he ran the red weal under the cold tap.

'I just singed myself,' he replied. 'Nothing serious.' At least he had retained his clumsiness, which was all his own.

When the meal was ready they moved to the table. Colin ran his finger over the wooden surface as Magnus set down the wok and the bowl of rice. 'What happened here? It looks brand new.'

Magnus was slightly embarrassed. 'Actually, that was me. I sanded it and put some oil into it. I hope you don't mind.'

'Not at all,' Colin replied.

'He's been through the flat like a dose of salts,' said Rosie, spooning out some rice. 'I've never seen it so clean. Have you ever seen it so clean before, Colin?'

The question, sweetly enunciated, sounded loaded nevertheless.

'Not in a very long time,' he answered, then made a lunge for the wok. 'Now this does look tasty.'

It was true. Magnus had been unable to keep his cleaning fetish to his own bedroom and, with the exception of Rosie's bedroom, had set about sanitising the whole flat (restricting vacuum-cleaning to daylight hours). During his diurnal cleaning purges, particularly when passing her room, he had suffered from a persistent and throbbing urge to conduct a search for a piece of the baboon that Isabel wanted so badly. But he had stopped himself, just as he had refrained from mentioning the carving to Rosie, because he didn't want to find it. He resented the pressure Isabel had put on him, which was not only unreasonable but uncanny. He vividly remembered her pale, angular face in the darkness at the wedding venue, and the comment he had not been able to shake off: *Don't you want her back?*

What a question. To which the honest answer was no. He was happy to keep Claire where she was: stored lovingly in his memory, and casting a warm shadow over his thoughts and actions. Surely that was where the dead belonged. He just hoped that Isabel wouldn't spoil it.

Colin filled his plate and started eating with nervous gusto. Between mouthfuls he asked, 'So, how did the filming go?'

'Good, mostly.' Magnus wasn't sure whether he should own up immediately to the omission of the best man's speech and the mess-up at the altar, but in any case he was saved by the phone.

'Sorry. I'd better get that. I'm expecting a call.'

Rosie, who had been watching Colin's rapidly emptying plate with pique, touched Magnus's arm as he stood up. 'Why don't you take it upstairs in that case?'

He picked up the call in his bedroom. At the end of the line was the soft voice of a drama teacher called James Langley at Ashton School in Northamptonshire. He apologised for phoning out of office hours. 'I've been rushed off my feet. You see, we're putting on a theatre production of *Titus Andronicus*, and only today the head told me that it would be a good idea to film the production during dress rehearsals. It's all frightfully last-minute, but do you think you could do it? It would have to be tomorrow.'

Magnus did not know how to respond. He was furious that his parents had gone ahead with setting this up for him, despite all his efforts. It was quite a long way to go, but could he really afford to turn work down? 'You're right, it is very last-minute. Just hold on, I have to check my diary.' Magnus went through the motions of flicking through it, although he already knew that it was more or less empty over the next two weeks. He had to make a decision. 'Actually, I probably can do it, so long as it isn't in the morning.'

'No, it's late afternoon. Is that a yes?'

'It is.'

'Oh, good, I am glad.' There was a pause. 'I understand that you have a connection with the school.'

Magnus was not sure whether he referred to his father or his sister. 'Yes, my father runs the Old Ashtonian Association. And my sister Claire taught there briefly. She was involved in the theatre side, too.'

'Before my time, I'm afraid. But it's good that you know the ropes. Shall I see you tomorrow, then? Just call in at the headmaster's office when you arrive and we can meet at the theatre later.'

'Yes, all right.'

Magnus hung up, then instantly phoned his parents' number. He got the answering-machine and shouted at it: 'I told you not to phone the school and you did anyway. Well, I'm going to do the job but I'm totally pissed off. Goodbye.'

He slammed down the receiver. Of course, going to the school meant that Isabel would expect him to track down the other piece of the carving that was supposed to have been sent there. It then occurred to him that maybe *she* was behind this commission. Had she, in fact, collaborated with his parents? If so, he was going to be spitting. Lending him money did not justify ganging up on him like this. He headed grumpily downstairs, but halted before he reached the bottom. Rosie and Colin were arguing in the loudest of whispers.

'You're the one who invited him to move in,' he said, 'and now you're the one who has the problem.'

'I don't have a problem,' she hissed back. 'Not with him, anyway. It's . . .' Her sentence stopped short, and instead she made a squawk of frustration.

Magnus knew what she wanted to say. She wanted to say 'Claire', but she couldn't because it didn't make sense. He felt sorry for Rosie. Her flat had been annexed by Claire's cleanliness, Claire's cooking, Claire's brother. The only thing missing was the person to point the finger at, because she happened to be dead. Or perhaps she regretted her drunken confession that she wasn't happy with her husband. Unhappiness and bad decisions could be lived with, but regrets were best kept quiet.

He heard the creak of a chair as Colin leant back. 'Well, it's only temporary. Cheer up, we'll be away to Sicily tomorrow and moving into the new house when we get back.'

Judging that it was time to advertise his approach, Magnus crept back to the top of the stairs and came down them again with heavy footsteps. When he entered the kitchen they looked up and gave him a big corporate smile.

'Everything all right?' Rosie asked.

'Absolutely fine. But I've got a long drive to a job tomorrow, so I'm off to bed. Goodnight. See you in the morning, hopefully.'

In fact, they did see each other the next morning, at about four. Magnus had no idea where he was, or what he was doing, only that a light had come on and he was sitting in the downstairs study in a pair of boxer shorts, surrounded by open cupboards, spilt papers and disgorged drawers. He blinked and turned round.

Colin was standing in his pyjamas by the light switch, surveying the damage. 'Good morning,' he said. 'Are you all right? I heard you bumping around outside our bedroom door, and then noises coming from downstairs.'

Magnus rubbed his eyes and looked around him once more. 'I . . . don't know. Who did all this?'

'You did. I've been watching you, you were fast asleep but with your eyes half open, going through a drawer.'

'You should have woken me up.'

'Are you supposed to? I said your name a few times. Were you looking for something in a dream?'

Magnus groaned and ran a hand through his hair, still spaced out. 'God, it's happened again. I'm a sleepwalker. Just ask Rosie. She found me at the bottom of the stairs . . .'

Colin finished the sentence for him. 'In your pants with the vacuum-cleaner about to blow up. I know. She told me.'

'Yes.' Embarrassed, Magnus got off the floor and brushed himself down. 'I can't remember what I was dreaming. I can only apologise. I'll clear all this up.'

Colin smiled. 'That's okay. Since you do the cleaning, I think you're allowed to make the occasional mess. I don't expect you found much of interest. There's only old bills and cheque-book stubs as far as I know. Anyway, if you don't mind, I'm going back to bed.'

'Right. Me too. Maybe I should get a lock for my door. Sorry again.'

Colin turned round and plodded back up the stairs, leaving Magnus to put everything away as best he could.

Magnus released the handbrake, cranked from first gear to second, then braked once more and rested his head on the spindly steering-wheel of his mother's car. Pus-green and hopelessly underpowered, her 'runaround' was never going to mark him out as a leader of men, but it had been the only vehicle available to him at short notice and at least the petrol tank was full. The journey had been miraculously trouble-free until he had reached this point on the motorway, somewhere east of Coventry, about an hour ago. The Astra's grille was inches from the quivering tailpipe of a dun-coloured Mondeo, and would be for the foreseeable future, it seemed. He sighed and contemplated sounding the car's horn in what he understood was a Mediterranean expression of frustration. The morning sky was uselessly blue. It heated the black road surface, which in turn was baking the underside of his bare elbow where it rested on the window-ledge. At this rate he would not reach Ashton until about four.

He brooded. Having not been to the school since he tagged along with his parents to a centenary celebration over a decade ago, he was filled with vague apprehension about seeing it again. There was also an element of despair: how was it that in attempting to strike out on his own, free from the influence of sister and family, he found himself heading towards her old haunt, on a job fixed up by his father, with a secondary mission to retrieve a piece of carving that Isabel seemed convinced would 'bring her back' in some inconceivable way? Corralled by a combination of obligation and necessity, he sensed a conspiracy, except nobody had forced him to do anything. He was blaming other people and external factors for the situation he was in, but wasn't it also possible that some dark corner of his unconscious was determining his future? People used to call it fate. He, on the other hand, was tempted to call it Claire.

Drumming his fingers anxiously on the steering-wheel, he looked out of the car window, over the fields. He still had faith that his most private thoughts and feelings were his own, but his sleepwalking experience the night before had shocked him. It suggested that his will was under siege, to the extent that his body could be commandeered when he slept. He couldn't remember what he had been searching for when Colin found him, but he could guess.

The carving was calling him, and however much he resisted temptation it still found a way, at night, when his defences were down. It was becoming an icon in his mind, imbued with power and its own implacable will.

He pushed up his spectacles and pinched the bridge of his nose. It was scary how huge an impact Claire's death had made on his most fundamental ideas about the world. Amusingly, he had previously considered himself an atheist. Now the denial of god or gods seemed blindly dogmatic. Gav had been wrong to suggest that Magnus couldn't accept her dying: he could. But he couldn't close his eyes to the constant, irrefutable sense that her spirit was still with him in some way. Atheism couldn't explain that to his satisfaction. This did not mean, however, that he was about to discover organised religion. That would require faith. All he had was fear, and unease, and confusion.

For instance, if he believed that Claire's spirit had survived physical death, how was it that he couldn't think of her without visualising her in her body? It was incredibly difficult to recall her personality or opinions in isolation from her features and mannerisms, as this was how memory kept its grip. While he remembered with a smile how she fiddled with her hair-grip when impatient to make a point, her mercurial political convictions could no longer irritate or amuse him. He recalled that she had once fervently opposed private education until she tired of teaching at a north London comprehensive and accepted Father's help in securing a post at Ashton. It had scandalised Magnus at the time; now it seemed just, well, human. Arguments faded; posture remained.

He looked at his own hands on the steering-wheel. Hers had been weathered, almost masculine, but her arms were slim and freckled; they used to make him think of an adolescent with more growing to do. He remembered the set of her teeth, the way one lower incisor was slightly crowded out of alignment. And there were the moments when she was excited or passionate and the bridge of her nose would seem to grow taut, adding to the intensity of her eyes. In picturing her with such detail, he felt her presence once more. It was as if she was beside him in this hot little car.

But the momentary exaltation went as suddenly as it came, leaving behind a fresh sense of loss, and then perplexity. Had the person he saw at the church really looked like her? The mackintosh had made it difficult to judge the body, and the distance meant he could not see the face in detail. Hadn't she seemed smaller than he remembered? If she had been a product of his imagination, she would have fitted his recollection perfectly: the dead don't change. If only she had not been so far away, he thought; if only there had been another reliable witness. But then he realised that there was another witness: the camera. When he got back home he would check the tape and see if he could ascertain who it was – if it was.

The traffic edged forwards and this time the Astra's green bonnet swallowed two road markings in one go. Then he realised that he had used the word 'home' to describe India Street. Was this really how he felt? Only if Rosie was there. About now they would be touching down in Sicily with their honeymoon spreading out ahead of them. Except they were only there for one night, of course: Colin's schedule was awfully tight. The fool didn't know how lucky he was.

A smile crossed Magnus's face. Further ahead the road was clearing. Within minutes, his gloomy thoughts were blown away by the glory of movement. Soon the motorway became dual-carriageway. Swiftly the car cut through ugly villages that had burst out of their traditional boundaries and left grey ropes of settlement on either side of him. Then, at last, he found himself in more human countryside. The old villages in this part of the East Midlands had retained their shape and were built of crumbly yellow sandstone; he stopped in one. The weather was mild and the air smelt grassy after several hours enclosed in the Astra with a mildewed road map. The local people seemed archaically content and so did their dogs. Even better, Ashton wasn't far away now.

The first signs of the school were visible on the approach to town. Beyond the hedges on either side of him spread empty playing-fields. Rugby posts rose against the sky, each white H a totem that summoned a familiar tapping against his ribs and a tightening in his stomach: he was entering one of Claire's territories once more. Parking the car on a side-street, he walked along one of the main roads into the centre of the old market town.

The school's heavy Victorian infrastructure was every-where. The main concentration of classrooms was in a large stone cloister, whose arched passageways were thronged with pupils coming out of lessons. Across the road was a tall neo-Gothic assembly room, the Great Hall, according to the sign above the door. Other department buildings lined the main street, some modern, others older, and between the school's stone fingers squeezed the local service industries: two bookshops, a school outfitter's, newsagents and sandwich shops.

He was almost charmed by it all when a phalanx of girls approached him along the pavement, schoolbooks pressed against their V-neck jumpers and ankle-length skirts kicking out with every stride. Privilege on the move, thought Magnus, with amusement, until they shoved him into the gutter. A car hooted and brushed his ankle. More pupils followed and Magnus was being bumped left and right by satchels and children from lower forms. Open crisps packets combined with fag breath to stifle him. Islanded amid this stale-smelling stream of youth, unable even to move the few feet into a shop entrance, he remembered once more why he had left the teaching profession. The atmosphere of overfunding in this place seemed especially obnoxious.

A distant bell rang, and the street cleared. Magnus looked around, slightly disoriented. As other civilians came out of hiding and went about their business, he decided to turn back, hoping to find someone so that he could clarify arrangements for the shoot.

At the cloister, he looked up. He was being observed from one of the classroom windows by a boy made pale by sunlight hitting the upper storey. The expression on his face was one of mild, bored arrogance. Then he disappeared. Magnus kept his eyes fixed on the window for a moment longer. A wisp of inherited memory seemed to brush against him and he was left with the uncomfortable suspicion that this face had once held a significance to Claire.

He found the headmaster's office at the top of some brown stone steps and was given the necessary times and details. He was also given directions to the school sanatorium where his accommodation had been arranged. He drove to the edge of town, where he spotted two tall walls of conifers and a pebbled drive that curled behind them. The sanatorium's size surprised him. Surrounded by a large garden, it looked as if it had been built early in the twentieth century, with wooden gables that made it look more like a golfing residence or upmarket retirement home than a medical centre. He parked in front of its left wing, tolerating a passing pupil's sneer at the Astra, and pushed through some weighty wooden swing-doors reinforced with brass. They closed behind him with two great brushstrokes against the mat.

The entrance led him on to a long corridor with a marble floor. Several schoolboys in tracksuits and rugby jerseys were ranged against the wall, gossiping and picking dried mud from their boot studs. A couple of younger ones in jackets and ties turned to look at him; then everyone's conversation died. He sensed them judging whether he was a new member of staff. After all, he had the education sector's answer to a military bearing: here, his posture said, is a man accustomed to giving orders and having them disobeyed. Magnus rose up to his full

height and smiled at them all in a general way. Several
looked away. Then one of the older boys in a tracksuit
broke the silence with a long, liquid sniff, which he noisily
swallowed.

Facing the line of wooden chairs on which they sat
was another large door, presumably the doctor's surgery.
This opened and a boy of about seventeen emerged with
a prescription note in his hand. Beyond the door Magnus
glimpsed a doctor's grey head bent over a desk, and light
streaming in through a window that looked on to the
garden beyond. 'You can go in,' the boy said to the next
in line. Magnus recognised his face as the one he had seen
in the window of the cloister before lunch. The boy
returned his look with mournful grey eyes that seemed
uninterested at first, then flickered. At that moment he
saw a woman in a nurse's uniform bustle past into a
storeroom at the far end of the corridor, so he went to
ask her instead.

The matron turned out to be a small unorthodox-
looking woman of about forty. She had straight auburn
hair down to the nape of her neck, and an old-fashioned
fringe that didn't really suit her; her name was Marjorie.
Under the pupils' curious gaze Magnus introduced himself
and was explaining that she might have known his sister,
but she cut him short. 'Oh, yes, I know all about you.
Tell you what, let me give you a quick tour of the building
while Susan – she's the nurse – gets your room ready. Is
that all right?'

With some time to kill before his appointment at the
school theatre, Magnus agreed, and she led the way in

a brisk manner, pointing out the staffroom as they went towards the stairs and started to climb.

'This leads to the first-floor ward,' she said. Her hand, which ran up the thick iron banisters, was slightly chapped, but her body – despite the ugly uniform and dumpy shoes – was vigorous and well proportioned. She maintained a starchy demeanour until they reached a set of fire doors. At this point she stopped and turned, glancing at the watch attached to her uniform.

'If I'm keeping you from your work . . .' he said.

'Yes,' she replied. 'You're the perfect excuse.'

With that she pushed open the fire door for him, blocked it with a foot and took a last peep down the stairs. Carefully she let the door swing shut again and glanced at him conspiratorially. A packet of extra-length cigarettes and a shiny gold lighter emerged from her pocket and she tugged open a window that looked out over the drive. 'You don't mind, do you?'

'Not at all,' he replied.

'Keep an eye out,' she said, exhaling luxuriantly towards the window. 'I'm not supposed to set a bad example.'

With his extra height he could see down the stairs, through the wire-reinforced windows of the door. There was no one about. When he turned back he saw that she had been watching him, a soft smile on her face. 'I can see the likeness.'

He smiled back and looked vaguely around him. There was another set of doors to his right and what looked like a long, vaulted ward beyond. 'Magnus, I heard the terrible news about your sister. I didn't want to say anything in front of the boys but I am so sorry. We were good friends, even though we didn't know each other for all that long.'

'Thank you,' he said. He didn't know if there was much more to say. His eyes returned to the ward.

'Feel free if you want to explore. I'll just puff away.'

The ward was untouched by modernity. There were two lines of ten iron beds, with a heavy blanket folded at the foot of each. Through an arched window at the far end, the surrounding garden and more conifers could be seen. The wooden parquet floor had been freshly beeswaxed. Everything was immaculate and completely empty, as if in preparation for an influx of patients that should have arrived forty years ago.

'What does this get used for?' he asked, as the ward doors swung shut again behind him.

'Nothing much,' she replied, taking a small tin out of her apron and using it as an ashtray, 'unless a dormitory gets renovated in one of the school houses or something, in which case they get put here. This place was built when there were still epidemics.' She sighed nostalgically. 'Now it's just a case of giving them some antibiotics or sending them to hospital.' Magnus looked sympathetic, but her regrets about medical progress were soon dissolved by another long and pleasurable drag on her cigarette. 'Oh, do you drink whisky, by the way? I confiscated a half-bottle from one of the boys a couple of weeks ago.'

'I'm amazed it's lasted that long.'

She laughed. 'I can't drink the stuff, I'm afraid. Nor can Susan. So don't hold back.'

'Claire would have helped you with it.'

'Now that you mention it, she did like a tipple. She used to drop by and keep me company on the night shifts. Me with my fags and her with a bottle of Campari.'

They laughed.

'What did you talk about?'

'Oh, everything. She loved discussing the supernatural. All sorts of nonsense. I used to say she ought to have been a mystic. Reincarnation was her thing, wasn't it?'

'She converted me to Buddhism once.'

'Poor you.' Thoughtfully she stubbed out her cigarette in the tin, closed it up and put it back into her pocket. 'I asked her once who she'd like to come back as, and she said she'd be happy to stay herself, except she'd like a few bits from her best friends.'

A vision of Isabel's butchered face swam in front of him; he felt momentarily sick.

She continued, 'I thought it was quite a sweet thought, don't you? Although I never really knew if she meant physically or in terms of personality. "Anything's better than coming back as an earwig," I said.' She glanced up and put a hand to her mouth, mortified. 'I'm sorry, I must sound incredibly insensitive. Please forgive me.'

Magnus fought to recover his composure. 'Not at all. Did she specify which bits she wanted?'

She seemed relieved that he wasn't offended, and crossed her arms over her chest. 'Now, that would be telling.'

'Was there anything about you that she particularly admired?'

His question was genuine this time, so she answered straight. 'I think she saw me as the nurturing type. Can't think why, considering I don't have kids.'

'You've got that lot downstairs instead.'

Suddenly he was put in mind of something ambiguous that Colin had written in his letter to Claire, and reminded himself to read it again. 'Do you think she wanted children of her own?' he asked.

'I never asked directly. But there was a boyfriend, wasn't there, in Edinburgh? Perhaps he wasn't so keen.'

'Perhaps.'

'He must be devastated.'

'He just got married.'

She looked surprised, but his sharp tone discouraged her from enquiring further. The conversation had come to a close. Without fully understanding why, Magnus felt that he had touched on some kind of clue. Bits of her best friends; reincarnation; the baboon carving. It was no coincidence that Isabel had intended him to meet Marjorie, and that she had used his parents, behind his back, to make it happen. He felt like a marionette; but who was really pulling the strings, and what part was he playing?

She straightened. 'Anyway, we'll not put you in a dorm on your own. There are some cosy private rooms downstairs. Does it smell badly of smoke?'

'Not much,' he replied.

'Can we pretend it's you if one of the boys smells it?

Otherwise I lose my moral authority when I catch them behind the conifers.'

Marjorie showed him into a small room off the ground-floor corridor. It had a little fireplace, a window on to the garden, a basin and a wooden chair beside the regulation iron bed. She pulled the curtains wider apart and opened a window.

'A couple of boys are sharing the room next door, and there's another further down. I'll introduce them to you, if you like.'

'What's wrong with them?'

'Tom has a stitch abscess from an appendix operation. The older one, Paul, had glandular fever and gets relapses from time to time. But he's well enough to direct that play you're going to film, so maybe he just likes the room service here. I don't mind, he's nice and polite. There's a bathroom across the corridor. I'll tell the boys to keep out of it.'

'Thanks.' Magnus wondered when he should broach the subject of the carving. 'Are you around later on?'

'I'm off now, but we can offer you some supper this evening. I'll organise a cup of tea for you. If there is anything you want in the meantime just ring for Susan. She'll be around somewhere.'

With that she went out. He still had half an hour to kill so he laid out some of his new clothes on the chair and hopped up on to the high bed with Colin's letter, which he had retrieved from his bag. There was a soft crunch as the plastic-coated mattress took his weight. Bedwetter-proof, he thought, with a grimace, and the sheets slid into hillocks under his back.

He slid the letter out of the envelope and cast his eye over the now familiar lines filled with self-justification, self-pity and pleas for understanding. But one paragraph held his attention.

I know what you think my real reason was, why I felt we couldn't go on. To be honest, it was something that I had always expected to have in life. It seemed essential somehow. But now I know it's not the most important thing. You are.

It wasn't at all clear what he referred to, but children seemed most likely. Might it have been that she couldn't have them? He had no idea, but it might partly explain why the idea of reincarnation was so important to her. Everyone has the urge to reproduce in some form. And if children weren't a possibility, perhaps her mind had turned even more to thoughts of death and how to cheat it. But this was speculation.

There was a knock on the door and a pensioner with a hooked nose clanked in, carrying two coal buckets. Barely looking at Magnus, who had put the letter away, he went directly to the fireplace, pulled out the grate with a loud screech and swept up some old ashes. Then he began to lay a new fire with coal and kindling from the other bucket.

'Afternoon.'

'Afternoon,' the man replied, and shook on some coal. Magnus lay back again and listened as the man scratched a match, then blew steadily on to the resulting flame. It made the fireplace glow and sent up sparks. 'Who are you, then? Teacher?'

Magnus rose up on an elbow. 'No, not any more. I'm a filmmaker.' That sounded a bit fancy so he added, 'I make videos.' The man did not seem to understand. 'The school play,' he clarified.

The man looked back at the fire with regret, as if his efforts had been wasted. Slowly he rose from his knees, gathered his buckets and clanked out. The door closed heavily and Magnus heard him head down the corridor. He knew he ought to check his equipment before going to the theatre, but right now he couldn't be bothered. He put his hands behind his head and listened to the birds tweeting in the garden outside, and asked himself what significance that baboon carving could possibly have. He closed his eyes and he seemed to sense the green-painted walls bulge towards him, lugubrious with a knowledge they would not share.

There was scuffling in the corridor outside his door and the clinking of a tray or trolley. 'Fuck off, Hopkins, she said I should carry it!' The voice was piercing and pubescent. Something made of plastic clattered to the floor.

'Fuck off yourself, Bingham, you little shit. Now look what you've done.' There was a timid knock on the door.

Not wanting to face boys on his back, Magnus sat up. He flattened his hair and put on his spectacles to lend the necessary air of gravitas. 'Come in,' he called. The door-handle turned and, very slowly, the door opened. The curly head of Bingham (if he had got it right)

Peter Jinks

appeared. He looked in with an uncertain grin on his face. Magnus sighed. 'Come on, in you come.'

Bingham opened the door wider and another boy entered with the tea-tray. Ferrety-faced and pimply, Hopkins had a broken-heeled slipper that clapped with each step. Both were about fourteen and brought with them a primordial scent that put Magnus in mind of semen mopped up with an old sock. Did young people always smell this bad?

'Matron said to bring you this,' said Hopkins.

'Right, thanks.' He received the precariously rattling tray with a curt smile. The boys were in no hurry to leave. Bingham looked around the room at Magnus's scattered personal items, then they glanced at each other and tried not to laugh. Hopkins swayed with suppressed amusement. What were they laughing at, he wondered, but experience had taught him not to ask. 'Your names are Bingham and Hopkins, is that right?' he asked.

'That's right, sir,' said the first, stifling his laughter and glancing over towards the bedside chair.

Magnus saw what it was. They were looking at the spare clothes he had unpacked, specifically a pair of designer underpants. 'Thank you, Hopkins and Bingham, you can go now.'

They turned towards the door with narrow shaking shoulders and the corridor echoed raucously as they returned to their room. Magnus poured his tea, then decided he didn't want any. Perhaps, he thought, he would have a quick snoop round the building. With a squeak and a crunch, he dismounted the plastic mattress and stepped out into the corridor.

It was quiet and the staffroom door was shut, so he knocked on it and, receiving no answer, popped his head in. There was some cheap furniture and shelves full of magazines. Checking that the nurse was not about, he entered and closed the door behind him. Confining his footfalls to the worn rug, he took a closer look at the shelves. There were postcards from various European destinations, a small stuffed donkey, a thank-you card from a former inmate and, poking up tantalisingly behind the magazines, the top of a dark wooden ornament. He felt a twinge of excitement. He reached over to pick it up. But it turned out to be an abstract figurine, and not the mid-section of a baboon.

The door opened behind him. Turning rapidly with a guilty excuse on his lips Magnus saw, instead of the nurse, the older student he had seen earlier.

'You made me jump then,' he said, with a nervous laugh.

The young man looked suspicious and faintly amused. His gaze was on the ornament in Magnus's hand. 'The matron said you might give me a lift to the theatre.'

'Are you Paul by any chance? My name's Magnus. I'm going to be filming your dress rehearsal today.' He held out his hand and Paul, mildly surprised by the gesture, shook it. 'Why don't you wait by the car? I'll be with you in a minute.'

Paul withdrew. Magnus took a last glance around the room and carefully replaced the ornament where he had found it.

Eleven

The Astra was nosing towards town when Paul, who was slouched in the passenger seat, cut short Magnus's admittedly ungripping comments about the weather (which he thought clement for the time of year). 'Are you really here just to film the play?'

For a moment the car's puny engine noise was all that filled the silence. 'What is that supposed to mean?' Magnus flicked his eyes to the rear-view mirror as if another query might be speeding up the rear to buzz him. He needed a moment to figure out how he should answer.

Paul had been watching his face but now turned to the front once more. 'I heard that Miss Calder was dead. The school didn't announce anything officially, though. Obviously.'

Magnus wondered whether he should read something into the pause that Paul inserted before the word 'obviously'. It seemed to imply a common understanding of what had been left unsaid. Did Paul simply mean that the school never informed students of such things, or was there a specific reason why Claire's death had not been officially mentioned? Magnus let it pass. Having expected the boy not to know about Claire's death, he now answered the initial question in a way that he hoped sounded as frank as possible. 'You're right. I suppose it isn't just work for me. I wanted to see this place again. My sister spent a happy year of her life here. When someone's gone, someone you love, you often want to learn a bit more about them, see the places they saw, get a flavour of their life. For the memories, I suppose.'

Paul seemed unmoved by his words of wisdom. 'You were looking for something in particular, though, weren't you, in the staffroom?'

Magnus frowned, and the Astra droned onwards, bumping over the manhole covers.

'Don't worry, I won't say anything,' he said, leaning forwards with a comradely smile. 'You're Miss Calder's brother, we're on the same side. I was in her history class. She was *amazing*. She used to teach extra classes on anthropology and stuff that was off the curriculum, *and they would actually be full*.'

Another of Claire's disciples, Magnus thought, with more than a trace of professional jealousy. He decided that honesty was the best policy with Paul. 'Yes, I was looking for something, as a matter of fact, but I can always ask the matron about it. It's part of an African carving that my sister arranged to be sent on to the school here, but it's one of a set of three and it seems a shame to have them separated.'

'What is it? Some kind of ritual ornament?'

'I'm not sure. Nobody's sure.' Magnus was slightly surprised by the educated question. Perhaps all those extra lessons with Claire had paid off.

'But you want it back.'

'Yes. If Matron doesn't mind. If she's still got it.'

'What if she does mind?' he asked slyly.

'I . . . I don't know. I suppose I'll just have to go back empty-handed.' Somehow he knew that this was not an option. 'Have you seen anything knocking around the san that looks like a baboon's belly?' Of course, Marjorie might have taken it home, but it was worth asking.

Paul leant back in his seat and attempted to stretch his legs out, which caused a sandwich carton that Magnus had discarded earlier to crunch in the footwell. He looked bored. 'Yeah. She never showed it to anyone but I saw the package arrive. It's in the dispensary, which is locked. You're not allowed in.'

Magnus sensed that this obstacle did not necessarily apply to his young passenger. 'You seem to know your way around, don't you, Paul?'

Paul stared at him frankly. 'You look like her.'

Magnus settled back and exhaled. They were approaching a traffic junction. 'So they say. Which way?'

'Turn right here. How did it happen?'

Paul's blunt way of putting the question left Magnus in no doubt about what he was referring to. Inexperienced teenagers talked about death in the same way as they did about sex: harshly, naïvely. 'It was a car accident.'

'Was there anything funny about it?' The question was quickly put.

'Funny?'

'I mean the circumstances. Anything unusual?'

There was silence, punctuated only by the percussive click of the indicator, which had acquired a back beat because something was broken; its rhythm sounded tastelessly cheerful – like samba at a funeral – and Magnus quickly silenced it once they had negotiated the corner. He didn't particularly mind Paul being direct, but if he kept asking questions like they were in a detective series, he might consider getting offended. 'No, nothing unusual.'

He was damned if he was going to inform Claire's pupil that she was burned to death, but Paul seemed to sense a cover-up: he slowly turned forwards again. Magnus was nettled, despite his best efforts. 'Why are you so curious?'

Paul blinked, correctly reading 'ghoulish' for 'curious'. 'She spent a lot of time at the dramatic society. We talked about ideas I had for directing this play. But really. You do know why she had to leave here, don't you?'

'*Had* to?'

He waved his hand. 'Okay, not officially, because that would have meant publicity.' He paused. 'You don't know?' Paul's tone, superficially disbelieving of Magnus's ignorance, was accompanied by a weird leer: he couldn't disguise his pleasure at being in the know, any more than he could resist the cruel sport of suspense.

'What are you talking about?'

Paul sat back and looked out of the window, as if the conversation was over. Perhaps this was his idea of retaliation for Magnus not being full and frank about the crash. He probably thought he was being patronised. It was too much. Magnus stopped the car abruptly at the side of the road and turned to him, angrily. 'Go on, then, spit it out.'

Paul didn't respond. He just looked back at Magnus as if he was being unbelievably crass.

'You can't do this, Paul. You can't say that and then clam up.'

Paul faced front. 'Ask the matron. Ask the headmaster. We're not supposed to know.'

Magnus took a deep breath. Despite appearances, he guessed that behind the boy's haughty expression there was at least a glimmer of compassion. 'Please, Paul, none of this is easy for me.'

His face didn't alter. 'Keep driving, or we'll be late.'

Reluctantly, Magnus obliged. He pulled out into the road once more and waited for Paul to explain. But all he uttered for the rest of the short journey were three words: 'Turn left here.'

Caught unawares, Magnus glimpsed the sign proclaiming, 'Redmond Theatre, Trade Entrance', about to pass by. He slammed on the brakes and spun the wheel, but since the Astra always gave the impression of going at sixty miles per hour when it was doing thirty he managed to strike the kerb before the gate and they bounced their way into the drive with Magnus cursing and Paul laughing. With the engine safely turned off, Magnus found that he was shaking – and not just from the bump. Claire had never said anything about being forced to leave for reasons that had to be hushed up. All he knew was that she had declared herself sick of teaching over-privileged brats and was joining VSO to do something useful. He had sympathised with how she must have felt but at the same time felt exasperated by the way the teaching profession protected its own, even if it meant bending the rules. It was strange: he had thought he would come away from this visit to Ashton knowing his sister a little better, but he was already experiencing the opposite sensation. And this, he suspected, was just the beginning.

'Are you coming, then?' Paul had already got out of the car and was waiting for him.

Ahead of them was the stage door and a larger garage entrance for props. Magnus told himself to wake up and began to climb out, only for the near wheel to squash his heel as he had forgotten to put on the handbrake. 'Idiot,' he told himself, and yanked on the brake. Then he slammed shut the Astra's door, which bit on the metal tongue of the seat-belt, causing it to bounce back and catch his knee. 'Ow! Fuck!' He rubbed his knee and noticed that Paul was staring at him as if he was a lunatic. He straightened up with difficulty and tried to sound composed. 'Could you go in, please, Paul, and see if anyone's around? I'll unload.'

Paul shrugged his assent and strolled in. By the time he returned a few minutes later, Magnus had organised himself a little better, suppressed the anxiety about his sister's alleged dismissal, and was determined to focus on his work. He would get to the bottom of it all later on.

'Langley's in the green room, arguing with Sanders, the stage manager,' said Paul. 'Do you want a hand with anything? Otherwise I'll get on and talk things through with the cast.'

'No, thanks, on you go.' Magnus slung the camera-bag over his shoulder, picked up the tripod and followed Paul into the theatre's backstage.

It was small in size but appeared to be very well equipped. Paul signalled towards a green door at the end of a corridor from which a raised voice could be heard, then went to check the progress of a boy who was ripping open sachets of fake blood and pouring them into a paint-pot. Mindful as ever of schoolboy thieves, Magnus thought he would hide his bag and tripod behind an array of ropes that rose up behind the backdrop's scaffolding. He took care to cover them properly, then glanced up and saw, several feet above his head, the toes of a pair of schoolboy's shoes poking out between the ropes. Frowning, he stepped back. Was someone on the scaffolding further up? A breeze came through from the stage entrance. A rope creaked and the tips of the shoes slowly rotated.

Light-headed with horror, Magnus jumped forwards and parted the ropes. He couldn't see anything at first. Then he heard the slithering sound of something falling. The shoe struck him on the head, bounced and fell to the floor. A second later it was joined by the other.

The laces had been loosely tied to the rope. He had fallen for a practical joke. He rubbed his head where the heel had struck, and kicked the shoes into a corner. 'Brats.'

He approached the door with the camera in his hands. The shouting temporarily stopped and he recognised Langley's voice from their telephone conversation, uttering soothing words. 'Now, come on, Tom, you always knew there were plans for someone to come and do the filming.'

'Nobody gave me any formal notification.' The manager's voice was stubborn. Magnus had a hot flush; the blood left his face, then bloomed once more over his cheeks. The sensation was remarkably similar to the first time he had seen Rosie, only this time it was definitely not love at first sight.

'Well, I'm telling you now, Tom. This is his only chance to do the filming. I know time is short but I'm sure he won't want to get in the way. Why don't you discuss it with him? He should be arriving at any minute.'

'What's the name of this clown, anyway?'

'Magnus Calder.'

'Calder? You're kidding. He's related to that bloody woman, is he? What did they call her? The Thane of Calder? Thank God she got her marching orders.'

'Tom, lower your voice. Don't you know she's dead?'

'Eh?' There was a short pause. 'She can't hear, then, can she?' There was a short bark of mirth.

'Magnus has been commissioned by the headmaster—'

'String-pulling once more, was it? Daddy must have put a word in the right ear.'

Hearing this, Magnus felt a powerful rush of hostility that was all his own.

'Absolutely not,' Sanders declared. 'No way is he coming into my theatre.'

The idea of having spent several hours in Midland traffic jams for nothing did not appeal. Magnus lifted the camera to his eye, edged the door open and began to film the backs of the two men, who had not yet noticed his presence.

'I am sure the headmaster would be very grateful for your cooperation. He did say——'

'I don't care what the bloody headmaster says,' shouted the manager. 'I'm the stage manager and it's me that's responsible for safety in this building.'

Using his shoulder, Magnus opened the door a little wider and stepped inside. They both turned simultaneously. He guessed that Langley was the short, red-bearded man in mustard-coloured corduroys and a hairy jumper. The other man was in a lumberjack shirt with a pot-belly and a heavily laden key-ring that seemed determined to tug down his jeans.

'Oh, hello,' said the bearded man, looking relieved, 'I'm James Langley. I expect you're Magnus Calder. I must introduce you to Tom Sanders, the stage manager. Tom, Magnus.'

Sanders was briefly speechless as Magnus fixed his features, similar in some respects to those of Kingsley Amis, squarely in the frame. There was definitely something familiar about him. 'So, Tom Sanders, stage manager, are you feeling optimistic about this forthcoming Ashton School production of *Titus Andronicus*?'

Sanders's jaw dropped, causing his chin to dimple. 'I'm . . . Yes, I'm – I'm—'

Satisfied, Magnus let the camera drop. Sanders's comments had only made him more determined to make this film flawless.

Twenty minutes later Magnus had erected his tripod in the central aisle of the auditorium and sat down next to it. The young director was still talking to his cast so, with a few minutes to go until everyone was ready, he found his mind returning to the mystery of Claire's dismissal. But then, remembering the disaster of the wedding video, he concentrated on work once more. Someone had left a copy of the Shakespeare play on the floor in front of the seat. He picked it up and began to read.

'You chose exactly where she used to sit.'

Magnus jumped. Paul had sat down next to him. 'Did I?'

Paul nodded slowly, eyes on the stage. Magnus lifted the text. 'I've never read *Titus Andronicus*. Is it any good?'

'It's my favourite Shakespeare.'

Magnus was going to ask why, but Langley appeared on stage, clapped his hands and tried to marshal the spear-carriers, who were milling about in Brechtian boiler-suits.

'Isn't that your job as director?' Magnus asked.

Paul sniffed. 'I let him do the menial stuff.' He

then looked pointedly at Magnus. 'Are we ready to go, then?'

It took a moment for him to process the hint. 'Oh. Yes. Of course.'

Magnus went to his post behind the tripod, allowing Paul to sling a leg over the armrest and sprawl more comfortably. Langley raised his voice to address the cast. 'Now then, everyone. Before we start I want to introduce you all to Mr Calder who is going to be filming the dress rehearsal for us today. He has specially requested that no one look into the camera when he is filming, and please try not to be distracted because he will be moving around.'

The cast looked over towards Magnus who waved and smiled, then busied himself with some technical double-checks. Satisfied, he gave the thumbs-up to Langley, who looked to Paul, who in turn regally inclined his head.

The stage lights dropped. Magnus crouched with his eye to the camera. Instinctively his hand crept down to the tripod screw and gave it another little turn. Ready. In the darkness a voice whispered, close enough to his ear for him to feel the moistness of its breath: 'That remark of mine about the Head had better not make it on to the film.'

It was Sanders. Magnus wiped his ear. 'It won't. So long as you're nice.'

Sanders considered this unpalatable demand. 'Don't even think about blocking the fire exits. And keep away from the set. We don't need another catastrophe, do we?'

Magnus shooed Sanders away and returned to the

eyepiece. Claire must have hated that man's guts, he thought.

It took a while, preoccupied as Magnus was with the business of filming, for him to register what was being acted out on the stage. But as the action unfolded it became apparent that Shakespeare had penned a slasher play. When Lavinia held out to Titus the two dripping stumps after her hands had been amputated and opened a gory, tongueless mouth, Magnus grimaced and zoomed in. The special effects were not exactly sophisticated, but he found that, all the same, he was beginning to feel impressively nauseous. Isabel's mangled face returned to him; so did the sound of creaking ropes and the feet poking out, shifting gently left and right. The walls of the auditorium seemed to advance in the darkness. He kept his eye pressed to the camera, but the teenage performance acquired a menace out of all proportion to the actors' skill. Magnus's fingers quivered slightly as they sought out the screw on the tripod, to check that it wouldn't slip. It didn't matter that he wanted to run screaming out of this stifling theatre, or that pressure was building in his throat, strangling his breath. The job would be perfect. It would see him through. Weakly, he leaned against the armrest of the nearest seat and continued to watch.

The lead actor playing Titus was apparently a school prefect called Hendry. He had been doing his seventeen-year-old best to depict the tragic old man but at this crucial moment in the play, poised to deliver the lines he must have read through a thousand times, he dried up.

"'Speak, gentle niece,'" he pleaded of the ketchupped

actress, a big-boned girl who looked like a school-teacher's daughter. '"What stern ungentle hands hath . . . hath . . ."'

In the long pause that followed Hendry turned and looked up towards Magnus, who was now covered in sweat, heart beating laboriously. The words wouldn't come. Another three or four seconds passed and Lavinia involuntarily shot a glance towards Paul, who was seated nearby. Unperturbed, Paul did not need to consult his text for the prompt. His RP voice rose up loud and firm. '"Lopp'd and hew'd!"'

The actor sagged with relief and continued, '". . . lopp'd and hew'd/And made thy body bare/Of her two branches."'

Paul glanced over at Magnus and indicated that he should keep filming, despite the mishap. Magnus felt better. A slight draught cooled his neck; the rest of the dress rehearsal went smoothly enough, so far as he could tell.

The lights came up, there was some half-hearted bowing from the cast and Paul clapped. Magnus unhitched the camera from the tripod and climbed the steps at the side of the stage. He was heading for the wings, planning to capture some footage of the actors returning backstage. As he turned with the camera to his eye, Sanders popped up in the frame, pointing at some overhead lights and shouting at one of the schoolboy stage technicians. Magnus stepped forwards and his foot hit something, but he kept filming. Hendry went past with a grin. 'You kicked the bucket,' he said. Sanders returned from the far side of the stage, still preoccupied with the overhead lights.

'Watch out,' he heard someone say, but he noticed the spreading puddle of stage blood too late and there was nothing for him to do but keep filming when Sanders slipped acrobatically and plunged off the side of the stage.

'I'm so dreadfully embarrassed,' said Magnus once more, as Langley shepherded Sanders to his car with what looked like a broken arm and extensive bruising.

'Accidents happen,' remarked Langley mildly. 'It wasn't your fault. The blood shouldn't have been left in the wings like that. I'd better get going to the hospital. I think poor old Tom is in quite a lot of pain. Oh,' he added, 'by the way, your father called. He wanted to know how everything was going. Perhaps you could call him back.'

Magnus was doubly embarrassed. 'Tom, really, I must apologise.'

But Sanders, pale-faced and with gritted teeth, avoided even the slightest eye-contact until he was safely in Langley's Honda and pulling away, at which point he sent a look of almost superstitious fear through the passenger window. Perhaps it was the likeness to Claire he recognised.

Sadly Magnus turned back towards the rear entrance of the theatre and saw that Paul was waiting there, keeping guard over his equipment.

'Thanks,' said Magnus, and picked up the bag.

Paul followed him to the car. 'Can you give me a lift, please?'

'Sure.'

Magnus put the equipment in the boot and they made their way back towards the sanatorium. Paul broke the silence first. 'Someone said it looked like you did that on purpose.'

Magnus blanched. 'That's absolutely ridiculous. Why would I?'

'I thought it unlikely too. But in any case, it's made you very popular. Everyone thinks he's a total prick, and he always said dreadful things about Miss Calder. I can't say I'm sorry.'

Magnus shot a glance at Paul. 'It wasn't intentional.'

They continued to drive. He scowled. Of course it hadn't been intentional. He just hadn't seen the pot at his feet. He'd been too busy filming.

'Didn't you like it, then?'

'What?'

'The production,' said Paul, peeved. 'What did you think I was talking about?'

Magnus tried to think of something to say. His critical faculties seemed to have abandoned him. 'You've done a great job with the actors. I'm sure it will be a success.'

'You didn't like it.'

'I wouldn't say that, but it's the sort of thing that gives me bad dreams. Take it as a compliment.'

Paul beamed and sat back. 'I just did.'

'But . . .'

'What?'

'It's not the production, it's the play. Poor innocent Lavinia getting hacked up like that. I know it's a tragedy and everything. Maybe I'm going soft.'

Paul bridled immediately. 'Well, Lavinia isn't strictly innocent, is she? Back then the family bore collective responsibility. In that play Titus is getting punished and his niece gets butchered as part of his punishment. She's a victim, certainly, but she's guilty too. She's his family.'

'She didn't commit a crime.'

'Guilt doesn't require it. Don't Germans feel guilty about what their grandparents did? Haven't you ever felt guilty for somebody else's actions?'

The last question sounded a little too personal, possibly even pointed. Magnus glanced over at Paul, but couldn't decipher his intent. He would have to get to the bottom of this mystery about Claire, but he wouldn't give Paul the satisfaction of begging for information again.

'I thought I saw her, you know.'

Paul's comment came out of the blue. There was no doubt whom he meant. Magnus lost his focus on the road for a second. Then it returned, only everything was brighter, at one remove. He tried to sound normal but his mouth was dry. The root of his tongue rasped against the back of his throat as he tried to coax out some saliva. 'Really?'

'She passed by in a car, on this road, just a few days ago. Same clothes, same hair, same sort of manner. I thought it was her, until I remembered the news.'

Paul's voice petered out. He picked at the cuticle of his thumb and chewed at it nervously.

Twelve

So he definitely wasn't hallucinating. Or if he was, someone else was hallucinating the same thing. On top of Gav's semi-verification of having seen someone in a mackintosh at the wedding, Paul's testimony gave further weight to the reality of these sightings. Although there were the usual infuriating margins of error to be taken into consideration, Magnus was exhilarated by this affirmation. Perhaps too exhilarated. He resisted a delirious urge to spill out to Paul all the things that had happened to him in the past weeks, and went straight to his room, where he splashed water on his face and hopped up on to his high, crunchy mattress. He breathed deep and considered the situation more calmly. If this person was real, who were they and what the hell were they up to? The implications of reality were more disturbing than he had given them credit for. Fantasy had its limits, after all. Madness was contained within the brain. Feeling hungry, he looked at his watch and saw that it was nearly eight. Time to seek out dinner down the corridor.

'The boys eat in their rooms,' explained Marjorie as she led Magnus into the staffroom. Some solid institutional crockery was laid out on the coffee-table, green like the Astra against the nicotine brown of the lacy tablecloth. 'I hope you like fish-fingers,' she said, and put down two tin platters.

'I think so. It's been a while.'

He lifted the first lid to reveal some orange-breadcrumbed brickwork, while the second exposed a large orb of mashed potato, flattened on top by the cover. The platters themselves put Magnus in mind of medical specimens rather than foodstuffs, but his mother's catering had long hardened his appetite to demoralising presentation: he took it as a challenge.

She served him, then put a hand to her mouth. 'The whisky!'

She went to the sideboard and took out a half-bottle of Famous Grouse from behind a box of plastic medicine spoons. Two chipped glasses were set on the table and filled.

He smiled. 'I thought you didn't like whisky.'

'You're right, but I just want to make sure,' she said. They raised their glasses and he watched as she took a sip. She put it down with a small grimace. 'How did the filming go?'

'We got there in the end. Although there was a mishap.'

He told her about Sanders's injury, but omitted that he had been responsible for knocking over the pot. Her comment, 'Poor thing', did not sound heartfelt; Sanders was not a favourite among the staff either.

'Also,' he continued, 'I was the victim of a practical joke.' He told her about the shoes sticking out from behind the ropes backstage.

She looked appalled.

'In poor taste, I agree. It gave me a fright, though.' He laughed, but stopped when he saw her expression. 'Is there something I don't know?'

She picked at her fish-fingers. 'It doesn't matter.'

He groaned. 'Please, not another mystery. I just heard that Claire left under a cloud, but I wasn't told why. Is that true?'

She put down her cutlery, exhaled. 'Yes.'

'Well?'

'The joke they played on you was in very poor taste. A boy died in the theatre. He was found hanged.'

'Hanged? It was suicide?'

'Nobody could be sure. There was no note and he didn't show signs of being particularly unhappy, although he had been ill previously and stayed here at the san. Misadventure was the verdict at the inquest. He had been helping with the props, but nobody found him till late in the evening when they realised he was missing.'

'My God. Who found him?'

'The stage manager. Sanders.'

'He got the blame?' Once again, Magnus had to read Marjorie's face. 'Claire?'

'She was the last person in charge that evening. She had the keys.'

Magnus ran a hand through his hair: his first thoughts were for Claire and how she must have felt. Then he asked himself if his father had known. Perhaps, although he knew how adept these schools were at hushing up scandals and bad news.

'I can't believe it. She never said a word to me.'

'It wasn't her fault,' said Marjorie quickly; perhaps even a little too quickly. 'It was an accident.'

Magnus looked at her sharply. Her last comment had a certain resonance. It was more or less what Langley had said to him that very afternoon, as he headed off to hospital. He remembered Sanders's frightened face once more, staring at him through the window of the departing car. And what about that silly nickname of Claire's he had overheard: the Thane of Calder. Macbeth's title was Thane of Cawdor. Why had they called her that? Or was he reading too much into stupid details?

'How did she take it?'

Marjorie sighed. 'Of course she was extremely upset, although obviously it wasn't her fault. She left so soon afterwards we didn't have a chance to talk. I can't imagine. The next I heard she was in Africa.'

Thoughtfully, he speared a fish-finger but he couldn't put it into his mouth. He had yet to ask Marjorie about the carving. Maybe it was time to change the subject in any case.

'Did you happen to receive an African carving that my mother sent?'

Her face brightened, relieved at the change of topic. 'Yes, I did. Please thank her for it again, although I did send her a card.' She paused, delicately. 'You don't happen to know what it is, by any chance?'

He laughed to vent the tension that had built inside him. 'Up to a point. It's part of a baboon. There are two other pieces, although we're not sure of their significance, exactly. It's probably religious or something.'

She seemed politely interested. 'Well, I'm glad to have something to remember her by, even if it is a bit peculiar. I'm sure she would have given a very colourful explanation.'

Magnus was about to speak when Marjorie continued hastily, 'Do you know, it's the only thing I have of Claire's? She even ducked out of the school photo somehow or other.'

This did not make his task any easier. He felt his resolution fade but his obligation to Isabel drove him on. He had made a promise, after all. Then when he got home he would bite the bullet and ask Rosie about the other piece. Maybe then Isabel would leave him alone. He joined his fingertips together and looked at Marjorie over the top of them. 'What you've said puts me in rather a difficult position.'

She asked him what he meant and he explained that a close friend of his sister was keen to reunite the three carvings.

'But, you see, Claire meant it for me. Your mother said so.'

'Yes, I know.'

'I do sympathise with your friend, but surely she can understand how I feel too.'

Magnus applied some more pressure. 'Let me explain the situation a little. This friend, her name is Isabel . . .

How can I put this? She's unstable. Particularly since she heard the news of Claire's death. She has utterly fixed her mind on bringing together these pieces. Don't ask me why, but I am never going to hear the end of it if I come back empty-handed. I won't say it's going to tip her over the edge, quite, but . . .'

'Is she mentally ill?'

'Clinically speaking, no, not as far as I know. But I'm worried for her and I want to do everything possible that might help.'

She did not take long to make up her mind. 'Magnus, I am going to say no. It's my property now and I don't think it is fair or reasonable of her to demand it. Nor do I believe that a wooden carving will magically solve her problems, whatever they might be. Also, I think it's a bit shabby that she sent you to come and get it on her behalf. She had asked already, you know.'

If Magnus was going to return empty-handed with a clear conscience then he would have to try again. 'Of course, you're right, it does sound unreasonable. But please, if you did do me this enormous favour and gave it up then I could certainly have my mother send you something else of Claire's to remember her by.' Her face did not soften. Her lips pursed stubbornly, so he accepted defeat and helped himself to some more mashed potato. 'All right, all right, I give up.'

She nodded curtly as if to say, 'Good, at last.' After several attempts he managed to dislodge the adhesive mash from the serving spoon, and with a rattle of cutlery the two of them addressed the fish-fingers: he

with a dull sense of foreboding about facing Isabel; she
– judging by her expression – with a certain amount
of indignation. But then she stiffened: her eyes had slid
towards the closed door. He opened his mouth but she
held up her hand to silence him. Slowly and stealthily she
crept towards the door and grabbed the handle. From the
other side came a stifled giggle and the sound of two pairs
of slippers skittering down the corridor and around the
corner. She waited for them to escape, then pulled the
door open and went out. 'What's all that noise I heard?
If I catch anyone out of bed . . .'

A distant door slammed shut. She came back. 'I'm sorry
about that. I'd better dose them before lights out.'

Magnus stood up. 'Yes, I'm going to turn in too,
I think.'

He followed her out of the room and towards the
locked door of the dispensary where the medicines – and,
according to his intelligence, the carving – were kept.

'Is there anything else you need?' she asked, over her
shoulder.

'No, thanks.' He waited behind her as she fumbled in
her pinny for a key. Then she turned and feigned surprise
that he was still there. 'Do you mind if I see in there? It's
such an interesting old building.'

She seemed a little wary. 'No, I don't mind.'

She opened the door with the key and the strip-light
blinked on to reveal glass-faced cabinets containing medicines and a refrigerator in the corner. There was a strong
smell of disinfectant and cold-cream soap. Although it
was tucked into a dark corner at the end of a shelf, he

immediately spotted the carving. The big round belly was made of the same dark, notched wood and was shaped like a bowl or gourd, only it was sealed. His heart jumped with excitement. Marjorie shot a look in his direction. He pretended not to have spotted it. Stepping forwards, she blocked his view of the carving and unlocked a cupboard from which she took some medicines. But then, in an apparent shift of strategy, she pointed towards it as she arranged pill bottles on a tray. 'There it is, safe and sound. At least you can tell your friend you saw it.'

A plastic beaker containing a thermometer had fallen to the ground and as she bent down to pick them up he noted her breasts pressing against the uniform. He watched her put the key on the tray beside the pill bottles.

'You're welcome to watch the telly in the staffroom if you're not sleepy.' She was shaking the thermometer's mercury reading down. A ring on her finger made a ticking sound against the glass as she did so, but it wasn't a wedding band. He realised that he didn't have a clue about her private life, whether she was single or divorced, restless or settled, lonely or surrounded by friends.

'I hope you're not woken too early tomorrow morning – there's surgery and it can be noisy with all the boys and girls.'

'That's all right, I'll be off first thing. I've got a long journey back to Edinburgh.'

'In that case, I'd better say goodbye now.'

She had picked up the tray and was about to put it back down but he told her not to bother and pecked her on the cheek, the tray pressing between the two of them, holding them apart in a way that was awkward but also — for him, at least — poignant. His hand had strayed to the key at the edge of the tray but he found that Marjorie's thumb was pressed down firmly upon it. He patted her hand and pulled back.

She smiled as if nothing had happened. 'It was very nice to meet you, Magnus.'

'And you too. Thanks for everything.'

'Even the fish-fingers?'

'Even them.'

'Drop by again if you're ever in the neighbourhood. And I'm sorry to be the one who told you about that dreadful episode. It could have happened to anyone.'

She stood and watched as he returned to his room. Perhaps she was drawing out Claire's likeness from him to replenish her memory. He understood, having been through his own crises of forgetting. He shut the door, poked the dying fire and leant against the repulsive crunchy mattress. He sighed and looked out of the window at the blue-black evening sky, which shaded into the vegetal gloom of the garden. He stayed that way, immobile, for some time. A blackbird sent a last salvo into the sinking evening, though it seemed too late for song. Some older boys' voices could be heard on the path beyond, prefects perhaps, making their way back to their houses through the playing-fields. One of them loudly mimicked a master. Their laughter drained away off to the right and a lorry rumbled by on the road beyond.

A hanged boy. The belly of a baboon. A broken arm.

Intuition

He laid them out like tarot cards in his mind, hoping for a sudden revelation. But why should they hold meaning? He pushed up his spectacles. The dead didn't explain themselves. The living had to make sense of things for themselves, and right now he didn't have the strength. The cards remained a meaningless sequence. The world was ruled by chance. Death was obliteration and there was no such thing as fate.

Everything was still. The only movement in the room was tears. They sledged down his cheeks one after another and dropped on to the ugly bedspread between his thighs. He did not know why he was crying. Was it grief? No. Not loneliness either. These tears were about failure. A few minutes later he pulled off his clothes and crawled between the sheets, exhausted. His back ached, but the thought of Rosie's hands sent him to sleep.

Thirteen

Marjorie takes off her clothes in front of him. At first it seems to be an erotic game – her smile is knowing – but as she opens her dressing-gown, his eyes move down and he sees that her belly is enormous and her breasts, which he remembered to be compact in her uniform, are heavy and distended. Is she pregnant? Alarmed, he looks up: she confirms his ownership with a nod and a smile. Bizarrely, he is pleased. Her dressing-gown falls to the ground. She steps forward, naked and vulnerable. Moved, his hand goes to her belly, to cup it. The skin is warm but the bulge feels odd; not like flesh at all, but solid, like wood.

Her eyes compel his attention. She takes his wrist and guides his hand down to her right breast. She presses his palm down on her dimpled nipple, then with her own hand encourages his fingers to sink into the side of her breast, to take a grip. Her fingers tighten over his. Her eyes implore him: she wants him to tear. Her face is changing, there is movement under her skin: her features are becoming simian. The baboon is under Marjorie's skin; it wants him to strip away the flesh and free it. The grip on his left hand is incredibly strong, and holds him as he pulls away. His right hand feels the notches on her belly. He is filled with horror. With all his strength, he punches her stomach but his knuckles bounce off it with a hollow thump. His other hand, clamped helplessly to her breast, is forced to rip, and her breast comes away like a great clod of dough. In the wound he has made of her chest, through the seeping blood, he sees that the wood is lustrous and new.

Magnus came tumbling out of his dream with a short yelp. Disoriented, he panted in the darkness as the image of the carving circled dizzily in his mind. Then his hands shot up to his face and touched the skin: it was damp with sweat but he felt his fingers — he wasn't numb again, thank God. The sheets felt revolting: the mattress did not let the skin breathe and the linen was wrinkled under his buttocks. Groaning, he twisted on the bed and tried to kick off the blanket. But he couldn't. The sheet and blankets were taut over his legs, as if he had been tucked in tight after he had gone to sleep. This was strange, as was the small downward slant that the mattress seemed to have acquired. It was too dark to see; so dark that he was not sure if his eyes were open or shut. The heavy sanatorium curtains kept out even the faintest street-light. Had he closed them himself? Unable to remember, he tried to lift his knees, but only gently, as if he didn't want to disturb whatever was on the bed. No luck. Resisting a surge of panic, he decided to wait for his eyes to adjust and his mind to find its co-ordinates. The dream seemed to hang heavy in the room, with its stifling odour of medicine and coal dust. He remembered the weight of Marjorie's flesh as it came away in his hand, and shuddered. *Titus Andronicus* was partly responsible for this: Paul *would* be pleased.

He felt calmer, and attempted to think positive. At least he was still in bed and not standing at the bottom of some stairs with a screaming vacuum-cleaner in his hands. More good news: he was now most certainly awake. Which meant there was just one uncertainty to be cleared up. Once more, he tried to wriggle free of the taut sheet. Whatever it was didn't shift. He lay back and thought again. Had he left his bag on the bed, perhaps? No.

He waited. Very gradually the darkness pressed against the furniture and revealed its shapes: next to him, the chair; beside it, the table; beyond, a milky outline of the basin. But could he really see them, or was he sketching his recollection of the room on to the blackness? He reached for the light, but he didn't find it.

Time did not operate normally in such darkness. Were they seconds or minutes that he was counting? His back itched. He thought that he might reach down and untuck the sheet where it was tightest. Heart hopping stupidly in his chest, he sent his hand down the side of the bed. It met nothing, but by then the mattress had already lurched.

A weight had lifted. The sheets had loosened. Someone had been sitting on the bed. He heard a ticking sound. It sounded vaguely familiar: a bit like Marjorie's ring when she shook the thermometer. God knew what she was doing in his room.

The dream pressed down on him: the wound full of red shining wood.

'Marjorie, is that you?'

And just as the fragile query left his mouth, he remembered precisely where he had heard that sound. Claire's hair-grip: she would fiddle with it nervously and it would click exactly so. Abruptly, the noise stopped. Adrenaline streamed through him. His eyes strained to see and the effort caused black sunflowers to bloom in the darkness. The petals were fringed with tiny veins. He could even make out the circling corpuscles as they throbbed in time with his heart. He pulled himself up and the sweat-dampened sheets creaked softly under him. He had been hot, now he was cold.

The curtain, shifted perhaps by a draught, opened a fraction. A thin streak of street-light came through the conifers and allowed him to make out the figure that stood at the bottom of his bed. His whole body spasmed in shock. She had her back to him.

'Claire!'

He reached out for the bedside lamp. His hand was still groping for the switch as she turned towards him. Her eyebrows were arched, her face strangely different from the way he remembered it. Death had changed her, or was it the shadows? She walked out of the room, soundlessly.

His flapping hand now found the switch. Yellow light burst across the empty room. He squinted and once again asked himself whether it was possible that he had been dreaming. But the door was half-open, and he had shut it behind him before going to bed. It could have opened by itself, he supposed. Or one of the boys might have been playing another practical joke. But reason gave paltry comfort. He pulled up the covers. He had to admit that he was scared of Claire now, or whoever that was. Perhaps death did turn people bad. He had promised that he would never run from her and here he was, tempted to hide under his sheets.

He made a decision. It was time to confront whatever he had seen. Not going after her now would mean capitulating to fear, and after that there would be no hope of recovery. He let the covers drop. Enough of panic-attacks and sleepwalks. Enough of fear. He was awake. He wanted his own life back. Swinging his legs out of the bed he turned off the lamp again so that his eyes would readjust to the dark. He pulled on some clothes – trousers without socks, jacket without shirt – and opened the door wide.

The corridor was empty. A few oblongs of white light from the sanatorium's main entrance flowed through the frosted glass near the ceiling and helped him see. To his right were closed doors where the boys were asleep. He turned left and began to walk. It was very quiet. He could hear the soles of his feet squeak over the cold marble floor. He tried the door to the staffroom but it was locked. He stopped at the dispensary. The carving was in there. It had woken him up, invaded his dreams, insistent that he honoured his promise to Isabel. He tried the handle; it was locked. But the dispensary had a window facing the garden as well.

There was a movement. He swung round, but saw only the stairs that led to the ward. That and a glimmer of light on the brass door fitting.

His fright fell away. He gritted his teeth. If this was Claire, why was she playing games with him? Why was she waking him up and scaring him? Angry, he left the dispensary and rapidly climbed the stairs, but at the fire doors he paused. Slowly he slipped through and advanced to the window where Marjorie had smoked a cigarette and chatted to him during the day. He looked down on to the driveway. There was no way a car's headlamps could reach inside this corridor. So he waited. Time passed. His fear was euphoric; he felt light-headed, alive.

The wire in the windows of the ward door throbbed once, faintly yellow. He crouched down, approached it, and edged it open. Seeing and hearing nothing – the beds seemed empty – he slipped silently through. Immediately he dropped behind the first bed on the right and peered along the ranks of iron bed legs that ran the full length of the room. The view was unimpeded to the far wall. The left side appeared to be clear also until he noticed that the white skirting-board, which was just visible on his side of the ward, was obscured by something on the other. Taking to his hands and knees, he crawled forwards, and stopped. He had seen the flicker of a torch beam across the parquet floor and also its reflection in the dark panes of the arched window, which was ajar. Closer now, he could see that a thick blanket had been hung down from the last bed to block the view from the door. From the corner he heard a scrape.

His excitement passed away. It could only be boys. One of them must have come into his room for a dare, and his imagination had filled in the rest. He straightened up, cheated and annoyed. But curiosity remained. If he was going to see what they were doing — and he already had his suspicions — he would have to see them before they saw him. Crawling wasn't the dignified approach, so very carefully he rose to his feet and stepped slowly to the far wall where he could get a view without coming too close.

There were three boys in dressing-gowns. Bingham and Hopkins were sitting cross-legged with their backs to the blanket screen while a larger boy — it was Paul — was against the wall. He held a torch whose beam was directed on to a downturned glass. Around it was a circle of letters on a square piece of chipboard, with a 'Yes' and 'No' set on opposing sides. It was a ouija board and each boy had a finger on the glass, which was positioned by the letter D. Magnus was about to speak but he noticed that the boys' eyes were fixed on the glass: something had grabbed their attention. He watched, lip curling in mockery.

The glass edged to E. Paul followed it with the torch beam, which quivered slightly on its target. It had not been a long way for the glass to move — the letters, alphabetically positioned, were close together on the board — but then it began a longer journey towards R and stopped.

'Calder,' said Paul softly. 'Miss Calder.'

After initial disbelief, Magnus was filled with indignation that he had to control. On one hand his sister's name and memory was being turned into sacrilegious dormitory entertainment for spotty teenagers. On the other hand, was he in a position to judge when he was prowling the corridors in search of her ghost? He reached for his reserves of hypocrisy and tried to compose the words with which he would break up the party. Meanwhile Paul glanced up at the nervous faces of his companions and put a malevolent smile on his face.

'If it's really Miss Calder, tell us how you died.'

Despite himself, he held back to watch. The glass moved slowly back to D. And then to E, and then towards R, at which point Bingham groaned. 'It's just repeating itself.'

'Shut up,' said Paul. The glass continued from R to M.

'Derm?' There was a small giggle. The glass continued, this time to U, and then R, and then it stopped.

'Dermur,' said Hopkins. 'Is that a medical condition?'

'It's murder, idiot,' snapped Paul. 'Just the wrong way round. Some kind of interference.'

There was, Magnus had to admit, a perverse pleasure to be got from doing the scaring rather than being scared. He chose his moment and took a heavy step forwards. Immediately the torch beam flicked across the ward, from bedcover to painted brick wall to iron bedstead. He took another step forward and put his hands on his hips. This time the beam went straight into his face and he flinched, shielding his eyes. There was a collective squawk of terror. Magnus's likeness to his sister must have contributed to the impressive effect he had on the boys. They scrambled into the corner and cowered, and he couldn't deny himself a certain satisfaction at their eyes bulging out of white faces — until he realised that their attention was directed behind him, not at him.

Immediately he twisted round, but it felt so slow; his vision described a huge, leisurely parabola. And when he saw what he did, it took even longer for him to lurch forwards, reach out and grab. His fingers closed on thin air because already she had disappeared, not in a puff of smoke or in the blink of an eye, but out of the window, with a bang on the window-ledge and a short slithering descent to the garden below.

He had seen the mole, and the painted face, and the wig with its clip.

'Stay exactly where you are,' he said to the boys, although the command was not necessary as they were still centrifugally plastered against the wall. He ran to the window and looked down on to the ink-coloured lawn. It was empty.

'Isabel!' He did not expect an answer. He waited a moment longer, then ran his hands through his sweaty hair, and leant his elbows on the window-ledge, panting softly. It was as if he had known all along, but hadn't been able to accept why. Because it was a question that applied equally to him. She, too, was a marionette, playing the part of the dead.

Remembering himself, he dashed back to the ward

entrance to cut off the boys' escape, and turned on the light switch.

'Come on, come out, all of you.'

The two younger boys stood up in their tartan dressing-gowns and stepped out shakily from behind the bed. The rumpled stripes of their pyjama trousers stopped short of two sets of bony ankles. Hopkins's red hands were hanging loosely at his sides while Bingham's were joined behind his back. Both looked hopelessly guilty, and pale from shock, although the appearance of an adult had neutralised the terror. They squinted at him, then stared down at their acrylic slippers, seemingly hypnotised by the lurid tartan fur.

'Someone was playing a trick on you. Back to your rooms, both of you,' he said, sternly.

They looked up at him and then at each other. His ire could not have been very convincing. They were aware that he was in no real position of authority, and this made them unresponsive if not rebellious. He tried once more. 'I said bed!'

They tried to repress hysterical giggles, then looked to their senior, Paul, who was still hidden behind the bed. Obeying an unseen signal they filed past Magnus with flushed cheeks and eyes glowing with excitement. The door flapped softly behind them and he waited coldly for Paul to emerge.

Paul was in no hurry. With a slow sigh, he got to his feet and straightened his dressing-gown in an attempt to restore some composure. He then stooped and picked up the ouija board. He put it under his arm and the glass in his pocket, turned off the torch and made his way towards Magnus with an air of bored resignation, even though he was shaking all over. He stopped in front of him and met his eye.

'I am going to get you expelled,' said Magnus. 'Tomorrow morning I am going to tell the headmaster about this.'

Unexpectedly, the threat seemed to relieve the boy. He smirked. 'That would be interesting. I'd like to see that.'

Magnus wanted to beat Paul's skull against one of the iron beds, mainly because of his insufferable insouciance, but also because he was right. Of course it *would* be interesting to see him complaining that students were contacting his sister beyond the grave. He suddenly felt very tired.

'Who was that, by the way? She moved pretty fast. Assuming it was a she.'

Magnus leant against a bed. 'Someone with psychological problems.'

'A friend of yours?'

He didn't answer. It was time to ask some questions of his own. 'I spoke to the matron. She told me the reason why Claire left.'

'All of it? About this?' Fractionally, he lifted the board.

Magnus frowned. 'She told me about how they found the boy at the theatre. So tell me the rest of it.'

Paul shrugged. 'I can tell you what I know. These sessions are a sort of tradition. Normally they happen on Matron's night off. That way there's only the nurse on duty and she leaves you alone unless you ring the bell or cause a racket. Your sister used to cover for her sometimes so she could go and see her boyfriend. One night she caught them red-handed, like you just did. Jones was one of them. The boy who died.'

Magnus started to have a bad feeling about this. 'Go on.'

'She caught them but she didn't send them to bed. She asked them what they were doing and if they really believed in the occult. Obviously, they didn't have a clue, really. It was just for a laugh. But she knew all about it. She said there were people in Africa who believed that when you die, your spirit doesn't go to heaven. Instead it sticks in someone's heart, someone close. And if someone really wants them to come back, they can do a spell.'

Magnus began to shake. 'What kind of spell?'

'She said there was no point in telling, because it required special ingredients.'

'Which were?'

Paul glanced up sharply. 'She didn't say.'

'You were there, weren't you, Paul?'

'No. I just heard.'

'Then what happened?'

'Then nothing. She said she'd supervise, but nobody wanted to go on with it. They said it wouldn't be fun with a teacher there. But it wasn't just that. Something about her.' Paul paused. 'Jones died a week later.'

'Jesus,' said Magnus, under his breath.

Paul leapt to Claire's defence. 'Look, it wasn't her

fault. He did it himself. His mother had just died. When they found him hanging there he was dressed up like it was the end of term. Overcoat on, satchel with his homework and a banana, some clothes. He missed her. Maybe some of the things Miss Calder said gave him ideas. But she couldn't have known.'

Magnus could guess the rest. 'But someone got scared. Someone who was there. And he told someone. The house-master, or the headmaster, and Miss Calder was out. But ever so discreetly. Right?'

Paul didn't reply, but for the first time Magnus saw his expression drop its guard. He glanced over at the arched window. 'Someone wants her back, don't they?'

Magnus took a step closer. 'What ingredients were they?'

Paul dropped his eyes to the floor. Quietly, he said, 'You want the carving, but Matron wouldn't let you have it.'

Magnus forced the answer out of his dried-up throat. 'Yes.'

Paul's face suddenly brightened with desperate help-fulness. 'I can get it. I can get it for you.'

'You've got the keys?'

'Yes, but you've got to promise . . .'

'I'm not going to tell anyone. So long as you keep your own mouth shut, and those other two boys' as well.'

His lifted his hand tentatively, as if to touch Magnus's arm, but it stopped short. With this gesture he shed about five years. 'I want to know. Is she with you? Can you feel her?'

Magnus became angry. 'That's none of your business. Anyway, what the hell were you doing up here again, playing with that thing?'

'I couldn't not. The others wanted to. And they're all younger. I had to.'

DERMUR. The mangled word had caught in his mind. He paused, straightened up, and eventually nodded. 'Get the key.'

Relief streamed over Paul's face. He nodded, almost laughed. But Magnus grabbed his arm before he could leave. 'One thing, Paul. Are you dyslexic?'

Paul blinked once. 'A little bit. Why?'

Magnus smiled and let go. 'Nothing. Go on.'

Five minutes later Paul was relocking the door to the dispensary. The key, he had explained to Magnus, was part of a set that opened various parts of the school's properties. Nobody knew how they had been acquired (or most likely copied) but for nearly a decade they had been handed down by a member of the departing senior year to whomever was prepared to pay for them. Magnus had the carving in his hand, which he held securely against his side, while Paul's dressing-gown pocket bulged with stolen items. Magnus didn't ask what they were, but he stared.

'They'll change the locks after this. It's my last opportunity.'

'Just make sure you don't leave those keys in your room.'

Paul's look suggested that the advice wasn't necessary. 'They won't be worth much after this, anyway.'

They parted company. Magnus went directly to his room, turned on the light and shut the door behind him. The mattress crunched as he lay on it, but this time he even smiled at the gruesome noise as he stretched his back and flexed his cold toes. DERMUR was merely an attempt by Paul to scare his juniors; it had his dyslexic fingerprints all over it. Claire had been a fool; the death of the boy was coincidence. None of it seemed to matter. He closed his eyes, his hand reached out for the carving and he placed it on his chest. Its weight felt reassuring; his thumbs stroked the dark polished wood and he exhaled, long and deep, through his nostrils. He had taken possession of it. His fingertips explored the notches on its belly. Warmth rinsed his system; that, and a tingling sensation at his extremities. It was a sensual fear. He didn't need to sleep any more. He thought of Isabel with a smile. He thought he understood her now, just as he was beginning to understand himself. But there was more to learn. This piece of the carving would be bargained for some answers.

With an hour or so until daylight, he decided to get up and wash the dried sweat off his body. Tiptoeing across the corridor into the bathroom, he found a deep old bathtub mounted on short bandy legs. The taps' heavy jets of water filled it rapidly and soon he was immersed, barely touching the bottom when he filled his lungs with the steamy air. The tub's ancient enamel had been worn away so that a rusty patch of iron was exposed on the bottom, and the metal winked like a lucky penny as he dried himself off. Then he noticed that a watery ray of red light had pierced the small window above. Dawn: it was time to leave.

Magnus let himself out of the sanatorium and went to the car with the carving in one of his bags. Everything was quiet as he put them into the boot, apart from the first birdsong from the garden. He was tempted to take a parting stroll over the lawn and see the window from which Isabel had escaped. He breathed the fresh air and walked along the rank of shaggy conifers until one caused him to stop and stare. Standing out from the rank of drab green fronds was a single golden-brown tree, made exquisite by drops of dew that glimmered all over its needles. An autumnal evergreen in late spring? No, it was dead.

With a single finger, he bent a branch and let it spring back. It sent a shower of crystal and russet to the grass. He smiled, charmed. Then he shoved both hands in, gripped the tree's trunk and shook it with all his strength. With each push and pull he was covered by a torrent of needles and water droplets. He continued even when the cascade stopped, until his arms burned and he looked up and saw the very tip of the tree swinging against the sky in a great figure of eight, bald as a whip.

Panting, he stepped back. He shook some of the needles out of his sodden hair, brushed down his shoulders and wiped his eyes, then turned back towards the sanatorium. A pale face was visible from the ground-floor window. Paul was staring out. His gaze fixed on the skeleton of the tree, and the golden piles of needles that lay among the grass on all sides, and his gaze didn't even flinch when Magnus walked past, heading for the car.

Fourteen

Guilt met him on the motorway. He had already stopped at a service station for something to eat, and upon setting out again had turned up the radio to block out thought. Unfortunately it didn't quite work. It was safe to assume that about now Marjorie would discover the theft of the carving. He cringed as he imagined the cheerful smile wiped off her face when she opened the dispensary. First there would be disbelief and then, perhaps, recriminations visited on the boys. Only then would suspicion swing round to him. He had deceived her. He was a worm, worse than a worm. Then he realised that a whole guilt tailback was waiting its turn.

Flagellating himself about Marjorie only made things worse, because it reminded him of all the other moral crimes in his past. It didn't matter that they lacked a common theme or that some were over a decade old. Time did not wither their capacity to torture him, in fact quite the opposite. The older guilts kept themselves sprightly by competing with the younger ones. Naturally they varied, although many revolved around broken promises, lost tempers and drunken indiscretions. A couple of teenage infidelities still packed a formidable punch. He hated himself for never having visited in hospital a friend who had once paid his rent for three months straight. He'd run over a cat a few years ago and didn't have the guts to finish it off.

Of course he had big guilts as well as the relatively petty ones, but strangely they required much less attention. He never fretted much about being a bad son, for example, although he knew perfectly well that he was. And he realised now that there was not much to be done about the fact that he was alive and Claire was dead: it merely generated a sense of unworthiness. No, the little guilts were the ones that constantly demanded his attention: a kind of arduous mental paperwork. His conscience produced huge amounts of the stuff. For each accusation he had defences, justifications and mitigations, which he annually and fastidiously updated, and which (guilt being guilt) never quite amounted to a convincing rebuttal. The carving would cause a new case to be opened. His best defence, he calculated, was that he had been constrained to commit the crime by Isabel's emotional blackmail. But by annulling one guilt (about Isabel) Magnus had simply given rise to another (about Marjorie) and he was unsure which would prove the most burdensome. Thus the process began, and it would continue under its own impetus, he expected, for the duration of his natural life. He just hoped Marjorie wouldn't report him to the headmaster. This was unlikely, he concluded, mainly because it wasn't her style and also because she had no evidence that he had committed the crime. Unless Paul was interrogated and pointed the finger at him, which he wouldn't.

He concentrated once more on driving. Having barely slept the night before, the rapid passage of road markings worked as a mild but cumulatively effective tranquilliser. Guilt exhausted him almost as much as recalling embarrassing moments, of which there were legion. The staffroom pass, the teenage royalist poem (unbelievably published) . . . and then there was dancing. He sucked in air through his teeth. Embarrassments: these, too, hunted in packs. Urgently he turned up the radio and slowly — mercifully — the music did its work. When he woke up it was to avoid collision with a cattle truck.

Five minutes later the Astra pulled up at a North of England service station and Magnus stepped out, vein-eyed and wobbly. There he bought a can of cola and a small mountain of sugar-rich confectionery, which he took back to the car and sloshed down his throat. Amid all his thoughts about death the small matter of his own mortality had somehow slipped out of the frame.

He felt better as he pulled out of the service station. He was alive anyway. Pushing towards the Scottish borders, he was actually calm. Half an hour later Edinburgh's grey outskirts rose up and the weather sagged down. His mood returned to normal — that was to say, tolerable. He looked around and wondered if, one day, he would think of Edinburgh as his city rather than his sister's. Certainly that would only happen once he had put certain matters to rest. Delivery of the second piece of the carving was surely a step in the right direction. However, as he steered into Bellevue his equanimity was only disturbed by a broken word that must have tailed him all the way from the south, and now flapped bleakly around the outer fringes of his mind: DERMUR.

The Astra rumbled over cobbles and drew to a halt outside Isabel's flat. It could be assumed that she was waiting for him. He took the camera-bag out of the boot, checked that the carving was still in it, then went to her door and buzzed the intercom. It hissed briefly, but before he could announce himself the door sprang open. He stepped in and climbed the tenement steps.

When he got to her floor he saw that the flat was wide open. He waited a moment, then tapped on the door. 'Isabel, it's me.' He waited. Nothing. 'Don't be scared. Let's talk.' Timidly, he put a foot into her flat and looked down the corridor. 'I've got something to show you.'

At last she appeared, but he hardly recognised her. Her face, beneath the limp blonde hair, seemed strangely shapeless, while her pale blue eyes lacked all animation, even of pain. Wearing a nondescript grey tracksuit, she was drained of colour and character, as if her own identity had been horribly sapped by the guise. She said nothing and barely looked at him. All the same, he smiled encouragingly. The situation required some normality.

'Hi, Isabel. Do you want to see the video I shot at the school?'

She blanked him, but her gaze went to the bag on his shoulder. 'I've got that piece of the carving, too.'

Suddenly she became alert, hungry-looking. 'You have?'

'Did you think I'd break my promise?'

She darted forwards. Involuntarily his hand gripped the bag and he turned to keep it from her, only to find that she had gone to shut the door behind him. She had noted his reaction, but did not say anything as she led him back up the corridor towards the sitting room. He saw that she was limping slightly, and she didn't seem to care that he saw it either. She had presumably got the injury when she jumped out of the dormitory window. She was lucky: it might have been worse, unless she'd had the escape route planned beforehand.

Nothing had changed in the sitting room: the baboon's head was on the mantelpiece, showing its fangs between raised paws. The poster of her triumphant *Macbeth* kept its pride of place on the wall: the high point of her non-existent career. Except now he knew it had been mere preparation for the role that she would truly make her own: that of director.

She turned to face him, waiting. He was not invited to sit down. Her eyes were creeping over his bag so avidly that he laughed nervously and put it down on the sofa — within reach, however.

'So, would you like to see it? The film, I mean.'

Understanding that she would have to observe some

basic politeness before he gave her what she wanted, she forced some scratchy brightness into her voice. 'Yes. Would you like a cup of tea?'

'Yes, please.'

Pursing her lips, she went into the kitchen. She made him feel like he was playing a cruel comedy of manners. Perhaps he was. But his cruelty to her was dwarfed by what she had dealt out to him. Laying bare an obsession required a certain formality, he believed. She had nearly sent him mad.

He waited to hear her fill the kettle before he opened the bag and took out only the camera. He zipped the bag securely once more, rested the camera on his lap and waited. A couple of minutes later she came back with a mug of tea and sat down next to him, meticulously averting her eyes from the bag. She even smiled. He thanked her, sipped some tea and put it down on the floor.

'Did the shoot go smoothly, then?' she asked, squeezing up to get a view of the camera's mini-screen.

'More or less.'

Suddenly, unexpectedly, he found that he was nervous. This would be the first time that anyone had seen his work, even if it was in unedited form and on a three-inch screen. He had not even found the time to look at the footage himself. 'There's not much to see,' he stammered. 'It's just a school play. Nothing fancy.'

She nodded and smiled encouragingly. He hesitated, then picked a random spot in the film. She shifted closer to him so that their shoulders touched. He could feel the movement of her breathing as they began to watch.

Despite initial nerves, it only took a few seconds to see that his expectations of catastrophe were unfounded. Never a man knowingly to overestimate his talent, Magnus had to admit that his work verged on being professional, even craftsmanlike: Lavinia's stumps looked most convincing, and so did the set. He glanced over at his audience of one. She seemed politely engrossed – or was her interest genuine? This was good work, after all. He sat back and felt rather pleased with himself. But as his fears about the quality of the filming receded, a new anxiety took its place, and this related to Isabel's arm, which had moved along his back and was about to encircle his waist. Indeed, her fascination with this excellently filmed theatre production seemed to require that she lean ever closer, causing her to press against his arm. He let the camera droop.

'What is it?' asked Isabel, her face close to his. 'I was enjoying that. What's the matter?'

He put the camera aside and stood up. 'That's enough for now. You can see the rest when it's edited. We need to talk about last night.'

Her eyes swerved left and right. She didn't look evasive so much as slightly disoriented. 'Okay,' she replied, in a small voice.

'It was you, wasn't it, dressed up as Claire?'

She hunched forwards, hopefully. Her eyes sparkled. 'Did it seem real, though? Was it convincing?'

'It was, quite. In the dark. Certainly the first few times.'

She sat back, glowing with satisfaction. 'I did a course in stage makeup, but it has its limits. Surgery's the only real way. Anyway, none of that matters now. Or soon.'

He almost lost track of what he wanted to say. 'It was you, then, was it, the first time? On the bus, when you went into the café?'

She grinned happily, half closed her eyes, and hunched her shoulders, as if she was curled up in a cosy blanket. 'I was as surprised as you when I saw you there. What did you think?'

'I thought it was her. But when I followed you into the café and you weren't there, I thought I was going mad.'

'I knew you thought it was her. I saw the love in your eyes.' She sighed nostalgically.

'But . . .' He was groping for the words. 'Where did you go?'

'I told the waitress you were my ex-husband and that you were breaking a court order. They let me out through the kitchens at the back and promised to cover for me.'

That explained the hostility he'd felt. 'And the other times?'

'I followed you, of course. I nearly got caught in the rain on the way to the wedding, had to grab a waterproof from a second-hand shop. It wasn't always easy, you know.'

'Isabel!'

She seemed a little confused. 'But you really didn't know it was me? I thought we understood each other in a way.'

'Why did you do it?'

She looked at him softly. 'Because I missed her. Because I wanted her life instead of mine. Because I saw the way you looked at me when you thought it was her. Because I want you to love me.'

'And that was the way to do it?'

'It was the only way. You're not interested in me as myself.' She looked sad, but then her face lit up with a memory. 'The boys as well. You could tell they loved her. How they stared! And Colin's letter. Love. Love.'

'But there's more to it, isn't there?'

She nodded seriously and confidently, like a schoolgirl who knew exactly the answer to the question. 'I couldn't let you forget what you had to do. Now, show me what you've brought.'

He continued to glare at her, but he wouldn't get another word out of her until she saw. He reached over to the bag, unzipped it and took out the carving.

She took it reverently in her hands, but he did not let go of it. 'Tell me what you know about this. Claire's thesis told you something, didn't it?'

'I'll tell you when you get me the last piece.'

She tugged at the carving, but still he held on. 'No. Now.'

With a great wrench she tore the carving out of his hand and sent him sprawling on the floor. He looked up, shocked by her strength, and saw her place the baboon's head on its midriff. They fitted exactly. With a sharp cry of satisfaction she stepped back, only to stagger slightly. He felt it too: a great wobble, like sickness or the surge of a drug taking effect. Like the first time, when he had brought her the baboon's head, only now there were no malaria pills to blame, no jet-lag either.

It lasted a couple of seconds, and Magnus recovered first. He clambered to his feet and ran out of the room, up the stairs, towards the bedroom. If she wouldn't hand over the thesis then he would take it for himself. He barged through the door, saw a writing-desk and tore open the drawer. Nothing, only bills and scrap paper, ribbons and address books. He went to the wardrobe, sending a glance towards the door, expecting Isabel to come charging in at any moment. He gripped the handles and pulled it open.

Claire's clothes. The ones he'd seen her wearing on the bus, at the wedding, on the street. A wig of straight brown hair, like hers. The beret. Some shoes. But he wasn't looking for these. There was a box behind the shoes. The thesis? He pulled it out, tore it open, and swore. More clothes. But then he looked closer, and frowned. Baby clothes. What on earth was Isabel doing with those? He rummaged through them. They looked old but in good condition. From their colours – pinks and pastels predominating – he assumed they had been bought for a little girl. Perhaps they were Isabel's from when she was a baby. He lifted out a cotton bib, opened it up and found that a name had been elaborately embroidered on to it in High Victorian style: Claire.

He came out of the spare room with the bib in his hand. In a daze, he went into the sitting room, but found that Isabel had moved into the kitchen where she was listlessly rinsing his mug in the sink. 'I've put it somewhere safe,' she said. 'One day I'll let you read it, when you're ready.'

He dropped the bib onto the work surface. She glanced at it, but failed to react.

'I want to know what this is about.'

She sighed and put down the mug on the draining-board. 'They're Claire's things. Your mother gave them to her when she moved away from home. She left them here when she went abroad.'

'Claire didn't keep her baby clothes.'

'How do you know?'

'I know my sister.'

She took the bib to the kitchen table and folded it carefully, then looked at him with dry amusement. 'So what are you suggesting?'

He hesitated. 'I'm not suggesting anything. I'm asking.'

'You're asking some leading questions. Leading some-where rather — suggestive.'

His cheeks burned, and he didn't really understand what he wanted to say until his mouth did it for him. 'You think you can get her back.'

There was a silence. Then she twisted round and the blood rushed to her face. 'If you love her then you'll finish what you promised!'

Magnus stared. He had stumbled on something, but he could not see where to take it. Outrage blinded him to any further investigation, but his voice didn't co-operate to express his anger: it clogged. 'I did love her,' he managed to gasp.

'Did? Past tense?'

'If you're saying I've forgotten her.' He was stumbling, anguished, through a forest of cliché, trying to find a phrase that could express how he felt. Tears pricked his eyes. 'Her memory means everything.' It was trite.

She sighed, then addressed him calmly, patiently. 'Magnus. There is a way, but I can't do it without you.'

She made him feel like he was being stupid or immature, yet she was the one sounding deranged. 'What on earth are you talking about?'

'To have her back, alive again. In the flesh. Don't you want it?'

'I don't want what I can't have.'

'Perhaps you don't want what you could have.'

Magnus now knew for sure that she was losing her sanity. 'Isabel, listen to what you're saying. Nobody can bring back the dead.'

For a moment her eyes were fanatical, but the next they were brimming with tears of release. The tension went out of her body. At last she was facing up to reality.

'I'm scared,' she said simply. 'Scared of what I've been thinking. Scared of what I've become. She's not just a memory to me. She's my life.'

Magnus came forwards and held her in his arms, which were shaking. He rocked her slightly. Compassion and relief filled him equally. He closed his eyes. 'We're not that different, in the end. It's been the same for me, only it's locked up inside, in my head.'

'Really?'

The question was muffled by his shoulder, but then she pulled back to look at him. What he had said was true, but now he wished that he hadn't opened his mouth. A tear dropped off her chin. 'Do you believe in anything, Magnus? An afterlife?'

The answer was still no. There was no religion to comfort him, or the security of obliteration; only superstition. He was terrified of an afterlife. Atheism was wishful thinking.

He held her at arm's length. 'The two pieces of carving. Something happened when you put them together. It wasn't just me who felt it. I saw.'

'You've felt other things too, haven't you? Your dreams. The numbness when you were taking on her spirit, the feeling that you were being guided or possessed. I've seen you struggle against it, Magnus. I've felt the pain you're going through. But you have to stop. You have to follow the path you've been given. Once we've united the three pieces it will be over. You'll feel so much better, I promise.'

His shoulders drooped. 'You have to explain. The carving.'

She looked at him, as if weighing him up, then took his elbow and led him to the sofa where they sat down together.

'This carving is an icon from a cult that Claire wrote about in her thesis. Each part represents one of the properties that make up a person. You give them to people you care about, and the carvings draw out certain properties from them, ready for when they're needed.'

'Properties? What do you mean?'

'The head denotes the mind, religious feeling, fidelity. The chest relates to the heart, the emotions and nurturing instincts. While the lower part . . .' she hesitated '. . . the lower part represents the sex. That is to say, sexual powers of attraction.'

He thought it through. The head went to Isabel. The middle went to Marjorie. And the third piece, presumably, was with Rosie, drawing off her sexuality like a sponge.

'When the ritual is ready to be performed, the spirit's closest relative collects the pieces and brings them together.' Her face was lit with ardour. 'Magnus, the people she found in Africa were miracle-workers. Everyone in Africa believes, even doctors, lawyers. She wrote about it so well.'

He pressed the palms of his hands to his temples. 'She didn't believe. She can't have *believed* this stuff.' He was trying to get his head round the information. 'It's as if she anticipated the crash. Her own death. But she can't have.'

'I believe that she sensed it. Claire was special like

that. Everyone she met could feel her spirit, her power.' She smiled at him with pity. 'Apart from her brother, perhaps.'

'She sent back all sorts of things. It doesn't mean anything.'

'Magnus.' Her face remained placid, her voice firm. 'You're going to bring me the third piece of the carving, like you promised.'

He stood up. 'There's something more, though, isn't there? There's something you're not telling me about these African miracle-workers.'

She nodded sadly. 'It's true, I'm afraid, that the *sangoman* are persecuted. The witch-doctors, I mean. And the women who associate with them particularly. There are burnings, murders all the time.'

He gasped, his eyes widened. 'You're suggesting . . .'

She raised her hands. 'I'm not suggesting anything. I don't know. But you're going to bring me the third piece of the carving, aren't you? You'll do it for her, won't you? Magnus!'

But he had already shoved the camera back into its bag, and a moment later he was out of the flat.

Fifteen

The tenement door boomed shut behind him and he paced down
the street, struggling with the terrible implications of
what Isabel had hinted at. Could Claire really have been
murdered? It was possible of course. The question was,
how possible? Magnus felt his whole future hang in the
balance. Was he prepared to devote years of his life
to uncovering the truth, however horrible or futile it
might be? The answer, decisively, was no. He didn't
want to chase ghosts any more. He wanted peace. And
so the choice was made. He would cling to the official
explanation of Claire's death with all the fervour of a
man evading his responsibility.

But he was also angry with himself. He had gone into
the flat wanting to confront Isabel with the games she had
been playing with his head, and to bring her back to earth,
perhaps even encourage her to seek help. Instead she was
pulling him into her own deranged universe where the
living served the dead, and where personal autonomy
was relegated to the status of disloyalty and selfishness.

The thought that his future had been plotted in advance repelled him. The baby clothes caused him to shudder. He ought to resist more. His ears burned against the cold air and his shoulders bent forwards, cramped with anxiety. He was heading towards the bar where he hoped to find Gav. He had known Claire. Perhaps he could shed more light on what Isabel wasn't telling him.

Ducking out of the blustery wind, he went down the pocked steps and found the bar largely empty, but he couldn't see Gav. Then the toilet door flapped open and he emerged, running a hand over his shaven head and taking up station beside the till where a packet of cigarettes lay, along with a pint of lime cordial. He took a slug of his drink, then turned round lazily to regard Magnus. 'Hello,' he drawled. 'Did you enjoy the wedding?'

Magnus came up and sat down on a stool. 'Gav, I'm sorry to be abrupt, but something's worrying me. Do you remember at the wedding, you mentioned *muti*, and a baboon cult, and an article? Please, is there anything else that you remember?'

Gav ran a finger over his grey chin and took a long, contemplative drag on his cigarette. 'Yes, I think I told you about the *muti* murders, didn't I? They were happening all over southern Africa. Bodies were getting found with pieces cut off them. Particularly children. Apparently the flesh gets dried or cured, and is then ground down for use in potions. *Muti* is the Zulu word for "medicine", but I don't know if it's the same thing.'

Was flesh the special ingredient that Claire had said

was needed when she spoke to the boys? 'Anything about baboons?'

Gav bent his duck-like lip into a smile. 'I don't recall anything specific, Magnus, but I know that people use witch-doctors all the time in Africa, businessmen, taxi drivers, the lot. It could be just to buy lucky charms, or herbal cures, or something for heightened virility. Are you all right?'

Magnus was not all right. He felt faint. His head was boiling. 'I think so.'

'You don't look well.' Gav leant forwards and put a hand on his shoulder, the picture of a concerned undertaker. 'Has this got anything to do with what we talked about earlier? You said you kept seeing Claire in crowds. It sounded quite upsetting.'

An ancestral British reflex required him to deny emotion in a bar, in the company of another man. 'No, it's okay. As I said, Claire left a statuette behind, and we're trying to find out the story behind it.'

'Sounds like a case for *Antiques Roadshow*.'

Magnus looked up at his face, which was deadpan, and got off his stool. He would not break down, he would keep his cool as far as the exit. They shook hands. 'Thanks, Gav. I'll see you around.'

Magnus reached the Astra, walking with the wind so that his shirtfront and trouser-legs flapped in front of him, as if they were keener than he was to reach the car. He pulled a wet flyer from the windscreen and threw it up in the air where it was caught by the breeze and sent fluttering down the street until it slapped against another car. He climbed in and spent a moment getting his breath back. Murders, mutilation, cults, the carving. Panic bubbled away inside him, but he still had it under control. Too late, he realised that it would have been better not to ask any more questions. The answers didn't lay worries to rest, but instead fuelled a growing sense of dread and disorientation, which only made it more difficult to distinguish between what was real and what was being inflated by his overheated imagination. Better simply to fulfil his obligation and ask Rosie about the third carving, if she still had it. With that done he could wash his hands of the whole business. Yes, that was the thing to do, once he had returned the car to Mother, as promised. He knew he was a bad son, and a failure, but he kept his promises and Mother needed the Astra for a ladies' golf challenge this afternoon. He turned the ignition, manoeuvred the car out of the tight space, and set off in the direction of Inverleith Row.

Magnus sat back in the parental sofa and watched the dark red blob that was Mother's twinset as it spread across the dimpled glass of the partition between the kitchen and the sitting room. Claire's photo had been restored to its silver frame. A clock was ticking somewhere amid the ceramic crowds of statuettes that were ranged, bucolic as ever, across the shelves. Beside him, the car-keys rested on a drinks mat to avoid scratching the gleaming lacquer of the coffee-table. He was relieved to see her approach as he had been obliged to wait over fifteen minutes while she finished waxing the interior of her golf-bag. She wanted a word. Could it wait, he had asked, to which she had replied, no, *he* could wait. Twice already he had got up defiantly to go, only to mutter impatiently and sit down once more. He knew it was going to be something ridiculous.

She came in and smiled. 'Cup of tea, dear?'

'No, thanks, I have to go soon.'

'Is the car in one piece?'

'Ye-es.'

She sat down on the other end of the sofa and joined her hands together on her lap. 'Your father told me that the stage manager had an accident at the school theatre during rehearsals. He said he left you a message earlier, but you never called back.'

Damn, he had forgotten. 'For Christ's sake, it wasn't my fault. Someone left a pot of fake blood in the wings. It got spilt.'

'I didn't say it was your fault. But you might have returned your father's call. After everything he did for you.'

The choice was to react or absorb. Magnus chose the latter. He sighed, and dropped his head in limp assent. 'Yes, you're right. I am sorry.'

'Good.' She smoothed out the wrinkles of fabric that had formed on her lap. 'And how is Isabel?'

The question, so casually put, had Magnus on alert. Normally he would have rebutted the query with an inscrutable 'Fine', but anything connecting Isabel with his parents now made him paranoid. Call it marriage or

239

diabolic union, they were all pulling him in the same direction.

'Well, Mother, since you ask, she is becoming deranged. And so am I.'

Her visage softened. 'Is it serious?'

'Actually, yes. We both think we're possessed by Claire. Isabel favours reincarnation, while I – typical male, I know – remain undecided.'

'Clearly.' Mother sighed. 'Don't fret about that, dear. I think Claire would have been delighted to see you two together.'

'But that's precisely what I'm worried about.'

She didn't follow, but it didn't seem to bother her particularly.

Then he remembered that he had something to ask. Best to do it casually, however. 'Oh, that reminds me, do you still have Claire's baby clothes somewhere?'

She opened her mouth to answer, but then hesitated. She folded her hands together and smiled innocently. 'I'm sure I don't remember, dear.'

'Mother.' His voice was threatening.

Suddenly, she edged forwards on the sofa. 'Go on, do tell. Is she pregnant already, or are you just planning?'

He was horrified. 'What are you talking about? No!'

But her bright eyes were looking to the future, which contained a solvent, settled son, and the slow creak of a rocking cradle. 'Perhaps I should have a word with the minister,' she said.

'Yes, we could book an exorcism.'

'Excuse me?' Mother's expression darkened; she didn't

like him being rude about the church, or indeed any institution, golf club included.

'Oh, nothing. I'm off now, Mother. Thanks for the loan of the car.'

She called after him, 'Keep us updated, then, won't you, dear? Please?'

Magnus tramped over India Street's wet cobbles with his bag bouncing on his shoulder. He was glad to have reached the flat: darkness seeped from the grates in the gutter and when he looked down on to Stockbridge the rain – threatening for some time – had already begun its sweep in from the Forth, drenching the city street by street, making the slate roofs shine.

Having climbed the stairs he went to lie down on his bed. Blissfully it didn't crunch. He stretched out his spine and loosened his shoulders, which were stiff with tension and sore as ever. Through the skylight he saw clouds moving at great speed, propelled by the strong winds. He unfocused his eyes and let them settle on the ceiling. His nightmares made him wary of sleep, but soon his breathing came steady and close. He liked being surrounded by the familiar technology in his room. Its office smell soothed him: it suggested that things could be explained. That, he supposed, was what the modern world was all about. It sought to destroy the unknown and acquire, if it could, certainty and control. He closed his eyes and a mushroom cloud rose up silently in his mind: it said apocalypse had been wrestled from divinity. Then came a sheep: the rights to creation had been acquired by man. He smiled drowsily. A cloud, a sheep. What next? Perhaps it would be the conquest of death. He remembered a magazine article that he had read about the isolation of the gene responsible for ageing. Would eternal life be tolerable, he wondered. On this free-floating speculation of clouds and sheep he was lifted away into unconsciousness.

Quite soon afterwards, he woke up to discover that the ceiling had started to bend. It stretched around the edges and sagged before returning to its original position. He almost missed it: the warp was quick enough for him to doubt what he had seen. Then it did the same thing again, except that in the centre of the sag he could now discern the outline of two human feet. The effect was like lying under a trampoline at the moment in which the gymnast has struck the fabric from a great height. For a fraction of a second even the toes showed, pressing down with disproportionate weight, and then sprang away, leaving the ceiling to vibrate.

He blinked and it happened again, except now the trampolinist came down on her front and – even in that split second – the shape of the breasts reminded him inescapably of Marjorie. There was another impact, this time the serrated edge of a spine that curved on impact. Then the force increased greatly. A pair of knees indented itself to the point where the ceiling strained terribly and emitted an odd sound, like a thick rubber rope at the point of snap. He clearly saw two hands, the fingers grappling for purchase, sunk in so deep that the ceiling almost fitted them like gloves before the rebound sent them away. Then, after a clear two seconds, a face surged down towards him. The force of its downward journey brought it within inches of his own. The nose was bent sideways, he saw the shape of the eye socket and the jaw wagging at him. For all the distortion he recognised the face as Isabel's, but it was changing, the bones and features were realigning under the skin. With a vicious crack the face, too, was propelled back to where it had come from.

Magnus did not move: he was fixated. The ceiling was flat once more but, as he feared, it was only a short respite. Now all the limbs that he had seen pressed down simultaneously. He had assumed them to be part of a whole but they were dismembered. Arranging themselves in a circle they began to nuzzle one another, as if seeking their correct position. They made little progress at first and the effect might conceivably have been comic as well as disgusting until suddenly they sprang together.

It was a grotesquely partial human form – trunkless – with the spine flicking left and right and all the limbs joining just below the chin where the breasts formed a strange ruff. He could see clearly now that the features of the face were Claire's but they also appeared subtly different, like those of an identical twin. The form scuttled within the confines of the ceiling as if it was looking for the missing part of itself. Then the eyes, which had hitherto been shut, opened and stared down at him. Like those of a marble statue they seemed blind, but the frowning brows made him feel accused, as if he was responsible somehow for its incompleteness. In growing frustration, the fingers and toes gripped the material of the ceiling and tore. The sight of this spiderish monstrosity seeking an exit at last caused Magnus to react. He wouldn't let it out into the world. He couldn't. With a soft cry he twisted on his bed.

He sat up, awake now, and his face was tingling. Had he heard something downstairs? His mind was still foggy. He was shaking and his back ached terribly. He felt that he could not handle this for much longer. The third carving. He must find it, if only to destroy it. The front door slammed shut, followed by the scrape of wallpaper, further bumping and some mild curses.

'It's me, I'm back!' shouted Rosie. 'Magnus?'

'I'm up here,' he replied as he levered himself off the bed and sat down on the creaking swivel-chair.

Rosie appeared at the door and grinned. 'Hard at work?' she asked.

He flattened his hair at the back, still shell-shocked. 'How was your honeymoon?' he asked at last, and it took an effort.

'As expected. We argued.'

'I'm sorry to hear that.'

However, he wasn't that sorry. Presumably the tiffs had been followed with some form of grisly reconciliation. He rubbed his sore neck and bent it from side to side. He was going to ask her about the carving.

'What's wrong?' she asked, immediately stepping forward. 'Turn round.'

With a screech the chair swivelled. Her hands investigated his neck, his shoulders and upper back. 'My God, what have you been doing to yourself?'

He groaned as her fingers found a fresh knot that had formed under his shoulder-blade. She kept going, working her thumbs deep into his yielding back. He emitted a long, soft whistle, but did not cry out. She made a noise that suggested she was impressed: he was a natural sufferer.

'Rosie,' he said, as she worked, 'did you ever receive a piece of a carving in the post a while ago, from Claire?'

Her fingers hesitated for a moment, then continued their painful progress. No answer came.

'Rear end of a baboon, dark wood. Maybe it didn't arrive.'

'Yes, it did,' she replied. 'It was addressed to me. A baboon. So that's what it was.'

'Where is it?'

She sighed and stopped her massage. She spun him round in the chair so that he faced her. 'I'm sorry but I got rid of it.'

The news jolted him. 'You threw it away?'

'Yes. I don't know how to put this.'

She looked up at the cloudy skylight and back to him. 'We already knew that Claire had died when it arrived, but that made receiving it particularly awful. I couldn't understand why she would have sent something so ugly to me. I suppose I thought the worst, that there was something insulting about it, or even malevolent.' She looked down. 'I feel very guilty telling you that. You're her brother. But she hated my guts.'

He was not sure what to say, but he nodded slowly. 'I understand.'

'Please don't think that Colin was behind it. He was

here when it came and he wanted to keep it. He even put it on a shelf. Maybe that made me jealous. Definitely it did. He went out and I grabbed it and dumped it in the bin.'

'So it's gone.'

She ran a hand through her soft brown hair. 'I should have sent it back to your mother, I know. Colin was furious when he found out. But I was angry too.'

Slowly, he looked up at her and felt a great infusion of relief. His obligations had been fulfilled. He had tried and failed to unite the three carvings, but the failure was not his fault. It was over. That hideous creature clawing at his ceiling would have its access denied for ever. Isabel would have to accept that Claire was never going to come back, and would then begin the long-delayed process of mourning and recovery. His sister would gently fade in their memories. The living would get on with life and nature, thereby, would proceed. His back immediately felt better. 'Rosie, you work wonders.'

'You're not angry? I mean, have I dumped part of a priceless artifact or something?'

He moved his head from side to side and marvelled at the lack of stiffness in his neck muscles.

She gulped. 'Of course, the sentimental value is much more important. I'm sorry if I sounded—'

He cut her short. 'Rosie, don't worry about that. It's fine. I forgive you.' His mood was only slightly dented by the prospect of breaking the news to Isabel. Down belo.v the front door opened again.

'That will be Colin,' she said. 'He was on the phone. We're going to start moving stuff over to the new house today. The builders have cleared their stuff out at last.'

'Oh, yes?' replied Magnus, dreamily. It was such an ordinary conversation; banal as blue skies. Life was returning to normal.

Rosie heard Colin traipsing along the corridor and went to the top of the stairs. 'We're up here,' she called, on the way to her own room where, by the sound of things, she got on with boxing up belongings.

Colin reached the landing and smiled drearily. 'Hi, Magnus, how's the wedding film shaping up?'

'Good.' Silently he gestured Colin to come into his room. He obeyed somewhat warily and Magnus shut the door. He hesitated to ask how the honeymoon had gone, so Colin came straight to the point.

'When's the film going to be ready?'

'I've not had a chance to work on it yet. That's not what I wanted to talk to you about.' He took a step closer and drew out Colin's letter from his bag. 'I've been meaning to give this back to you.'

Colin snatched it, looked inside the envelope and put it into his back pocket.

'Whatever happened between the two of you, I think she would have wanted you and Rosie to be happy. In the long run.' Colin's sceptical expression caused him to laugh nervously. 'Let's hope so anyway. Look, I know I was a bit screwed up. I felt like I had to take up Claire's case. But it's over now. Time to move on.'

Colin took a moment. 'Okay. If we've cleared the air, I'm glad.'

And then they shook hands. Magnus didn't enjoy this bit. Manly accords always made him feel foolish. Thankfully Colin broke the silence. 'How did the job go down south?'

'Fine, except for the stage manager. He slipped and broke his arm.'

Colin wrinkled his brow. 'His name wasn't Sanders, was it?'

Magnus nodded, and saw Colin's face darken. 'Why?'

'Nothing. Except . . .' He paused, as if he was not sure what Magnus knew.

'Go ahead. I know the story.'

'It was him who told me what happened. The boy's death, I mean, and what they were saying about Claire. I'd phoned the theatre, expecting her to be there.'

'She didn't tell you herself?'

He pursed his lips. 'No.'

'And what happened?'

'I was angry. And freaked out. Things weren't going well anyway.'

'You mean that was when you broke up?'

'Not immediately. Not definitively. But it was the last gasp after that.' Colin leant back against the wall. 'Sanders was a complete shit. You could tell he enjoyed breaking the news to me.'

Magnus felt his stomach perform a slow revolution. So Claire might have partly blamed Sanders for the breakup. The bucket of blood was no accident: she had used him to take revenge. And if she was prepared to cause injury to Sanders, what else was she capable of doing, and who else did she want to punish? He had better stay on his guard. Unless it was coincidence. He prayed that it was coincidence.

Meanwhile Colin had brightened and opened the door on to the landing. 'Any chance that you could lend a hand with the removals? We can show you the house.'

Colin's attention switched to the camera and equipment. 'Why don't you bring that over and we can have a look at the rushes?'

Even through his befuddled mind, this seemed like a bad idea. 'Sorry. Work in progress and all that.'

'Come on, we can have a glass of *cava* while we watch.'

No way, he thought. Impossible. 'I'd much rather show you the finished product.'

'Oh, don't be such a pussy.'

Magnus required a moment to identify this mild insult as a sign of their new bonhomie.

Rosie appeared, having overheard. 'Oh, yes, come on, I'm dying to see some of it. Any of it. Please, Magnus.'

His sense of elation under Rosie's hands flipped back to doom. He was being used like a puppet by everyone. It made him fatalistic. What was there he could do? Even when he tried to strike out on his own, he ended up fulfilling someone else's plan. This wedding video was going to be a disaster, without a doubt, so there was little point in delaying it any further. The omissions and technical incompetence could never be disguised and this might be the best, most forgiving mood he would find Colin in for some time. He smiled reluctantly, and was knocked backwards on to his desk when Rosie bounded up and hugged him excitedly.

Colin was watching with a smile. 'Someone's lending me a van to shift our stuff. Do you want to chum me?'

As it happened Magnus preferred Rosie's company, especially with her warm arms round him. Here, he felt, he was safe from monsters buried in the ceiling, and Isabel's ominous demands, and all the other horrors of warped grief. Sleep would be safe here. But, from Colin's expression, yes was the required answer.

He regretted it the moment they stepped out on to the street. The city climate spotted them immediately and quickly organised some unpleasantness. As they descended the steps to Stockbridge, light but accurate rain streaked their clothes while the breeze, funnelled by the passageway, made chilly windsocks of their trouser legs. The tall windows bearing down on them were not all lit because the evening was still a couple of hours distant, but gloom dwelt at the edges of everything as they tramped the pavement. Edinburgh's grey flesh seemed oppressively close, even as they reached the wide street, and with Colin by his side Magnus felt Claire's presence more strongly than ever, but in a way that seemed to have outgrown itself. This was an open contest with the elements.

They turned left up a cobbled back-street to escape the main force of the wind and the triangle that Magnus had traced on the map of the New Town glowed dimly in his mind: India, Bellevue, Drummond. Warmth spread through his limbs despite the heavier rain and a fresh pain formed along his spine. Yes, Claire had walked this way many times before, with Colin at her side just as he was doing now. Some traffic sluiced past and they were obliged to wait. Magnus looked up at the sky, and was punished by a sharp squall. They put their heads down, crossed the road and cut up past a disused town hall towards cover, which presented itself in the form of a small mews that Magnus, wiping rainwater from his face, came dimly to recognise. He scanned the low buildings, which in turn were encircled by higher tenements. It was the first place he had stopped having come off the coach from London. Colin shook some raindrops from his jacket and pointed towards the far building. 'They've left the van keys with a neighbour in there. I won't be a second.'

At that moment the rain let up, but Colin did not take the opportunity to run for the door. Magnus glanced at him, impatient to be left alone on this dry patch of slabs where he could listen to the sound of the rain. To his dismay he saw that Colin's damp white forehead was creased by nostalgia. His lips – which seemed livid in the premature gloom – moved towards a smile and Magnus already knew that their newly cordial relationship was about to be pushed too far. Was this why Colin had dragged him along?

'This place reminds me of Claire when we had just started seeing each other,' he said, and gave Magnus a confidential nudge. 'A friend of ours rented the place over there. There were parties in it most nights, a lot of dope and dancing and talk. It was a good time.'

The last sentence was put in a way that suggested understatement. So this was where they had fallen in love. He could imagine them making plans, discussing their engagement and the house they would live in. But then he stopped himself. He disliked being involved in this furtive act of remembrance. He did not want to bond with Colin over Claire, but he found that he particularly disliked being party to the disloyalty this nostalgia showed Rosie. It seemed like a minor development, but for the first time Magnus discovered that in his thoughts Rosie had come before Claire. And why not? Why should he show allegiance to his sister when she manipulated him for her own bitter ends? This was how it should be. The living displaced the dead; it was a law of nature.

Colin's friendly smile faded away, ignored. Fresh rain swept across the courtyard and Magnus watched the cobbles fry. Only when a dark figure hopped across his line of vision, jacket over head, did he turn and find that he was finally by himself.

Sixteen

'We bought it partly because of the gardens,' Rosie explained, from the front of Colin's four-wheel drive, her husband having gone ahead with the fully loaded van. Magnus was sharing the back seat with two suitcases, a golf umbrella and a large pot plant. The latter was squeezed between his knees and its fleshy leaves tickled his face. Peering through the foliage, he could see a hat-stand rising out of the passenger seat and the edge of some antique coffee-tables, which were lodged against the dashboard. All the props of a civilised future were crammed in here, jabbing him every time they went over a bump. He felt hopelessly unevolved.

'We thought about the country, but Colin thought that could wait until we decided about kids. That's the big "if",' she added, posting a slightly crooked smile via the rear-view mirror.

He grunted as she turned a corner and one of the hard-edged suitcases banged into his hip. 'Reproduction's all the rage,' he said.

She sent several short glances his way, or were they aimed at the traffic behind them? A leaf-tip entered his nostril and he batted it away.

'What are your longer-term plans, Magnus?'

He took a moment to answer because he was digging out something uncomfortable from under his leg, which turned out to be a pile of cardboard folders tied up with string, one of which, he discovered with a jolt, had 'Pension Plan' scrawled across it in Colin's handwriting. The future? He was having enough trouble with the present. He swallowed and tried in vain to think of a serious answer. Nothing came. 'In the medium term, a fish supper. In the long term . . . bed?'

She laughed. 'Don't feel like you're being evicted, but we're putting the flat in India Street up for sale quite soon. Obviously you've got the full length of the notice period to make other plans, although if you're interested in buying it yourself . . .'

The idea was ludicrous, unless he persuaded Isabel to loan him a quarter of a million, which seemed unlikely in the light of the news that he would have to give her about the carving. They turned right off Royal Crescent into Drummond Place and pulled up outside the house number that had been marked on Claire's map: the third point of the New Town triangle. She stopped the car behind the van, opened the rear-seat door and helped deliver the pot plant from between his legs.

'Easy does it,' she said, and her hair floated in the wind as she carried it, flapping, to the doorstep.

Magnus was beside her with the two suitcases when

she rang the stained brass doorbell. They heard Colin's footsteps approach, then the door opened and spilled light on to them. Colin slipped past for another load, leaving Magnus free to gape. The entrance hall was enormous, and it seemed even larger due to the absence of furniture. Far away, over a tundra of black and white tiles, boxes were waiting to be unpacked. Given a little shove by Rosie, he walked into the cavernous hall with the suitcases and his footsteps echoed as if he were in a mausoleum. He stopped at the bottom of the stairwell. A modest high-rise would have fitted snugly into the unused space.

'The suitcases go upstairs,' she said. With difficulty he ascended the broad steps, while the rib-tap of his sister's presence matched time. The familiar feeling startled him. He'd hoped it had gone for good.

'So, what do you think?' she asked.

'Nice.' Reaching the landing, he saw that there was another floor, possibly even two.

'Left.'

He turned left on the landing and dropped the suitcases inside the door of what he guessed would eventually be their bedroom. The shifting treetops of Drummond Place gardens filled the old window-panes. No doubt Claire had stood here, too, and looked into that great mass of leaves, thinking of a possible future.

A shout from Colin snapped him out of his brief reverie. 'Take the other end, would you?'

He went to the top of the stairs and saw that Colin was attempting to drag up a Persian rug, but had got stuck on a curve. Magnus took the other end and soon they were staggering on to the landing. 'Room on the left,' said Colin, and they let it drop in front of the television. They unrolled it, then went downstairs for the sofa. Once they had emptied both the van and the car Colin called a halt. This was the moment Magnus had been dreading. 'Why don't we have a breather and watch some of the wedding?'

Magnus was about to declare that he had forgotten the camera but Colin pointed to the bag, which was sitting beside the television. 'I brought it over in the van.'

'Well remembered. But the tape.'

Colin took out of his pocket a tape with 'Wedding' written on it. Conceding defeat, Magnus unpacked the equipment while Colin moved the sofa round and set up the television. Blocking out trepidation about how his work would be received, Magnus concentrated on the practical task in hand. He wired the camera to the mains supply, then attached two audio leads and a third visual one into the out-jacks. They led, yellow, red and white, to a special adaptor. This he inserted in the back of the television and, with Colin, spent a while finding the right channel. So the bit they did see before Magnus reset the tape to the beginning was part of the way into the film. On the soundtrack the minister could be heard droning his preamble, then the picture steadied to reveal a relative nodding to sleep in the pew. The camera zoomed in close on his fluttering eyelids and drooping lip. Colin smiled. 'I see you haven't been too reverential.'

Magnus cleared his throat nervously and put the film on hold.

'Darling!' called Colin over his shoulder, causing Magnus to twitch — at the word more than the volume. 'We're about to start.'

Rosie entered with a bottle of *cava* and three glasses on a tray. She smiled at the little corner of domesticity that had been arranged on the rug, while the rest of the room remained barren. She put down the tray on the coffee-table and Colin stepped back to inspect the arrangements. 'We're missing one thing. Magnus, come with me.'

His playful tone made Magnus's heart sink, but obediently he plodded downstairs and into the flying drizzle outside. Colin opened the back of the van and hauled out a huge yucca plant that had previously been stationed in Rosie's room by her portable television. 'Just to complete the picture,' he said, with a grin.

Magnus returned the smile wanly. Despite his fresh start with Colin, and the man-to-man chat, he found his charm contrived, and his manner subtly condescending. He took the yucca by the trunk and, with great awkwardness, they carried it through the front door and up the stairs. Half-way up, they heard voices from the wedding: Rosie must have turned the film on again while she was waiting. Then came a loud slam from the door of the *en-suite* bathroom. Both men froze.

'The wind?' said Magnus, hopefully, but Colin's worried face suggested that Rosie had slammed it in a distinctive and eloquent way.

Magnus closed his eyes for a second and prepared for a showdown.

They entered the room and Colin, seeing that Rosie had indeed shut herself into the bathroom, hefted the plant into Magnus's care. He tottered under its weight and carried it, caber-wise, to the far corner. Then he turned towards the television and glimpsed a close-up of Colin's mother picking at her knicker elastic after a reel. Quickly he turned it off again.

Colin tapped gently on the bathroom door. 'Rosie, we're about to sit down and watch. Shall we wait for you?'

'Fuck off.' Her voice was hoarse, upset.

'Can I come in?'

'Watch it by your fucking self. Go on, watch it!'

Magnus suddenly felt protective of his work. Surely it wasn't that bad. Perhaps he had gone slightly over the top on the irreverence front, but those moments could always be edited out. Rosie's sense of humour must have let her down. But what, he wondered, could she have been so upset about at the start of the footage when all the worst stuff came later on?

Colin sighed and glanced coldly at Magnus, who attempted successfully to look humble and respectful. He returned to the sofa and sat down.

'So play it,' Colin said, with resignation, 'from the beginning.'

Magnus sat down at the other end of the sofa, pressed rewind and then play. He expected to see external shots of the church and the first interviews with the guests waiting outside, but the film started earlier than that. They were in his bedroom, before the wedding, when he met Colin for the first time. Colin was squarely in the picture, shirt unbuttoned in the doorway, with Magnus's shoulder just visible to the left. How was this possible? He remembered fiddling with the camera before Colin came to the door and then, as his recollection went, he had put it down, but he was sure he hadn't turned it on. Unless by mistake. And it had to be coincidence that Colin was placed squarely in the middle of the screen. Except that malevolent coincidence no longer existed in Magnus's world. Or if it did he called it Claire. He watched with growing horror as their conversation unfolded, hearing it with Rosie's ears. He heard his own voice ask the address of the house Colin had bought, the one they were sitting in right now. Colin replied: 'Twelve Drummond Place. Why? . . . What is it?'

'Was it a house you looked at once with Claire?'

'Well, yes, we did look at it, a long time ago. Just speculation, though, for fun.'

When Colin heard his own confession he groaned and put his head into his hands. But even worse was the letter. Colin and he were speaking again.

'Me and Rosie had argued. I was letting off steam when I wrote it. I wish to God I hadn't sent it.'

'Why? Because it was all lies? You didn't still love Claire? Rosie wasn't "a stupid mistake that had gathered momentum"?'

'I was angry. I might have meant it at the time.'

Enough. Magnus made a move towards the camera to stop the playback, but Colin grabbed him by the elbow and pulled him down.

'Colin, believe me, this wasn't intentional, it's a—'

'Shut up.' His eyes were fixed on the screen, his hand continued to grip Magnus's elbow. 'We're going to watch my wedding video. All the way through.'

Magnus closed his eyes and prayed for this to end. Not to God, to Claire. Only she could have organised this. Unless it was truly him, and he was blanking out his own worst actions. He found the thought of madness even more terrifying than a conspiracy of the dead. The film continued and he did not believe that it could get worse. In comparison to the opening, the rest was tame, just a hopeless mess of missed opportunities, ill-judged satire and wonky camera angles. It made little difference that he had failed to record the exchange of rings, or half of the speeches when, in the midst of the party footage, another rogue scene played itself out.

The camera angle framed Rosie in profile, from below, with Magnus's lower arm wobbling at the top edge of the picture. The camera must have been resting on his knee. She was sitting on the step outside the hall and ceilidh music cluttered the background. But her voice was loud and clear, and her eyes seemed to burn with sincerity.

'I've got the wrong man.'

'Post-nuptial depression. It's a passing phase.'

'I've fucked up, Magnus. What do I do?'

He did not dare look at Colin's face beside him. All he felt was the fierce grip on his elbow and it stayed that way until the film came to an end. Several seconds passed and neither of them said a word. Eventually, Colin sighed. So did Magnus.

'Your handing back the letter was a nice touch. And then delivering this. A real sucker punch.'

Magnus turned towards him. 'Colin, this is all an enormous *technical* mistake.'

Then he realised that Rosie was behind them, eyes still fixed on the screen. Colin glanced at her tearstained face and then he, too, continued to stare at the snowstorm on the television screen.

The grip tightened on Magnus's elbow. 'What is it specifically that you resent about me, Magnus? I mean, what motivated you to do this? Are you jealous of Rosie, perhaps, or is it revenge for Claire? I'm genuinely curious.'

In his moment of crisis, Magnus withdrew into dreamy abstraction. There was a high whine in his ears. Jealousy or desire for revenge? Both were plausible. But plausibility did not equate with the truth. He was not conscious of being afflicted by either. These charges were for Claire, not him. But the dead had immunity, and he must take the blame. The silence had lengthened to the point where he could no longer hope that Colin's questions were rhetorical. He was still waiting for an answer. It was going to be one that he didn't want to hear.

'I believe,' he began, 'that this is a rare case of supernatural intervention.'

Colin swung his free arm round and grabbed Magnus by the neck. Though he was bigger than Colin, and possibly stronger, he did not make any attempt to defend himself. He felt that Colin deserved to beat someone up. Furthermore, there was the guilt tailback that had never been fully addressed. Perhaps a beating would make him feel better: retribution on account, as it were, for Marjorie, and the tearstained teenage girlfriend, and the generous friend he didn't visit in hospital, and the cat he had failed to finish off. And the royalist poem. Yes, the poem was enough all by itself. He waited meekly for Colin's fist to clang against his nose, ear or jaw, but the enforcement of poetic justice was interrupted by Rosie.

'Get off him, Colin,' she said. Reluctantly he obeyed. 'Is that all true?'

Colin rose to his feet and faced his wife. 'You tell me.'

'Why did you marry me if you still loved her?'

His brow had fixed itself into a hard, horizontal line. 'Why did you say yes to the wrong man?' There was a pause. 'Anyway, why are we arguing in front of him, for Christ's sake?'

Rosie didn't answer. She turned and looked round the room. Magnus could guess what she was thinking: Claire's husband, Claire's house. She walked. Her footsteps went calmly down the stairs and out through the front door.

The two men stared at one another, then Colin ran. In five or six huge bounds he was down to the floor below and a second later flung open the front door. Magnus could hear their conversation from the window, but he wasn't interested in listening. Instead he packed up his equipment. Half-way down the stairs he heard the four-wheel drive pull away. Colin was sitting on the stone steps outside, chin in hand. Discreetly, he slipped by.

'I want you out of India Street. Right away.'

He nodded, and walked. Colin's eyes crawled over his back all the way down the pavement.

Leaving Drummond Place via Royal Crescent, he put down his bag on the pavement and swore. Aside from being mad, he was now homeless as well: a popular combination. He would have to shove everything into bin-liners and get out that day. But where to? His parents might offer him temporary refuge, or he could ask Gav for floor space. Both were short-term solutions at best. He would have to look for somewhere more permanent to rent, but where was the money going to come from? Isabel's loan was all but exhausted and payment for the school project would not be due for at least a month. Why had he spent all that money on labelled clothing? Inevitably, he thought of Isabel and the warm, rent-free room she had offered him. It was a temptation. He still felt disgusted by her grotesque annexation of Claire's identity, but it was a disgust he felt equally for himself. She had slipped into Claire's identity, while Claire had slipped into his. They would make a perfect couple.

He stopped walking. That feeling of being watched as he walked away from Drummond Place had not gone away. Was Colin following? He looked behind him but there was no one, only parked cars and the grey fronts of Georgian apartments. This town still felt hostile to him, possibly even threatening. Hurriedly, he resumed his journey back to India Street, and ten minutes later was standing outside number fifty-eight with the key in his hand. He hesitated. Rosie would be up there. He had just destroyed her marriage. She would be furious with him. And yet he desperately wanted to see her. Again, Colin's questions rose up in his mind. Revenge or jealousy? He felt sure that the former wasn't true, but jealousy – perhaps there was a little of that. Did this mean love? It was a word that justified a great deal of mental instability. But, no, it wasn't true. She had been kind, and understanding, and had opened up to him. He liked her, certainly. He found her attractive, too. But wasn't that mainly because she was denied him – by marriage, by decency and, most of all, by Claire?

How she would hate Rosie and him being together; even more than Rosie and Colin. He remembered the stiff resistance put up by the amoeba in the bar, seemingly bent on keeping the two of them apart. But the situation had become more complicated than that: Isabel thought that Rosie had the last piece of the carving, which would have been charged, according to her belief, with all the sexual allure that had ensnared Colin. Perhaps that was why Isabel had tolerated his move into India Street. She must have calculated that he would retrieve the carving and then, by dint of family and financial pressure, and a superstitious deference to Claire, gravitate towards Isabel. And thus the carving would be united.

He groaned and pressed his hands to his temples. Divining the motives of the dead was impossible; as impossible as spotting their ruses before you fell for them. Rebellion was useless. His video business – his cherished idea for independence – had been used as a weapon against Colin's marriage, and as a means to retrieve the carving at the school. What he thought he had done for himself turned out to fit into Claire's larger plan, whose objectives had been relentlessly pursued under the cover of false trails and the general confusion of a grief-stricken mind. Couldn't he perform even one act of defiance to show that, for all Claire's arts of manipulation, there were some things she couldn't determine? Surely the living had that right.

His hands dropped from his head. Strangely, he felt calm once again. There was a point to be made here. Pushing his spectacles up his nose and flattening his hair, he turned the key in the lock.

He opened the door to the flat and stepped inside. Footsteps moved hastily to and fro in the bedroom upstairs. Rosie was packing. Deciding that it was better to wait until she had come down, he remained in the corridor. Barely a minute passed before the bedroom door creaked open and a large suitcase began to bump its way down. The lower half of her body came into sight. It pressed against the stair-rail as she heaved the luggage. No doubt she was furious with him, and he coughed to announce his presence. She stopped, and Magnus stepped forwards to help. Her face was flushed, her eyes glittering with emotion and resolve. But she looked relieved when she saw it was him, not Colin. She was going, that was obvious.

'Are you going over with another load?' he asked, taking the weight of the suitcase from below and easing it to the floor.

'You could say that.' She descended the last few steps

and wiped a strand of brown hair from her face. 'Except this load is leaving town, along with me.'

'Hold on. Not so fast. Separation is supposed to be a long and agonising process.'

She stared at him, then laughed tiredly and sat down on the lower step. Her arms were balanced on her knees and her hands drooped at the end of them.

'The film,' he said. 'I don't know why, or how, it came out like that.'

A sharp glance told him to shut up, but then she looked at her nails. 'Well, it did its job.'

It burst out of him: 'You think it was done intentionally but it wasn't. I didn't know what I was doing. It was as if someone else was in control. The camera. Claire.'

She fixed him with her steady, brown-eyed gaze. 'Magnus, I'm not angry with you. It was a desperate thing to do but it doesn't matter, because I think I know why you did it. Only you haven't had the guts to tell me yet.'

Did she think he was besotted? It would seem everyone had the same impression. Perhaps it was true.

She continued, 'More importantly, you were right. It was stupid of me to go through with the wedding. The film confirmed it.'

She took a breath. 'He refused to talk about Claire, but she was always in his mind. When she died, I thought things might change. But it got worse. I was always the substitute.' She sighed and got to her feet. It hadn't been easy for her to confess that, but she looked better for it. 'I have something for you, by the way.'

Laboriously, she climbed back up the stairs and came down with a plastic bag containing an object. She held it out and snorted mirthlessly. 'Look what I found when I was packing up the room. Colin must have fished it out of the bins downstairs after I'd thrown it out. It was hidden away at the back of the cupboard. There's no getting rid of that girl.'

Magnus took the bag and looked inside. He saw dark, polished wood, and a set of haunches circled by a long tail that formed the outer rim of the carving's base. Slowly he leant back against the wall and his arm flopped so that the carving bumped against his leg. Fate had asserted itself once more. It had just been a matter of time. He had failed to find the carving, so the carving had kindly come to him. Claire had had it all stitched up.

'Presumably Colin told you to get out.'

He nodded, and sighed. 'What about you? Where are you going?' he asked.

'North. A friend is going to put me up while I think it all through.'

He looked at her intensely. 'I wish you weren't going.'

Suddenly they were paying close attention to each other. He remembered what he had thought on the street below, about one last act of true defiance. Here was the opportunity, right in front of him. He touched her hand, then stepped back so that she could leave. But she didn't move. She closed her eyes. 'I just want to forget it all.'

Magnus groaned. He wanted to forget too. Not just the past, which contained his sister's death, but also the

future, because that was where his own death lay. Poor
Isabel was all the evidence he needed of where this morbid
fixation might lead. Death's only useful instruction was
to grasp the present. Therefore he would give himself a
reprieve. Excitement tingled through his body and, for
once, he felt that the sensation was entirely his own.
He gloried in the moment because he felt that it would
not last. But the seconds kept ticking. These charmed
moments only ever happened to him with Rosie. Not with
Felicity, not with his previous encounters, and certainly
not with Isabel. He realised that he could only ever offer
the better part of himself to another person if he took
control of his own life. So this was how it felt to be
alive, he thought, to be free. Right then the possibility
of happiness stood in front of him, within reach. All that
prevented him was Claire and her stubborn refusal to
fade. She had taken control of his reason, that much was
clear. Which meant that there was only one part of him
that remained more or less his own: his physical desire.

He looked down at Rosie. Her hand took his and he
felt it warm and tight. Their lips crushed together. Their
bodies too. She already knew his body: where it hurt and
also, so it transpired, where it did not. The kiss ended and
he put a hand on either of her hips. He turned her towards
the stairs and watched as she climbed. He followed and
the bag dropped from his hand. The carving fell out of it
and rolled down a step, then another, and another until
it clattered to the floorboards and came to rest against
the skirting-board.

They fell together on to the bed but took their time.

They both knew that it might not last so they resolved to extract from this one encounter all the pleasure they could in defiance of the future. They lay back in their clothes and looked at each other. And soon the present tense became as plastic as their bodies. Memory and anticipation merged. The past offered promise, the future had occurred. He heard her say, 'I love you,' but she hadn't said it yet and, anyway, she was talking about a time before or a time to come. When he kissed her it felt nostalgic and also pioneering. Being undressed made him feel childish and potent and frail, particularly as he undid his own cuffs and she bent down to untie his shoes and he shrugged off his shirt and leant forwards to pull her blouse from under the belt of her jeans – it was already hanging loose at the base of her warm back. Particularly as he put his hand on the skin there, felt the smoothness and leant down to press his nose and cheek against it. Also when he held a breast in his hand, the nipple hard in his palm. And the time when one of her arms rested on his neck and their naked proximity seemed to require a careful and sustained act of verification. First he would test her mouth and tongue. Then his finger would gradually run down the checklist as far as her belly-button. His left hand would move along her side and pull at her belt. It would slide beneath the fabric and he would hear a gasp. He would mistake it for pain although in fact it was pleasure. And when he gasped soon after her she took it for the sound of a man who was happy that he had got something right. But she was wrong because the wetness that he encountered between her legs was like mud, and it was horror that he experienced as his fingers sucked out and tinkled over a Cupid's bow of raw pelvic bone before going down once more, unbelievingly, to dab at her tightly coiled intestine.

His hand was caught in a remaining band of her clothing as he tried to wrench it free of the wound. Her thighs were solid, like wood. Rosie had gripped hold of his shoulders, but Magnus writhed off her and tore his wrist free, causing her to yelp as her body was tugged forty-five degrees across the bed and her underwear ripped.

'What is it?' she gasped. 'Is someone there?'

He stared at his hand, which twitched, and he knew he was mad. He looked over to her. She scrambled up and grabbed the pillow to cover herself. Her own hand went down between her thighs to check, but there was nothing wrong. He remained by the wall quivering, looking left and right with rapid, jerky movements. He felt as if he had just awoken from a nightmare in a strange room and had yet to understand where and who he was. Slowly she rose from the bed and approached. This caused him to cringe away from her towards the door.

'Magnus, calm down, come here.'

'Get back!'

His own voice sounded alien to him: panicked, aggressive. He could feel the whole of his body twitching now. She retreated. Rapidly he grabbed his clothes, put them on, opened the bedroom door and went down the stairs in one unbroken rumble, stopping only to snatch the carving from the floor.

Seventeen

He leapt down four flights of stairs with the carving in one hand and the stair-rail sliding at speed through the other. At each corner his body flailed outwards but his left arm jerked, hooked to the rail, and pulled it back on to the descent. He panted and sobbed and his legs pumped, and together these noises formed a disorganised echo that rose to the top of the building from where he glimpsed Rosie watching with a cardigan clutched to her neck.

Magnus – or, more precisely, his legs – had decided to capitulate. While his mind was caught in a kind of quivering inactivity, the lower limbs propelled him as far away from the last hideous experience as it was possible to go. The door on to the street ripped open and he hit the cobbles coatless, running. Seconds later the New Town had swallowed him up. The first mossy patches of white light formed on the grey city stone. The evening approached.

His legs propelled him, but they did not know which way to go. At a corner he stopped to catch his breath and his mind made its first useful contribution for some time. Get away, it said. Get out of the city. The thought gave him heart. His hand went to his pocket, but the car-keys were not there. Of course, he had returned them to Mother. There were buses. He could leave the same way he arrived, but when he did turn in the direction of the station, instinct told him that something unbearable was coming for him from there. He dodged into an alley, down which he sprinted. His trajectory was once more determined by fear rather than logic. The mouth of certain streets offered refuge but at the last minute dread sent him veering away, and on. Opening doors, emerging figures, waiting cars: they were all reasons to run or hide. He was not travelling in circles but in sharp-angled triangles of disorientation, like a trapped fly. If there was an exit from the New Town he could not find it.

At last he summoned the exhaustion to stop. The wind filled his shirt with phantom flab. It was quiet here. He wiped his eyes and found that he was in the little mews that Colin had taken him to. There were only two exits: the little road by which he had entered, and another taking him towards Dublin Street. Although his escape routes were limited it seemed that he was alone, for the time being. He bent over, with one hand on his hip and the other still gripping the carving. He knew that this was as far as he could go. If something or someone was coming for him, they would find him there. A crisps packet skipped over the paving slabs, lifted on the breeze.

He waited and an almost religious calm settled on him. He looked up at the grey sky and the smeared windows of the surrounding houses. A few moments later he began to cry once more because he knew that they had arrived. The three of them: Isabel, Marjorie, Rosie. They were standing behind him but he did not want to look, and when he did the tears pulled their figures into horizontal lines and mingled them into an amorphous whole, glimmering like crystals.

At last he found the courage to look up, and only Isabel was left. She at least was real. The weather sucked at her thin cotton dress with such vigour that the fabric appeared tattooed to her limbs, until a sudden change of wind direction let it flap once more at her ribs and knees. Her gaze was intent on him. 'I've been looking for you.'

The mews skewed to the side.

When he came to, she was trying in vain to lift him to his feet. 'Come home with me, you're soaked through.'

He made the effort to stand. She took the carving from him and led him by the hand, all the way back to Bellevue.

As they climbed the steps towards her front door, he was still shaking. He crossed his arms, trapping his fingers under his armpits, holding himself close. He only realised how cold he was now that the prospect of warmth was at hand.

'Aren't you freezing?' he asked, noticing her thin dress.

Isabel let him in. She sat him down and gave him a blanket, put on the kettle, then took the carving from the plastic bag. Now that he felt safe, his mouth started

Peter Jinks

to babble. She put a finger to it. His hysteria fluttered and fell away.

'Accept the things you don't understand. You did what you had to do. It's nearly over now.'

She walked over to the mantelpiece. How he longed for her tranquillity. He sat forwards, fingers still shaking; the feel of the wound. 'You don't know what I tried to do. You don't . . .'

But his voice died away as Isabel united the last piece of the carving. With a soft clunk, the baboon was made whole. She stepped back to admire it. He stared too, mouth wide. He took off his bent glasses and polished the lenses with his shirt, then stood up for a closer look. Isabel went out of the room. He bent forwards and squinted. Its ugliness was oddly potent. He looked at it from another angle and was reaching out to turn it round when Isabel came back in, pushed him gently to the side, steadied the carving with one hand, and struck it hard on the head with a hammer.

It made a piercing crack. Magnus was sufficiently shocked not to move. A second strike caused the baboon's head to splinter.

'Stop!'

He grabbed her elbow but she yanked it away and kept hitting. The baboon's belly collapsed with the first strike, and she moved on to the base. Magnus stepped back, dumbfounded. After all his efforts and all her pleas to recover this precious thing, she was destroying it. Splinters flew across the carpet, shards of wood bounced

274

off the brass fire tongs. She paused for a moment, then gave the remains of the carving a couple of sharper, better-aimed blows. Satisfied at last, she put the hammer aside, brushed away some fragments, and fished out from the carving's remains what looked like three pieces of old leather. They must have been hidden inside, one for each section. They resembled biltong – cured bushmeat – which he had seen but not tasted on his trip to Namibia. 'What are they?'

She held them in her hands and smiled. Two of them were unrecognisable scraps; the third, however, was circular and marked in the middle by a small dark disc with a tiny dimple at its centre, about the size of a nipple. She didn't answer. She took them into the kitchen where a pan of water was boiling on the stove. 'Wait next door,' she said. 'Go on.'

He obeyed, and sat down. No more questions. He didn't want the responsibility.

Presently a peculiar odour came through from the kitchen. The smell reminded him of beef tea, but with a sharp whiff of the tannery. A minute later Isabel came in with two steaming mugs. She sat down next to him and handed one over. 'Drink some of that. It will warm you up.'

He waited until she took a sip from her own, then he did the same. It didn't taste of much. He got it down. When he had finished she took his mug and put it next to hers, which was also empty, on the floor. She turned back to him and smiled coaxingly. 'There now.' She came closer. It was clear what she intended.

'I can't,' he said. 'You don't know what just happened to me.'

She looked at him as if she did know. 'Were you doing something wrong?'

She took his hands. There was compassion in her eyes. 'It doesn't matter. I forgive you.'

'It was horrible. I touched Rosie, and . . .'

She squeezed him. 'You were being guided away from a mistake. You'll be guided now, if you stop fighting her.' He looked at her with curiosity. 'It's over. Over. Over.'

Her fingers joined behind his head and drew him towards a kiss. He thought that possibly he might want to do this, he was trying, but he was trembling all over. He remembered his fingers on the hot intestine and twisted away.

She sighed and stood up.

'I'm sorry,' he said, and lowered his eyes to the floor. He only looked up when a shoe struck him painfully in the chest. She had kicked it off her foot. He ducked as she sent the other in his direction.

'No. Watch.' Without any decorum she pulled off her dress, rolled it up and threw it at him.

'Stop it,' he said. It was not a performance, but he watched as the rest of her clothes followed. Within seconds she was naked, except for the elastic bandage supporting her sprained ankle. She lifted up her arms and turned about. Her body was solid and whole. The soles of her bare feet squeaked slightly on the varnished floorboards. Her eyes were grave and entirely without self-consciousness when she faced him again. He found that his throat was blocked: he identified it as a symptom of desire. He edged forwards on the sofa and she stepped towards him so that he could press his cheek against her belly. He could smell the not unpleasant fragrance of her skin. Stop fighting, he told himself. His whole body was burning. He knew there was no alternative now. It was out of his hands; at last, he obeyed the command.

Her bed was a wound and they were rolling in it. It was red and warm and not to be feared. Both of them were taking what they needed from its fertile creases. His loneliness had been transformed into a long and wide hunger that he sensed Isabel desired equally to fulfil. In the dark they squirmed and groped like newborn puppies. There were three of them now, or were there more? Limbs were difficult to distinguish; physical ownership became blurred. Knees bumped softly against his that might have been hers or might have been someone else's; there were scratchings and wrigglings and semi-verbalisations that echoed another's or were answered by his own. Isabel's nuzzles and sighs seemed to offer a resolution to all his anxieties and fears: they told him he was wrong to think that the living were controlled by the dead. No, the living *were* the dead.

They rolled and rolled, and Claire was with them: in him, in her. He let his thoughts roll too of their own accord and soon he was lying tranquilly in Isabel's arms, undisturbed by the heavy weather outside. In the kitchen below the tick of the window fan could just be heard. It was going so fast it purred.

Isabel lay and stroked his hair. When she stopped he glanced up. She was falling asleep, it appeared, with a look of satisfaction on her face that was not entirely carnal.

Epilogue

'She's certainly got the Calder blood in her, hasn't she?' said Mother to Magnus, peering down at the child who was swaddled and snoozing in Isabel's arms. They were in the back garden of the parental home, taking advantage (warily) of a sunny spell that had broken through the Scottish summer clouds.

'Thank you, Mother, I did assume that,' he replied.

Isabel heard the terseness in her husband's voice and gave him a look of warning, which he reluctantly acknowledged, aware that his grumpiness had been tolerated all morning, both before and during the christening. He had been against baptising their daughter from the beginning, but was defeated by the grand alliance of wife and mother. So he carefully hated every minute of the service: he had considered the minister unctuous, the local church squat, and the new organ – which noisily proclaimed its congregation's generosity – intrusive. But the ceremony was over now and he knew that Isabel's glance would be followed by a humiliating scene if he pushed things too far.

Mother ignored her son and continued: 'She's the spitting image of Claire at that age. Right down to the mole on her lovely little lip.'

'Yes, sweetie-poos,' Isabel said to her daughter, and she was about to continue in a similar vein until Magnus, who had forgotten his resolution to be more cheerful, interrupted through a frozen smile.

'Shall we speak English to her, dear?'

Making the necessary compromise, Isabel smiled tightly and rocked her daughter in silence. Mother stroked down a cowlick of the child's wispy brown hair. Over Isabel's shoulder, he saw the french windows open and Father emerge with a camera pressed to his eye. Inwardly he groaned. He hated being filmed. 'Look here everyone,' Father cried, and all of them did the dutiful thing.

Approaching across the lawn he aimed the lens at Magnus first, who showed his teeth. Thanks to his new hobby of chain-smoking the smile matched his yellow tie. It was the only colour co-ordination to be seen on him. His interest in fashion had faded when Isabel became pregnant. The shirt clashed with the shoes while the suit, which Isabel had snapped up in a high-street sale, accentuated a nascent pot-belly. He looked into the lens mistrustfully and struggled to find some unsarcastic words. 'We've been lucky with the weather, eh?'

It was enough. The camera swung to Mother. She was on one of life's plateaux and would go on looking like an indomitable middle-aged woman for at least another decade. She raised her salmon sandwich and said, weirdly, 'Cheers.'

Isabel's turn was next, but Magnus scuttled away in search of a lager without waiting to hear the tedious banter that would surely unfurl between Father and his daughter-in-law. Finding a snub-nosed bottle of cheap Dutch beer in the fridge, he twisted off the cap and took a swig. Then he lit a cigarette and wafted the smoke towards the french window to avoid rousing Mother's wrath.

Things weren't so bad, he reflected, as the infusions of nicotine and alcohol did their job. Since Isabel's pregnancy and their hasty marriage, life had become a great deal simpler. He had moved into her flat, he had worked hard to expand his business, and he had broken off all contact with Rosie and Colin who, to his sketchy knowledge, were living permanently apart. Most importantly, the nightmares had ended. He was able to sleep peacefully and without interruption, even after the baby had arrived, because the infant slept with Isabel and Isabel, from early on, had decided not to sleep with him. It was an arrangement that suited them both.

The kid was no trouble at all. Quiet and watchful, she hardly cried, not even when she was being delivered. This had worried the doctors, although everything had turned out to be fine in the end. He remembered how a nurse had remarked that she was one of those babies who seemed to have seen it all before.

He took another swig of his lager and another puff on his cigarette. In front of him the high garden fence framed the family in a comforting suburban tableau. Father was poking the camera right up close to the baby. Only then did a frown cross his face.

'Come on then, little Claire,' Father said. 'Smile, darling, smile.'